Scepter of the Fire Cat

~~~

The Legend

by Bob Nailor

ISBN: Book: 978-1-61877-183-4
ISBN: Epub: 978-1-61877-182-7

The Scepter of the Fire Cat ~ The Legend

Discover other titles by Bob Nailor at
www.bobnailor.com

Dedication

This book is dedicated to my wife, Violet,
who urged me to write down the stories I
would tell the boys at bedtime.

Cover by Bob Nailor.

Table of Contents

PROLOGUE: The Legend Begins 1

CHAPTER 1: King Arlyon 5

CHAPTER 2: The Dark Man 16

CHAPTER 3: The Dream 26

CHAPTER 4: Coronation 33

CHAPTER 5: The Promise 40

CHAPTER 6: Siblings 46

CHAPTER 7: The Rivalry Begins 53

CHAPTER 8: Enyra 60

CHAPTER 9: Nos'Hanlah 69

CHAPTER 10: A Twin Split 75

CHAPTER 11: Penance 80

CHAPTER 12: Betrothal 86

CHAPTER 13: A Wedding Return 91

CHAPTER 14: Cornear's Tale 97

CHAPTER 15: Namo-Ke and Namo-Hoj 104

CHAPTER 16: Innead and Namo-Ke 109

CHAPTER 17: The King's Health 114

CHAPTER 18: Nos'Nevel Dawn 119

CHAPTER 19: Nos'Nevel 125

CHAPTER 20: The Journey Begins 131

CHAPTER 21: Under-Lord Laminar 136

CHAPTER 22: The Conflict 142

CHAPTER 23: A Struggle of Power 148

CHAPTER 24: The Forest Over-Lord 154

CHAPTER 25: The Emerald 162

CHAPTER 26: Plots Appear 168

CHAPTER 27: Under-lord Letiman 176

CHAPTER 28: Jaren 183

CHAPTER 29: News, Good and Bad 191

CHAPTER 30: True Colors 197

CHAPTER 31: Curiosity 206

CHAPTER 32: The Plan 213

CHAPTER 33: The News 220

CHAPTER 34: Adavin 225

A Tease Read — Book 2: The Lost One 232

About the Author 247

Bibliography 249

PROLOGUE: The Legend Begins

Within the shadows of jungle green
Lay hidden from all to view, unseen
A beast, the cat, the man, foretold
Emerged aloud, look and behold
A cat of strength to a man so lean
The winds of truth have spoken, foreseen.

from The Ballad of the Fire

The Council of Creation listened and judged each of the chosen four. The Pillar Monkey, the Rainbow Snake, the Silver Bear and the Fire Cat each explained and expounded their worthiness. The Council communed, deliberated, and finally divined. "Seek ye each the proper creature to rule with justice according to thy own ideals. Always be aware of The Other, for he will bring sadness and ruination. For it is prophesied, only one of you may live to establish a regency. For the regency to live, there will be death with a promise of rebirth."

With the prophetic judgment passed, the Council of Creation dismissed them. The four departed in separate directions; each to fulfill the prophecy, each to seek a destiny.

The Pillar Monkey chattered among the tree tops with others of its kind, happy to have friends and play. The Silver Bear hastened to fish with his brethren in the rivers and sought his destiny no further. The Rainbow Snake approached many creatures, only to be reviled by them. Finally, he curled upon a rock to warm himself and continued to laze in the summer warmth.

The Fire Cat was a hunter. He prowled, searching for the proper creature. He padded through the jungle, his yellow eyes flickering red as he searched. The muscular, white-furred cat stealthily moved through the landscape. The mane was full and bristled in shades of amber and rust red, giving the illusion of flames, hence the name, Fire Cat. He ignored the other animals for they didn't meet the qualifications he'd set.

The sun shone brightly on the open area. The luxuriant growth of jungle ended barely and a verdant valley spread before him. The search included traveling many miles over several months. It was early morning when he stumbled upon the creatures. Humans. Perhaps these were the creatures he sought. He listened to their cheerful voices and singing in the far distance. As he neared, he noticed a group collecting berries, nuts and roots from the area. The younger children, naked, chased one another about the scantily attired females. The Fire Cat kept a safe distance, lurking in the shadows and underbrush, keeping a low profile from the wandering children and adults. Older children, both male and female, wearing basic coverings, assisted the bare breasted, older females in gathering food. A few of the young females nursed babies as they collected the edibles.

As the group moved closer to the heavy forested overgrowth, he followed them and now lay in the shadows of the jungle's edge, watching. Before him were the males, the simplest of farmers. They tended the small fields with rudimentary tools at the jungle's edge. His golden eyes darted to catch every nuance of the view. In the distance, beyond the small fields, were makeshift huts. The females and small children returned to the huts and milled about. Only the simplest of tools were visible. A peaceful group, he thought and was lulled by the serenity of the scene.

Approaching him on an almost direct course was a male. His first instinct was to charge the man, to attack this opponent who now approached. The male was of strong build, with a body deeply tanned by the sun. The cat watched the glistening sweat dribble and collect on the fabric covering the man from waist to mid-thigh. His heart beat faster. Should he attack? The man suddenly stepped into the jungle. Human scents, so close now, made his mind heady with a mixture of emotions. The man disappeared into the jungle trees and shrubs. He twitched his ears to listen for the human and heard the man relieving himself.

He lay there with his ears pulled tight against the top of his skull; eyes narrowed. His body was taut, muscles tightened to spring, his legs ready to pounce. He watched as the male hurried to exit the jungle. He watched warily as the human waved to his companions in the fields and yelled. He concentrated on their actions as they gathered their tools.

"They're leaving." he thought. "These are peaceful creatures. I will go to them and become one of them, to appear as they." He stood up on all four paws, lashed his tail and rolled back his head. He opened his mouth and as the lips pulled back from the fangs, he let loose a resounding roar. The mane of bronze hair glistened in the sun like a flaming aura as he stepped into the open, his white body glistening in the bright sunlight.

The men stopped. They turned as one toward the location of the sound. They stared at the great maned cat standing at the edge of the jungle. The humans watched as the cat reared up on its back legs and roared again. The transformation was incredible: the white fur turned to a golden tan and the mane became long flowing locks to careen carelessly along the perfectly chiseled human face. The once strong forelegs and body of a cat were now the well-muscled arms and torso of a man. The tail disappeared as the rear legs extended to become the mighty legs of an athlete. The only vestiges of resemblance to a cat were the golden eyes, and two prominent fanged teeth. He stood before them naked as he rolled his head back and again roared loudly one last time.

He watched the farmers who stood in awe. Finally, one of the men dropped his tools and fell to his knees while spreading his arms outward in adoration. "Arlyon," the man whispered. "Arlyon," another

4

repeated. The cat, now a human, listened as the voices swelled and gained volume. The farmers began to chant. "Arlyon. Arlyon. Arlyon." All the farmers were now on their knees in adulation, their heads bowed and their tools carelessly tossed to the side.

He approached them, padding confidently, quietly. As he neared the man whom first knelt, the man looked up. He smiled at the farmer, exuding a benevolence and kindness. The farmers face glowed.

"Arlyon," the man-cat said. "Why do you call me Arlyon?"

"It has been foretold that he who comes as a cat to walk as a man among us will be our leader. His name will be Arlyon," the farmer said and once again bowed his head, fearful to gaze on the cat-man.

"Then I shall be called Arlyon. Attend me," he said and held his hand out to assist the farmer to stand. "What is your name?"

"It is Reen, Lord Arlyon," the farmer said then bent down, picked up and handed Arlyon a dropped cloth. "For your nakedness, sire."

Arlyon smiled at the red-faced man as he took the cloth from the farmer and wrapped it about his waist to cover his manhood.

"Stand. All of you, and follow me," Arlyon said to the group as he headed toward the small gathering of huts. "Today is the beginning of our tomorrow."

CHAPTER 1: King Arlyon

One province lush, jungle green
Pure, a sparkling emerald seen.
One transverses to the sea
As a sapphire, blue can be
And third is fire, a land untame
Red, the ruby, blazes aflame.
One to touch, to rule them all
The Jewel of Air, attend the call

from The Ballad of the Fire

The sun was always full and bright, never changing as it arced across the sky each day from sunrise to sunset. The moon, in thirty days went through its cycle; growing smaller and smaller to disappear, only to re-appear and grow larger and larger; starting the cycle over. As Planting Time approached, the days got longer. It was time to rejoice in the newness of the land. As the Growing Time came, the days got warmer, and the planted fields grew. It was a time for festivals, visiting and lazing in the sun. The Harvest Time arrived when the days got shorter. The crops were ready to gather in. It was a time of color and sharing. During the Quiet Time there was the snow and cold, it was a time of rest, to reflect and plan. Time passed and the moon was the timekeeper. So it was that sixteen full moons created a Full

Circle; with four Moons to a Time and four Times to a Circle. Within a Full Circle were four celebrations, one each at the third full moon of a Time. The Planting Time was honored with Nos'Nevel, the Harvest Time with Nos'Hanlah, the Quiet Time with Nos'Dovel and the Growing Time with Nos'Rovlah. It happened that Lord Arlyon's appearance was during the Growing Time; therefore, to honor him, Nos'Rovlah was the longest celebration of the Circle. The Circles passed and the humans prospered.

The chamber space was opulent but reeked of somberness. Rich colored tapestries highlighted with silver and gold threads hung about the hall glittering in the late day sun. The tapestries were gifts from various lords of the realm or created by local merchants to exhibit their craft. The tapestries either honored a triumph of the king or showed mythical beasts with the Great Cat King. The sun filtered through stained glass windows with their colorful and intricate designs. The dust danced and reflected among the multi-colored rays of light streaming into the room. Massive columns of marble supported the polished cedar arches holding aloft the gilded tile ceiling. More marble and deeply polished woods could be found all about the chamber. The large throne, sitting on top of an eight-step dais, was the focal point within the room. This mammoth structure was fashioned of marble and onyx. Amber and red onyx was used to emulate the fiery mane of the Fire Cat around the back of the throne. Ivory was used for the fangs which hung from the arm rests. The throne was a gesture of love by the people, given to their monarch to commemorate his eightieth Circle of rule. Each step represented ten Circles; a time when all the lords gathered to bear homage to their king and re-negotiate contracts. Each step was inlaid in gold with the names of the new realms under King Arlyon's benevolent rule during that time. Adavin glittered alone on the top step. This was the small hut village where Arlyon first appeared. Vishalia, Clondine, and Yorel were on step two. The steps continued with other names, displaying the growth of Adavinya, the realm, and the rule of King Arlyon.

The Circles, a full one hundred and seven, had been kind to King Arlyon. He was no longer the strong determined man of his youth, but instead, a seasoned man living with the frailties of age. The old man rested quietly on the throne listening to the lilting music of the flutes, drums, cymbals and harps. He watched as Leear, his eldest son of thirty-five Circles, prepared for tomorrow's departure. The Great Cat King, Arlyon, was ready to relinquish his sovereignty, but had placed a challenge before Leear. He had resolved the first-born would assume the throne only after the realm's over-lords had conveyed their intent to accept the king-elect. Arlyon smiled inwardly realizing the amount of pomp and festivities Leear would suffer during the next Circle. This excursion would create a bond between the over-lords and the new king-elect and allow the new king-elect to appraise the lands he would rule. Arlyon knew one must be in contact with those which one rules.

Arlyon mused as Leear dismissed the group to put into action the plans that were made. As the massive oak doors closed behind the group, Leear turned back to face him. "Great Arlyon, my retinue will be ready for departure in the morning." Young Leear's voice resonated in the chamber, giving it an air of authority.

Arlyon smiled and looked at his son, noticing for the first time a confidence he had not seen in him before. "Who goes with you, my son?" He absently stroked his beard with the back of his fingers.

"I take with me Triesha, my wife."

Arlyon nodded approval while absently looking at the top step of the dais. Leear sighed relief at the knowledge his wife would be allowed the journey.

"Also, my children, Ralson, Anea and Obera," Leear continued. Arlyon raised his head and stared at his son, his hand stopped in mid-stroke of the beard.

"I would suggest, my son, you leave your children with me. I will entertain them. I feel young ones would not appreciate the pomp necessary to be endured by adults." Arlyon grinned at his son.

"Father, I know you will spoil the children. Triesha will not be happy with that decision."

Arlyon cut him off. "Triesha will have many duties to keep her busy. I will take the children under my tutelage." He paused. "Do you feel I did not raise you properly?" He watched Leear as the young man considered the question posed. He continued to watch, again stroking the beard, as Leear realized the question presented was the answer to Triesha's objections.

"As you wish, father. I also take Grel, my companion, and his wife," Leear continued. He moved from foot to foot as he stood there waiting.

"For what purpose," Arlyon asked as he stopped stroking his beard and let his right index finger slide under his lower lip and to push the lip upward. He watched, gold eyes beaming from under a slightly cocked eyebrow. Leear's left eye twitched. Arlyon expected and waited for the small tick of Leear's left eyebrow that occurred when his son was irritated or impatient. He waved his left hand absently in the air at Leear. "Amuse an old man."

Leear looked about the chamber, none were about except the musicians. He stepped closer to the dais and lowered his voice. "I intend to make Grel my main advisor when I am king. I felt his inclusion during this quest would be most beneficial."

"A wise choice, my son, but what of Kaltyo, my current advisor? He is the son of Reen, my first advisor. He is a man with many Circles of knowledge, both his and his father's. Surely you have use of him?" Arlyon's golden eyes watched Leear closely.

"Kaltyo, I had hoped would be advisor to Grel. Father, I would never discard any of your advisers. Only a fool would discard a filled vessel. Your advisers, I hope, will serve me also. The knowledge you have gathered about you is like a deep blue pool, refreshing and pure."

Arlyon narrowed his eyes to slits of pure gold. "I see you have attended and listened to your classes in the intricacies of diplomacy." He stood. "We need not be so formal, Leear. Let us go to my chamber, discuss your plans and my hopes, and share a flask of wine." He smiled at Leear as he slowly moved down from the dais, step by step, to greet his son. "Attend me," he whispered.

As he moved from the dais, Arlyon lifted his arm. Leear moved in under the arm and assisted his father from the throne room. As they passed the musicians, Arlyon nodded to them. "You played well today, I am pleased. You may leave now."

The musicians lay down their instruments, nodded to Arlyon and quickly left the chamber. Their exit was hasty and quiet.

"They have left, father." Leear whispered as he removed his shoulder from under Arlyon's arm. "Why do we play this game? Why must you act as an old man who cannot move without assistance?" They exited the chamber and entered the hallway leading to Arlyon's personal chamber.

"Dreams, Leear. Dreams. How many men in the town can remember my coming? How many men live who have seen eighty Circles? I have ruled over one hundred Circles. Ruled, Leear, not lived. I wish to allow you to rule. I have lived my life. There are none alive now who lived when I first walked from the forest. Your mother's journey to the Isle of Forgotten Sleep last Circle made me realize I have stayed too long." He watched as Leear looked away, to stare out the window of the bed-chamber they had entered. He knew if he forced Leear to face him, he would see a little boy with tears in his eyes. He allowed Leear his silence.

"Do you plan to journey to the Isle of Forgotten Sleep?" Leear's hand moved to his face with a small gesture. "We both know you are still very strong." He turned to Arlyon. "In fact, you are stronger than I. Why do you want to leave?"

"I will not depart until after your task is performed with the over-lords and I see you as the monarch of Adavinya. I promise to stay and see Ralson, my eldest grandchild, properly trained to rule. After all, with *four* grandchildren, I know there will be plenty of offspring to rule when my only son decides to step down from the monarchy." A twinkle in his eye, he watched as Leear allowed a small grin to cross his face.

"When did you find out? We have attempted to keep Triesha's pregnancy a secret."

"Kaltyo told me this morning before you assembled your group." He watched as Leear was about to question him. "Let me assure you, I know most of what occurs within my realm. The path of knowledge was from Triesha's maid-servant to others, to Kaltyo's wife, to Kaltyo, to me."

"I see now why you speak highly of Kaltyo. Will you permit him to journey with me?" Leear watched his father. "I mean to have him teach Grel his many clever methods to knowledge."

"Grel will have the time to learn. Upon your return he can spend time with Kaltyo and learn the mysterious methods of knowledge that Reen taught to him. He will not have the time for dreaming."

"Dreams. Father, before you again change the conversation, I ask. Why do we play this game? You spoke of dreams."

Arlyon went to the couch and sat down with his head bowed. Slowly, he looked up at his son. "Yes, there are the dreams. Your mother journeyed to the Isle of Forgotten Sleep last Circle. It pained me. I remember the day when the Council of Realms came to me on my seventieth Circle and told me I should wed and bring forth an heir. It was at the beginning of Nos'Dovel. I was taken aback by the idea I should be forced to marry. The Council even had the forethought to bring a varied group of young maidens from each realm for my inspection. They were a lovely group — young, nubile, and very skittish in my presence. They were not of the type to be my helpmate. Behind the over-lord of Yorel stood a young woman with a strong will, totally in control of herself in my presence. Yes, I noticed the red-haired woman you knew as your mother. Gaetta took my attention and my heart. We were wed the next full moon. Your mother had beautiful red hair which flared even more red with her anger. Her eyes were a deep emerald green, very similar to yours, Leear." Arlyon looked to where Leear now stood. "An old man wanders in his conversation. She was in my dream before we had met. I knew her from my dreams." Arlyon stood and walked to the table. "A little wine, my son?" He poured a rich, red wine into the chalices and offered one to Leear. "It was her departure which made me realize dreams end. I have ruled too many Circles." Arlyon again moved to the couch. "There have been dreams all my life — some I understand immediately, others still elude me. It would seem, Leear, I have lived a dream. All I have accomplished has been from dreams. Since your mother's journey, I have not been able to comprehend the dreams as well. Last night there was The Other." Arlyon looked at Leear, he could see the question on his face. "Do not seek an answer. Suffice it to say there is a power which plots now against me. It is immortal and evil. It has found me and will continue to foul my plans. It is time for a new monarch. I do not know how many more Circles I have left, but I feel I could out-live you, my son. I do not want to watch my grandson take the throne from me — assuming I journey to the Isle during his time." Arlyon again stared at the young man who had moved to stand before him.

"Dreams. All this is naught but dreams. I am not a dream, father. I am flesh. Are you a dream? Are you immortal, father?"

"Nay, my son, I am not immortal. Different, yes. I will not attempt to explain. Let it be I am as I appear. I shall continue this ploy of aging so the Council of Realms and the subjects of Adavinya will accept the fact a new monarch must come to rule. We will plan my journey another day." Arlyon stood again and slapped Leear on his back. "First, we must plan your journey. I will explain my desires as you explain your decisions for the journey."

Arlyon poured more wine and the two men discussed the plans and desires of each.

The morning sun cast hazy shadows on the open courtyard as the billowing, white clouds lazed in the light breeze. King Arlyon stood in a doorway and watched the group finalize the packing the wagons. Kaltyo stood politely to his side, unobtrusive, but ready.

Men and women moved quickly about the four wagons, three litters and six pack horses. One litter displayed the royal flag; a red trimmed white flag with a golden cat's head on a green tree. Leear appeared at another doorway. Men came running up to him. He listened then nodded his head in approval or disapproval as needed.

Arlyon watched, then turned to Kaltyo for assistance. Together they moved into the courtyard, Arlyon leaning on Kaltyo as they walked. The duo moved toward the litter with the flag of Adavinya. Kaltyo's messenger lad followed silently behind them.

"Triesha. Attend me, my dear," Arlyon called to the enshrouded litter.

"King Arlyon, you honor me." A soft radiant face with blue eyes and blond hair peeked from between drapes, her hand gently placed at the edge for balance.

"Nay, it is you who honors me. I know the task I have set before Leear will keep him from the castle for near a full Circle. I allowed your attendance to be with your husband, but my concern is now more for your welfare. I must consider my grandchild."

Triesha's face flushed with embarrassment. "It is true, sire. I have at most only seven more moons before I deliver. The journey will be long, but I shall remain with my husband and fulfill my duties as his wife to honor those whom we visit."

"And I say your duty is to your child. If you feel you need to return to Adavin before the journey is complete, please return. You will not disgrace, nor shame any. It would do more harm to not heed the safeties necessary during this time." Arlyon laid his hand on her delicate white hand and leaned over to her. "My blessing on you. Safe journey and hasty return. I await my grandchild." He kissed her on the forehead.

"Who is this person being familiar with my wife?" Leear's voice mockingly interrupted them.

"Only a lonely king who seeks a lovely unattended woman." Arlyon sighed heavily and winked at Triesha. "I was advising Triesha if she felt more comfortable here in Adavin, she could return at any time."

"We are now ready to depart, father. Triesha, make your farewell with the children. May they stand with you, father, as we leave the castle-keep?"

"An honor, my son. First, before you depart, I have one more ceremony to place upon you." Arlyon looked to Triesha. "Attend your children, my dear, then send them to me." He turned back to Leear. "Attend me, Leear."

Leear placed his shoulder under Arlyon's right arm and assisted his father to the doorway from which he could see all the courtyard. Kaltyo followed behind, he spoke quickly and quietly to his messenger. The lad dashed ahead and quickly disappeared into the portal in front of them. When they reached the opening, Kaltyo rapped his staff upon the stone steps as King Arlyon turned to face the assembled group. He removed himself from Leear's assistance and raised both arms into the air. A silence fell on the courtyard. The young messenger returned and stood breathless near Kaltyo.

"My friends, Leear is about to begin a journey. I have placed before him a task which must be completed before a monarch may ascend the throne. I have requested he travel the realm, visiting with under-lords and over-lord of each province to gain their acceptance. In order to know the over-lord will accept the new king, I now place the Jewels of Rule into his safe-keeping."

Kaltyo reached down and retrieved the scepter from the youth. The scepter was of carved ivory with intricate patterns weaving up and down its length. At the very top was the largest gem, a diamond, the Air Jewel. Below it was three gems: Earth Jewel, Fire Jewel, and Water Jewel. These gems represented the realms of rule. The forest and jungle area to the West and South was represented by the Earth Jewel, an emerald of the deepest green. The Water Jewel, a royal blue topaz, designated the coastline of the East and the island domains of the Great Seas. A rich red ruby, the Fire Jewel, alluded to the once highly fiery and volcanic mountains of the North. These were the features surrounding the province of Adavin and made up the kingdom of Adavinya. Each province had an over-lord who ruled the smaller fiefdoms within their province. Arlyon, himself, had chosen the jewels for the scepter. The four jewels glistened in the morning sun. Arlyon accepted the shimmering scepter from Kaltyo. All eyes of the courtyard followed the object as it moved in front of them. Arlyon plucked the diamond from the scepter and held it aloft for all to see.

"It is my decision Leear will travel and visit each fiefdom and then visit the over-lord of the province. He will remove from this scepter the appropriate jewel and place it in the hands of its designated over-lord. He must finish this quest and return to Adavin by the second moon of the growing time. Two days before Nos'Rovlah, the over-lords will assemble and your next king will be decided. If the over-lords return the jewels my son has entrusted to them, they and their subjects, accept the king-elect. If all gems are not offered as a bond, a new king-elect must be decided immediately by the over-lords and the process repeated. At the next Circle's Nos'Rovlah there will be a celebration of the new king. The final step of coronation will be to replace the diamond to bind the three gems as one. Until that time, I now give this jewel to the Royal Priest for safe-keeping."

The priest, in flowing robes, moved forward with hands uplifted and knelt before Arlyon. As the priest's fingers closed around the magnificent jewel, he turned up his face and gazed at King Arlyon.

Arlyon hesitated. For an instant he saw the priest's face change. At first it appeared like the Pillar Monkey, then the Rainbow Snake and finally the Silver Bear. As the bear's face faded, he saw The Other. Arlyon wanted to step back, to grab the diamond away.

"Is there a problem, m'lord?" the Royal Priest asked as he lowered the diamond to his chest.

Blinking, Arlyon took a deep breath. "None," he whispered.

The Royal Priest stood, cradling the giant diamond to him, and stepped back, away from Arlyon to disappear behind Kaltyo.

A silence permeated the crowd. Then, the soft murmuring began, swelling until finally a voice from the crowd asked, "What of you, King Arlyon?"

"I will remain to assist the new king until my time to journey to the Isle of Forgotten Sleep." He watched and listened as the crowd once more murmured among themselves.

"Leear, do you accept the challenge set before you," Arlyon asked.

"Yes, my liege." Arlyon watched with pride as Leear dropped to one knee before him, bowed his head and raised his arms, palms up, to receive the scepter. Arlyon placed it in Leear's palms and watched as Leear's fingers encircled the scepter.

"Thank you, father," Leear whispered, startling Arlyon. Leear stood.

"Safe journey. Return with haste." Arlyon spoke the traveler's blessing to the gathered group.

Arlyon watched, holding back a tear as Leear turned to depart before being rushed by his children. Ralson, at ten Circles, was awkward, unsure whether to hug his father or not. Obera, having just finished her fifth Circle knew exactly what to do. She jumped at her father, allowing him to catch her as she hugged him about the neck. Anea, who was nearing her eighth Circle nudged under his free left arm and snuggled against his chest. Arlyon smiled inwardly as his son disengaged himself from the arms while attempting to hold onto the scepter.

"Attend your grandfather. I shall return as quickly as I can."

Arlyon, with a smile on his face, lifted his arms and gathered the girls in and held them close to his sides, safe, secure. Ralson stood to one side of Arlyon, aloof, stiff, his eyes filled with tears that would not fall.

Arlyon watched Leear prepare to depart, riding the dark gray stallion, the white scepter with the three jewels, a ruby, a sapphire, and an emerald, nestled in the crook of his left arm. Leear lifted his right arm and motioned the gathered group to proceed out the main gate.

CHAPTER 2: The Dark Man

He moves with abandon, as a dance
Your mind to weave within the trance.
His laughter shrieks, the spine to chill,
A loathing sense your soul to fill.
Anger and hate within him dwell
Around you watch it grow and swell.

from The Ballad of the Fire

Arlyon watched as the last wagon slowly trundled through the massive castle gates. The populace danced and sang as they moved in and out of the parting group. He was glad the populace was pleased with the concept of Leear becoming the next king.

"Well, children, your parents are now—" Arlyon started.

"Grandfather. Who is that?" Obera questioned, her arm stretched out, a stubby finger pointing to the gates. Arlyon looked to the gate, then to Kaltyo who shook his head ever so faintly. Kaltyo had no idea of whom Obera spoke.

"Who is who, Obera, dear? Which person do you ask of?" Arlyon looked with haste between his granddaughter and the crowd. There was one in the crowd who caught *his* eye.

"The funny dancing one. The one with the black—"

"Obera! Must you tease grandfather with your nonsense?" Anea chided her little sister, shaking an index finger at her. She stopped then pushed back her long red hair as a mild, warm wind passed, rustling her hair and garments.

Arlyon looked to Anea, her mannerisms gently reminding him of Gaetta. "Hush, my dear. Let Obera speak." Falling to one knee beside Obera, he stroked her strawberry blond hair. "Tell grandfather what *you* see."

"I... oh, nothing, grandfather." Arlyon could hear the exasperation in her voice. He watched Obera as she looked sheepishly at her older sister. "Anea says I see things that are not there." Obera's blue eyes held a hidden mischievous gleam, her lower lip tightened in a small pout.

"Let me guess, Obera. I bet you saw a man who was wearing a long, black cape. He was dancing directly behind the last wagon." He watched as Obera's eyes opened wide with surprise. As he looked up again to Anea, she was about to speak, but a wink kept her silent.

"Yes! He danced this way," Obera said as she quickly jumped about in imitation of the man. "He wore a funny black hat with two points, like this." She placed her hands to her forehead and pointed her stubby index fingers upwards. "He was so funny, grandfather."

Arlyon watched his granddaughter bounce around in front of him. He quickly looked out to the gate. The man was gone. Arlyon frowned, his forehead furrowed in thought, his golden eyes darting to watch for any movement in the distance.

"Obera, stop at once." The command startled Arlyon as Ralson's voice shattered the silence. Arlyon turned to look at the youth as he stood there with his arms folded over his chest. "Your incessant chatter of the black man is—"

"Is between Obera and I, Ralson," Arlyon said softly. "The eyes of innocence are not veiled in knowledge and maturity. Have you forgotten your invisible playmate? Come," he continued as he stood up, "let us go in and prepare for a glorious day together. I am sure Kaltyo has already made some plans for us." He winked at the ever-present Kaltyo who stood to one side, unobtrusively watching. Arlyon watched as Kaltyo eyes rolled upward in silence before he moved to assist the king to walk.

"Sire," Kaltyo began, "you have two judgments this morning which have been referred—one from the Boscno region and the other from the Luyel region."

Arlyon stopped. "Referred?" He pondered the possible implications. "Have you any knowledge of the subterfuge regarding this referral?"

"Sire, the children." Kaltyo nodded to the three who stood in rapt attention to the conversation.

"It appears I have a duty to perform. Ralson and Anea, off to lessons. Little Obera, I want to talk more with you about this dancing man. Will you play in your chamber until I come?" Arlyon stretched his hand out and cupped the child's chin. He watched as the older children balked at the notion there would be no holiday today. Arlyon smiled inwardly, noticing the envy they displayed of their little sister.

"Off you go." He smiled at the children and waved his hands to shoo them down the corridor toward their appointed places. They walked slowly, almost begrudgingly, down the long corridor, their footsteps echoing in the loneliness. Anea hugged her little sister before Obera turned down a connecting corridor to her personal chamber, disappearing from sight.

Kaltyo moved forward and assisted Arlyon to resume the walk, moving silently down the corridor towards the personal chamber.

"Sire," Kaltyo's voice broke the silence. "You questioned this morning's judgments." Arlyon caught the quick shifting of eye movement Kaltyo did to see who was present before proceeding in a quiet voice with the information. "It appears there is one in Boscno who is causing a disturbance against Luyel. The Over-lord of Yorel has requested assistance."

Arlyon raised his eyebrows at the news. The under-lords of Luyel and Boscno were related through marriage, their wives were sisters. The only problems to come about in the last ten circles between the two regents were directly related to which wife had the best of everything. He shook his head remembering the last incident of jealousy.

"How is this person causing problems?" Arlyon questioned Kaltyo. "Or rather, I am assuming, just what do the sisters have to do with it this time?"

"At the present time I do not have that particular detail, sire," Kaltyo replied. "I assure you; I am at a total loss. My resources know nothing of this issue, both emissaries arrived late last night. I should also warn you, Luyel is requesting the same judgment."

"Truly?" Arlyon could no longer contain himself as he burst forth with laughter. "How is it two separate regents could find it necessary to send an emissary to me for a judgment and both arrive on the exact same day." Arlyon's eyes twinkled at the prospect of what would transpire. "I must say a wife can certainly, at times, create a situation of enormous size." He remembered his lovely red-haired wife and how she manipulated certain wives to attain special contracts or concessions for him.

Kaltyo smiled at the wry humor. "What I find very interesting is neither regent could bring this third party to justice. Apparently the person appears, causes havoc, then silently disappears, leaving the wounds to heal of their own accord. The claims are of theft, but nothing is stolen. There are rumors of harm, yet not one person has come forward to display damages. There is dissension; wounds if you will, which are not healing, but instead, are festering within the populace. It seems to be there, but not there. It is an enigma, my lord." Kaltyo shook his head.

"Let us have both emissaries in the Judgment Hall. They are both here and they are not an enigma. I shall prepare for them now. In fact, let them stand in the hall while I prepare." Arlyon eyed Kaltyo who knew the meaning. This was not the first time Arlyon had let someone fuss over a judgment while awaiting the king's arrival.

"Until your presence, sire." Kaltyo bowed, turned quickly and disappeared down the corridor. Arlyon entered his personal chamber to prepare for the judgment, a cold chill coursing his spine as he closed the door.

The scream startled him. The sound was quickly followed with yelling and shouting. Arlyon rushed from his chamber and darted quickly down the corridor toward the Judgment Hall. He entered, quickly assessing the chaos — several guardsmen attempted to separate both emissaries as they pummeled each other while tumbling and writhing across the floor of the hall.

Kaltyo was immediately to his side. "Sire," he started while scrutinizing the king who stood before him full stature, barely winded. "The emissaries seem to have started the argumentative portion of the judgment without you." Kaltyo pointed at the two men who were now restrained by the guardsmen. "I hope you have not harmed yourself, sire, in your rush to get here."

Arlyon realized why Kaltyo boldly stared at him. "I am fine." He waved his hand at Kaltyo to cease the conversation. He surveyed the hall. Something was different but he could not put his finger on it. "Let us be about this judgment before there are no emissaries to return a decision. Attend me, Kaltyo." Arlyon lifted his arm and Kaltyo assumed the position to assist in the walk to the throne, all the while frowning at the charade.

Arlyon left Kaltyo at the bottom of the dais as he started up the steps leading to the throne at the top. He moved slowly, reading the names of each region as he ascended. It was a ritual he had started doing since he first was given the throne and steps. It was a time for reflection and thought. There was Luyel, step four from the top; and Boscno on step three. He remembered each of their joining to Adavinya. He reached the top; the great seat sprawled before him, almost ominously. Arlyon turned and faced those in attendance, acknowledged them with a nod, then sat on the red marble throne.

The shadows moved at the edge of his perception, his attention elsewhere. The two emissaries shouted, cursed, proclaimed and promised as they expressed their views, waving their arms about. Arlyon watched them with a detachment. They appeared as nothing more than puppets flailing about without strings. It seemed the men moved as if each were in great pools of water; slowly, gracefully, their voices only a minor drone.

The shadow moved. Arlyon paled.

"Sire," Kaltyo spoke to be heard above the din of the two emissaries' verbal fighting match. "Sire, are you all right?" Arlyon watched as Kaltyo moved quickly towards the throne. All eyes were on them as silence blanketed the chamber.

"I am fine, Kaltyo. I only need a little fresh air. I believe it to be all the excitement of this morning." Arlyon let his head fall forward to rest while massaging his forehead with his right hand. "Let us resume this at a later time, perhaps after the mid-day meal." He lifted his head to look at the two emissaries, their bitter seething obvious at first glance.

"Yes, sire," they replied in unison, each bowing low as they spoke.

Arlyon watched the two men turn and be escorted from the hall. He shook his head and smiled as each man glared at the other through the armed guards surrounding each of them. A light hissing sound reached his ears. He quickly realized their exit was not silent by any means.

The shadow flicked at his left, but he saw nothing. Suddenly, the Luyelan emissary lunged at the Boscnoan dignitary. A quick flurry of commotion and the two men were separated at an even greater distance.

Arlyon stood. "Hold," he said with a loud, growling voice. "You are dignitaries representing your regents. If there is another outburst as such, I shall be forced to send each of you to your opposing regents without a judgment, leaving you to explain the reason. I expect, nay, demand, each of you to show proper respect while in my presence."

The two men fell to their knees groveling in the distance before Arlyon.

"Mighty lord, King Arlyon, I beg forgiveness. I must explain," the Boscnoan emissary seethed while using both arms to direct the attention to the Luyelan delegate, "The Luyelan verbally attacked me with vulgarities."

"Nay, m'lord," the Luyelan said. "I said nothing. It is the Boscnoan who verbally abused me with vulgarities."

"Silence," Arlyon again growled. "As you leave this chamber it will be in total silence. Guards, remove them."

"Sire," the lead guard bowed. He stood between the two emissaries. "May I state I heard no speaking from either delegate." He cast a glare at one, then the other. "I would have silenced them personally."

Arlyon watched as the other attending guards nodded agreement to that which had just been spoken. "Interesting. Acknowledged." Arlyon motioned them out of the hall.

Arlyon turned to Kaltyo who stood motionless, dumbfounded, behind him. "Kaltyo," he said as he lifted his arm for assistance. The hall emptied quickly and quietly.

"Yes, sire," Kaltyo mumbled as he moved forward to assist. "Forgive me, sire," he continued. "I have never seen such. You are truly the man my father described."

Arlyon frowned at Kaltyo. "What do you mean?"

Kaltyo stared into Arlyon's yellow eyes which still were laced with flecks of red fire.

"When you started to speak, your voice... I saw..." Kaltyo stammered then stopped. Arlyon watched as Kaltyo took a deep breath before beginning again. "Your anger, which I have never seen in this magnitude before, brought forth a transformation. I saw a cat, for just an instant. I... Forgive, me, King Arlyon, I babble as a young, foolish maiden."

Arlyon proceeded down the steps of the dais with the assistance of Kaltyo. The silence of the hall deafening as they stopped and Arlyon pretended to rest at the bottom of the dais.

"Anger." Arlyon said. "There was anger throughout the throne room chamber today. I felt the room seemed to be filled with hate, resentment, and anger. Did you not feel it, Kaltyo?"

"Yes, sire. I felt a coldness in the room. It was..." Kaltyo left the sentence unfinished since he could not describe it.

"Did not the coldness pass through like a unfelt wind, touching only your insides?" Arlyon watched Kaltyo's face for an acknowledgment. "I feel we have a foul presence in our midst, Kaltyo. A very foul presence, one which I was forewarned of and have been awaiting. Let us be out of here. I need sunshine, a smile. Help me to Obera. She waits for me."

As they entered the room, Obera sat kneeling on the floor, intent upon some item before her.

"Obera," Arlyon began. "I have returned as promised. Did you have fun while waiting?" He disengaged himself from Kaltyo. "You may leave us," he said, discharging Kaltyo.

The little girl jerked about to face him. "Did you see him? Did he come to the meeting?" Obera jumped up and ran to him.

"Did I see who, Obera?" Arlyon replied. A light scowl crossed his face. "Who was I to see?" Arlyon watched as his granddaughter's face, full of expectation, changed to one of despair.

"It was... it...," she stammered as she looked down at her sandals. "He said he would see you."

"Tell me, Obera, was this the same man you saw dancing earlier? You need not fear me. I saw the black man this morning, also." Arlyon knelt down beside her, grabbed her into his arms and lifted her up as he stood. "Let us go to the divan and talk about this stranger." He carried her across the room. The window behind the divan allowed the morning sunlight to stream in and brighten the chamber. Arlyon glanced out the window. The wind gently moved the tree branches, birds sang and there was the sound of hustle and bustle in the courtyard.

"You say the black man talked with you? He said he was going to come and visit me. Where was he going to visit me? In the Judgment Hall?" He spoke softly as he began the conversation with Obera. He gently placed her on the divan beside him and protectively wrapped his arm about her.

"I don't know, grandfather. I was playing and then he was sitting across from me. We played. He said he had to go and see the king, and he danced out." Obera fiddled with a ribbon on her gown.

Arlyon stared absently into the space in front of him. He felt her head shift against his arm as she looked up at him. Arlyon nodded.

Obera continued to stare at him, he could feel it. "Did I tell you he giggled when he left, grandfather? It was a funny giggle."

"A funny giggle?" Arlyon glanced down and smiled.

She smiled back. "A funny giggle. It was like..." She started an imitation. Arlyon listened as her voice kept getting higher and higher. He could almost hear the maniacal voice of the dark stranger. He felt the chill transverse his spine.

"Who do you think this man is, Obera," he asked his granddaughter. "You have talked with him."

"No." She looked up at Arlyon with innocent eyes. Arlyon glanced at her for such a sudden response. She smiled. "He speaks to me. He dances and he laughs. He is the happy man." Arlyon couldn't help but raise an eyebrow. "Ralson calls him the Black Man. Anea calls him the Dark Man. They can't see my Happy Man. Why?"

"I remember Ralson had a friend when he was near your age. He was the only one who could see and talk to him." Arlyon tried to remember if he had ever heard a description of Ralson's invisible playmate. He had no recollection of such then he started to question if Anea or even if his son, Leear, had had an invisible friend. His mind raced to answer the questions now surfacing.

"Grandfather?" Obera tugged on his sleeve to get his attention. "Grandfather, are you listening to me?"

"Yes, Obera," Arlyon answered. "I was just thinking about your dancing man." He attempted to smile at her as he squeezed her into his chest to reassure, but failed.

"Let us move out into the sunlight of the courtyard." He picked Obera up and tossed her into the air, her exuberant squeal filling the room

"Moreover," he whispered conspiratorially while holding her close, "let us go get Ralson and Anea. We will have a picnic today."

He watched as Obera clapped her hands. "Oh, grandfather, may we go swimming?" she asked as they approached the door to the room.

"Yes, swimming, too," he replied.

Obera burst into the corridor, singing, "A picnic, a picnic." Arlyon followed closely behind and noticed Kaltyo standing to one side of the hall, waiting, raising an eyebrow to the light-spirited walk.

"Sire, I..." Kaltyo started, but Arlyon waved a rejecting hand to him and quickly followed his skipping granddaughter down the corridor to where Ralson and Anea studied in the room.

"A picnic, a picnic." Another small voice echoed mockingly in the corridor. Kaltyo listened, his head slightly cocked in an attempt to ascertain its origin. Shadows moved and a chilling breeze rustled his garments. Then, it was gone.

CHAPTER 3: The Dream

He moves within the dark of night
To play in shadows with no light.
Always present, never there
Cannot be found anywhere.
It is The Other, as foretold
He plots and plans; he moves so bold.
Beware, fair innocence to keep
He steals upon you in your sleep.

from The Ballad of the Fire

He moves so none can see him within the shadows. Some may hear him, some may see him, but only when he decides. The Other slips through world, always hiding in direct view.

"Hurry, grandfather," Obera shouted to Arlyon. "The picnic tree is very near." She raced ahead to the tree marking where once the huts of Adavin originally stood.

Arlyon moved slowly, deliberately toward the children. The walking stick but a ruse to keep the image of being frail for all to see when in public.

"Toss the stick aside," a voice whispered softly in his ear. "You are not of these creatures. Why do you continue?"

Arlyon struck out with the staff, pushing the non-existent being from his side.

"Grandfather!" Obera shouted. "Careful! You may hurt him. He is trying to help you."

"Perhaps he is," Arlyon replied. "Still, I would rather do it myself."

"You lie to your grandchildren and all who know you," the voice whispered again to him. "You don't deserve these creatures."

"Do you deserve them?" Arlyon offered softly in reply.

"Grandfather! Look! The swing!" Anea shouted and ran forward, pushing Ralson to the side in her rush. "Hurry!"

Arlyon nodded his head and continued to trudge toward the tree and picnic grove built around it. He looked over his shoulder at the contingent of three who brought the food and drink for the festivities. Arlyon had hoped Kaltyo would defy him and come along, but his loyal advisor had remained at the castle to keep the emissaries at bay. He shook his head knowing full well he would need to resolve the issues upon his return.

Arlyon stopped short. He suddenly realized what had transpired this morning when the emissaries departed. He now understood what was happening in Boscno and Luyel.

"Push me, grandfather," Obera called. "I want to fly in this swing; to be like a bird high in the sky."

"Allow Ralson to push you, Obera dear," Arlyon replied. "I am old and tired." He sat on the grass and watched the children at play.

Ralson, the ever vigilant, protective older brother pushed Obera higher and higher, but never too high. Then it was a turn for Anea and she went higher than Obera. The three attendees spread out the foodstuffs and finally called the children to eat. The seven of them shared the food, laughing and enjoying the summer afternoon. Arlyon was swept into the moment and suddenly realized he no longer heard The Other whispering or could even see him dancing in the distance.

"Is your Happy Man here, Obera?" Arlyon asked as nonchalant as he could.

"Why, no, grandfather," she replied while casually flipping about the partially devoured chicken leg. "Didn't he tell you? He said he had to go back to the castle."

Arlyon cocked an eyebrow in surprise. "Oh, did he now? When?"

Obera grabbed a cookie and began to nibble then pulled the cookie away. "Oh," she let her eyes roll around in a pretend thought. "Just before we sat down to eat, I suppose."

"Must we endure all this make believe," Ralson asked and pushed his lower lip defiantly out in a pout.

"Why must you always pick on Obera?" Anea said. "Are you jealous just because your imaginary friend doesn't visit you anymore?"

Ralson glared at Anea. The frown was strong and he breathed deeply and slowly. Time passed. "Fine," he blurted. "She can have her friend. I don't need him anymore."

Arlyon glanced at Ralson, intrigued by the response.

"Sire," one of the attendants called and pointed to the path. "Someone approaches."

Arlyon stood and gazed at the lone person who hurried toward them. He recognized the guard; it was the one who had escorted the emissaries out of the Judgment Room.

"King Arlyon," he called, approaching the group. "Kaltyo has requested your presence." He hesitated, breathing deeply to get his breath. His face suddenly flushed red. "I beg forgiveness, my lord. Kaltyo asks if you will return to address an issue that has arisen."

"Immediately," Arlyon said. "We will take the horse and cart so you may rest. The children and attendants may walk back at their leisure." He turned to his grandchildren. "Will you oversee this, Ralson? I put you in charge."

"Yes, grandfather." Ralson pulled himself to full stature, his eyes wide with surprise. "I will make sure Anea and Obera get home safely." He sheepishly looked at the attendants. "With their help, I am sure I can do it."

Arlyon smiled and ruffled the curled locks of hair on Ralson's head. "You walk well in your father's footsteps," Arlyon said. "I will see you at home before the sun sets then. Stay and enjoy the afternoon of play."

The guard was in the cart and held the reigns of the horse as Arlyon stepped up into it. "Please," he said and the guard snapped the reigns. The horse trotted away and he quickly glanced back at the group: three adults, three children and a shifting shadow. Arlyon frowned as he heard the high pitched, maniacal laugh.

"King Arlyon." Kaltyo announced the king's attendance.

Arlyon hobbled into the Throne Room, the walking stick clicking loudly on the marble floor. His golden eyes flicked back and forth, taking in each nuance of the room. The guard had been silent of the event or events requiring his attention. Arlyon wanted to know what awaited him; why he was needed so urgently.

Kaltyo glided across the room to him. Arlyon cocked an eye at his advisor.

"Sire," Kaltyo whispered. "I found the emissary from Luyel..." He hesitated. "He was dead, hanging from a rafter in his quarters I assigned to him. I locked his door, immediately sent for you and told no one."

"Wise, Kaltyo," Arlyon said. "Wise indeed." He peered about the room. "What of Boscno's representative? I don't see him here."

"I also checked on him. He was fine." Kaltyo rolled his eyes. "I told him I was going to lock him in his quarters until your return. He balked at first, but when I explained it was for his own safety, he relented." Kaltyo offered a feeble smile and a shrug.

"Fine," Arlyon said, all the while frowning at his advisor's nervousness. "Bring him here. Perhaps he can shed a view of what has occurred."

Kaltyo fidgeted and hung his head. "My humblest apologies, m'lord." he whispered. "I did not set a guard." He paused. "The Boscnoan emissary is now also dead. In the same exact manner as the Luyelan emissary."

"How peculiar," Arlyon said. "Two emissaries find it necessary to die in the same manner. I have yet to make a judgment."

Kaltyo reached in and pulled two small parchment scrolls from within his robes. "Oddly, they left instructions," he said and handed the scrolls to Arlyon.

Tossing the walking stick aside, Arlyon started up the steps. "Attend me, Kaltyo," he said. "I wish to review these."

Kaltyo quickly assisted Arlyon and they preceded up the stairs. Arlyon sat on the throne and cast a glance at the room, noting those in attendance. He unrolled the first scroll. In clear, legible blue lettering, he read:

> My lord Urial, benefactor of Luyel,
> King Arlyon has ruled against you. I have failed.
> As requested, I give you my life. O.

Arlyon scowled at the wording. No emissary has ever been required to give up his life for a failed bargaining at the king's castle.

"You read this?" Arlyon asked Kaltyo, his free hand tapping the scroll held in the other hand. "Do you understand the implication?"

Kaltyo nodded his head. "Read the other, my lord."

Arlyon let the Luyelan scroll drop to his feet and opened the other scroll. He read the dark green lettering:

> My lord Tazon, benefactor of Boscno,
> King Arlyon has ruled against you. I have failed.
> As requested, I give you my life. P.

Arlyon dropped the scroll and stared at his advisor, his golden eyes searching for some answer, any answer.

"The exact same wording," Arlyon said. "I feel something foul is afoot. I never ruled either for or against them. I still don't know all the truths necessary to judge."

"Lords Tazon and Urial will not accept the deaths easily. I know the Boscnoan emissary has performed his duties for over ten Circles. I am most sure this is not the first time he has received a ruling against his lord."

Arlyon glared up at Kaltyo. "I did not set a ruling."

Kaltyo bowed low. "Forgiveness, m'lord. I did not mean to insinuate you had ruled, only that I am sure Lord Tazon has received ill-favored news before."

"When does my son visit these under-lords?" Arlyon asked, his voice sharp.

"Not until the beginning of the new Circle," Kaltyo replied. "He is first going to the west, to the forest realms, then to the north with the mountain realms where he will pass the Quiet Time and snows. Next Planting Time he will visit the sea realm and nearby realms then return home by Growing Time."

"Fine," Arlyon said. "I will go to Lord Tazon and Lord Urial to clarify these particulars. First, I did not make a ruling. Second, one does not request a death for failure."

A loud giggle reverberated through the chamber.

Arlyon glanced about the gathered attendees but none of them reacted to the sound.

"Did you hear that?" Arlyon whispered to Kaltyo.

"Hear what, sire?"

"Did you not just hear a giggling sound?"

"Nay, sire."

Arlyon pounded his fist on the throne's arm in exasperation.

Again, the giggle echoed and faded away.

Then, in his left ear he heard whispered:

Beware when the sun is double
It is the fall, the start of trouble.

"You didn't hear that, either, did you?" Arlyon snapped, glaring at Kaltyo.

"No, my lord," Kaltyo said and searched Arlyon's eyes for a truth.

Arlyon looked up and watched the dark man dance about while heading for the doors. Arlyon shook his head and slumped forward, catching his forehead in the raised palm of his hand. "It has begun," he whispered to Kaltyo. "The dream is over."

CHAPTER 4: Coronation

The old moves on, the jewels are bound
The lords have gathered, a ruler found
The prophesy filled, as foretold
A cat has dreamed a vision bold

from The Ballad of the Fire

Arlyon looked out over the hall, nodding his approval; all the under-lords and the three over-lords in attendance. He nodded to Lord Tazon and Lord Urial. It had been almost a Full Circle since he had last seen them when he resolved the issue with the dead emissaries. Leear had been advised of the incident and its final outcome before arriving. The sister wives intently watched the other wives to ascertain what the others wore, calculating what they should desire.

What or who Arlyon wanted to see, he couldn't, and it disturbed him. He knew The Other would be present. Each day since the incident with the emissaries, things continued getting more difficult. The Other was pushing a darkness upon Arlyon's reign. The Council of Creation had forewarned him. He now wondered if his was the chosen or if it was destined to fail.

"Princess Obera," Kaltyo announced and Arlyon's mindful wanderings re-focused again on the ceremony at hand.

Obera's entrance was grand. She was a Circle older and appeared no longer the little girl with who he crawled and played on the floor. The crowd moved back to allow her entrance and she glided in with the dignity as trained. Suddenly, she spotted Arlyon on the throne and was a little girl who tromped her way to the bottom of the dais. Arlyon held back a smile.

"Princess Anea," Kaltyo called out and she entered with a nod of her head to those nearby. She regally joined her younger sister and performed her duties with proper decorum.

"Prince Ralson." The words echoed throughout the hall and the young man entered and marched to the front.

He holds himself aloof, perhaps too much, but he is young and still has time to learn, Arlyon thought.

"Her majesty, Crown Princess Triesha and Prince Salzon."

Triesha moved into the procession area and nodded to the assembled lords and ladies. She cuddled Salzon close hoping to keep him asleep. Applauding began which soon swelled to a thundering roar. She held up her hand to stop the noise then quickly put a single finger to her lips. This was Salzon's first appearance in public and the populace was excited. They quickly realized the babe slept and Triesha was endeavoring to keep him that way. The noise abruptly ended and she proceeded into the hall, smiling and thanking those closest to her. She solemnly walked to her place at the base of the dais. King Arlyon sat at the top watching.

Kaltyo soundly stabbed the base of his staff to the floor three times. "The Crown Prince Leear." He bowed, holding the staff upright in the left hand while bringing his right hand to his chest in a large flowing gesture. He was setting the proper action for those gathered to follow.

Lords bowed and ladies curtsied with bowed head.

Leear walked slowly and deliberately toward the dais, all the while keeping his attention on the man at the top of the magnificent throne, his father. He held tucked in the crook of his arm the Scepter of Rule. Leear approached the bottom step of the dais, stopped, then knelt, raising his hands toward his father, offering the scepter in them.

"Father, King Arlyon," he said loudly. "I offer you back the Scepter of Rule. I have completed my assigned journey to visit the lords of Adavinya. As instructed, I have given each over-lord of the three realms a Gem of Rule. The Fire Jewel, a ruby, I gave to Lord Hintos, the Water Jewel, the sapphire, I offered to Lord Saltpe and to Lord Whiton I gave the Earth Jewel, an emerald. If it pleases them, they may return the gems to be replaced in the Scepter of Rule thereby signifying their allegiance to me, their future king."

Arlyon stood and momentarily looked out over the assembly. This would be his last time performing a duty from this position. He was glad, yet there was some remorse. Although he hadn't seen The Other, he knew an appearance was definitely assured.

Upon Leear's return, the first question from Arlyon was if Leear had had an imaginary friend, a dark man, when he was young. Leear had smiled and stated only for the shortest of times. Arlyon kept his face about him and didn't reveal it was of a concern.

Arlyon grabbed the walking stick beside the throne and slowly stepped down, leaving the throne he would no longer approach as monarch. He breathed slowly, but still a tear welled in one eye. He blinked to get rid of it. In his mind he repeated the names of the realms engraved on each of the steps as he slowly walked down them. He stopped in front of Leear and placed his hands on the scepter.

"I accept the Scepter of Rule," Arlyon said then gently took it from Leear's hands. "Arise, my son, and let us call forth the owners of the Gems of Rule."

Leear stood and gazed lovingly at his father. It was a moment he had hoped for, but also feared, for he knew his father was still young and only pretended.

Arlyon put an arm about Leear. "Call forth the first gem, the Fire Jewel," he said.

"Lord Hintos," Leear said loudly. "I call you to attend and show your intention." Leear shifted his footing, suddenly nervous.

"I am Lord Hintos." A gruff voice exploded a few people beyond Leear. "I am lord of oh, Bre! You know what I rule for you, my lord, King Arlyon." He pushed his way to the front. "I offer you my allegiance, sire." He knelt before the two and lifted up the Fire Jewel. The ruby glistened with a burning fire within it.

"I accept your fealty and loyalty to the crown of Adavinya," Leear said, taking the proffered jewel and handing it to his father.

Arlyon placed the jewel in the scepter.

"Call forth the second gem, the Water Jewel," Arlyon said.

"Lord Saltpe," Leear said loudly. "I call you to attend and show your intention." He stretched to see where Lord Saltpe stood.

"At your request, my liege," Saltpe replied and strolled from the back of the room toward them. He dropped to one knee. "Pardon, my lords, but I cannot offer you the Water Jewel."

Silence enveloped the room.

Arlyon narrowed his golden eyes at Lord Saltpe. "Pray tell me, good lord, what is your issue?"

Saltpe lowered his head even lower. "I fear a darkness is falling upon Adavinya. A darkness Prince Leear will not be able to contain, nor control. I do not wish to be in conflict with another realm, nor against you, young prince."

"Lord Saltpe," Leear said. "We discussed this lightly at our first meeting. I have since had time to review your issues and feel you are correct. There is, indeed, a darkness falling upon Adavinya. My father, King Arlyon, is with failing health. We have lived an idyllic life with a minimum of strife between realms. My father has taught me well and I will continue with his rule in his name."

"But what of the darkness, my lord?" Saltpe asked.

"The gods of Bre shall be with us, and together, we will overcome this darkness. I have discovered the darkness and given it a name." Leear looked out over the crowd. "Let this darkness we fear be named The Other and with a name it is no longer an unknown fear."

Arlyon snapped his head to stare at Leear. "Where did you..."

"Later, father," Leear hissed then looked down at the man bowing before him.

"Lord Saltpe," he said. "Look at me. I ask you to have a confidence in me, to allow me your allegiance so we may jointly fight this darkness you so fear. Let us join forces to fight The Other and keep Adavinya safe."

Lord Saltpe reached into a pocket and pulled the blue sapphire out and into the light.

"I offer..." Saltpe hesitated. "I offer you the Water Jewel and my allegiance, Prince Leear." He looked up and smiled at the young man before him.

Leear took the gem and handed it to his father. Arlyon nodded his approval and placed the stone in the scepter.

"Call forth the third gem, the Earth Jewel," Arlyon commanded.

"Lord Whiton, I call you to attend me and show your allegiance."

"My lords," Whiton said hustling then kneeling before them. "I offer you, without hesitation and in full admiration of your skills, Prince Leear, the Earth Jewel. May Adavinya prosper." He held up the large emerald for all to see.

Leear retrieved the gem and handed it to Arlyon.

"Father," Leear said. "As requested, and required, I have been given the Gems of Rule by the Over-lords of Adavinya. Both the Under-lords and Over-lords have agreed and sworn allegiance to me as the new king. We now need the stone that binds."

"Three gems," Arlyon said while lifting the scepter into the air for all to see. "Each jewel represents a realm of Adavinya. Earth. Water. Fire. Three realms, three jewels. There is a fourth gem. The Air Jewel, it rules all the gems."

The Royal Priest moved forward holding the great diamond before him. He knelt and offered it to Arlyon.

King Arlyon held the glittering diamond high above his head for all to see.

"The gem to bind and rule," he said.

The crowd applauded.

Arlyon placed the diamond onto the top of the scepter then held the scepter aloft.

There was cheering among the attendees and applauding.

"I now offer the Scepter of Rule to my son, Crown Prince Leear, to fulfill the obligations of ruler as Adavinya's next king. Do you so accept this responsibility?" Arlyon lowered the scepter and held it out for Leear to take.

Hands trembling and sweaty, Leear reached out to take the scepter.

"I accept," he whispered and bowed his head. He quickly looked up. "I accept," he repeated loudly.

The room burst into hand clapping and loud cheering: King Leear. King Leear.

Arlyon motioned for Leear to ascend to the throne. Leear slowly turned and walked solemnly up the steps of the dais to the throne. Queen Treisha nodded to Ralson and the young prince followed his father up the steps. She followed her eldest son while carrying the youngest son. Anea and Obera followed. Arlyon could feel a tear welling and turned aside so none could see him as he wiped it from his face.

Kaltyo thumped his staff on the floor to gain some semblance of decorum.

"A banquet will be held in the Great Dining Hall in honor of this coronation," he said. "Please move to the hall."

Arlyon nodded to those he passed on his way to the back and out of the Great Hall and back to his chambers. He had not seen The Other. It concerned him. He walked into his room.

"So, the great King Arlyon steps down," the voice said. It was a dark voice, one filled with hate, seething with anger.

Arlyon looked quickly in the direction and saw The Other sitting in a corner, huddling in the shadows there.

"Ah, Obera's dancing fool," Arlyon said. "I have been waiting for you to make an appearance. Why here?"

"And why not?" The Other said. "I waited for you. You did what you set out when the Council of Creation allowed the four of you to go forth. You, of the four, created a regency. If it had been the monkey or bear, I would have had no problem destroying it. But you, my dear fire cat, you chose another creature other than yourself for your regency. A very wily choice and it will give me many Circles of difficult work to destroy."

"Why must you destroy?"

"For every action is there is an exact opposite. You created. I must destroy." He jumped up and danced across the room. "And now

I must start my true work. Remember that which I whispered in your ear?"

"Yes, something about the sun and trouble."

The Other laughed. It was a hearty laugh, not maniacal, but there was danger within it.

"I said to you to beware when the sun is double, it is the start, it is the trouble."

Arlyon yawned. He felt tired and rubbed his temple. "I shall rest and ponder your words, then join in the festivities in the dining hall."

"Yes, dear, dear Arlyon. Rest." The Other whispered with a titter and danced about him.

Arlyon crawled onto the bed and could feel his breathing slow. He wanted to get up, to move, but didn't have the strength. Suddenly, he felt as old as he had been pretending he was. He stretched and growled — a very loud growl. He couldn't remember when last he had felt like that. Arlyon growled one last time and with it, lost his humanity.

A great Fire Cat lay stretched out on the bed, unmoving. The amber hair paled with white age. The magnificent mane of fire now dull reds and gold.

A shadow moved about the walls, a titter haunting the open space.

"My time is now! My time is now!"

Suddenly a bolt of lightning blazed within the room, singeing the walls and smoldering the woodwork. Arlyon disappeared in a shattered twinkling of starry lights and fiery flames.

The Other huddled in an upper corner, seeking shadows and darkness to hide within, afraid.

CHAPTER 5: The Promise

Beware to all when the sun is double,
It is the start, both the fire, the trouble.
The moon of love can touch but one,
And cause all plans to be undone.

from The Ballad of the Fire

And so it was that King Leear ruled almost forty-eight Full Circles before his son, Ralson, who had grown up to be a kind and gentle man, became king. Ralson ruled for forty-five Circles then his son, Aormu, ruled for forty Full Circles. The lineage of King Arlyon, the Cat King, continued for nearly six hundred Full Circles.

The Other would visit the children but the parents were aware of his presence and kept a close watch, at first. The Circles passed and The Other was forgotten since it no longer was seen and the Seasons passed with a blur. Then, one day, The Other decided to visit again.

Adavinya was a peaceful kingdom, there was no strife, no wars, no problem too large that couldn't be easily taken care of.

King Lanfeld came to rule. He was a very gentle man and was of the true blood back to King Arlyon. He ruled Adavinya and the world of Adavinya prospered. The only thing Lanfeld wanted was a child to take his place when the time came for him to journey to the Isle of Forgotten Sleep. Being childless became a burden on his mind and it darkened his thoughts.

At the beginning of each Moon, Lanfeld would approach his advisor to find if his wife was with child. Each Moon was the same and Lanfeld would go to the wizard for any possible assistance. The wizard, Innead, shook his head, sighed reluctantly, yet would concoct another potion to assist Lanfeld in hopes of siring a son.

Today, Innead shook his head, claiming to have no more potions.

"You must have something," Lanfeld shouted. "I am the king. I demand you make a potion for me."

"Sire," Innead whined. "I have tried many very strong potions, and all to no avail. Perhaps, if I were to make a potion for both you and your wife, it would work?"

"So be it," Lanfeld said.

"Also, I will make it twice as strong." Innead looked at Lanfeld. "It may taste bitter," he added and looked nervously about. "I will add a bit of citrus to help cut the bitterness. You could take it during an evening meal, sharing it with the queen."

"I said, so be it," Lanfeld snarled. "Now, get to work." Lanfeld slammed his hand down on the table, knocking over several vials and pushing a box of limion powder to the floor. "Do it!"

Innead nodded agreement and wondered at the king's sudden streak of abusiveness. He had never seen the king this distraught before.

Lanfeld stormed out of the wizard's room and hastened down the hallway to the Throne Room. Judgments awaited and he really didn't want to perform that particular duty right now.

"King Lanfeld," Aubrea announced and stamped his staff on the floor. "Rise for judgment all who wish such."

"I have a headache," Lanfeld said. "I will not pass judgment today. Come back another time."

Lanfeld waved his hand in the air to dismiss them, turned and walked out of the hall.

"Sire," Aubrea cried after him. "These people await your judgment. Even more will be in attendance tomorrow."

"Petty complaints," Lanfeld spat. "They are but mere peasants with no mind of their own. Must I make all their decisions? Who is there to help me? Where do I go to find judgment?"

Lanfeld stormed down the hallway toward his room where, he was sure, he would find his wife lingering on a lounge with a book or perhaps, she might be outside by the fountains. He hoped the latter.

"My dearest Miasi," Lanfeld started, holding an empty fork in his hand. "I hate to once again breach the subject, but are you not closely approaching your time for conception?"

Miasi looked up from her plate where she had been playing with the vegetables, pushing them back and forth. Her stomach churned and she knew he was right. It was the reason she didn't want to eat too much.

"Yes, my lord," she whispered. "Very close."

He looked up and across the table at her. The candles burned brightly to highlight her face and soften her features. She looked exactly as she did the night he asked her hand in marriage, and he thought would fulfill his dreams of a family. Lanfeld carefully moved the items on the table so there was a clear view between them.

"I have spoken with Innead, again," he said softly. "He has given me a potion for us to take together to aid us in our endeavor to produce an heir." He reached down by his foot and grabbed the flask sitting there. He placed it on the table. "He made it twice as strong and this time both of us are to consume its contents."

"Dear Lanfeld," Miasi said. "I love you dearly, but my stomach pains me tonight and I fear consuming one of Innead's concoctions..." She left the sentence unfinished.

"One last try, my love," Lanfeld whispered and poured the contents of the flask into two goblets. "Would you not like to hear the patter of small feet?"

Miasi smiled and nodded her head. Lanfeld stood and carried the two goblets to her end of the table. He offered her one. They held the drinks into the air in a toast, then drank. Two gulps down and Miasi coughed and choked on the potion.

"Ugh!" she sputtered. "This is disgusting."

Lanfeld agreed and stood there while chills coursed through his body. Finally, he took her goblet and placed the two on the table.

"Innead said he would flavor it with citrus," Lanfeld said. "I don't think he did and I will speak with him first thing tomorrow morning."

"Lanfeld," Miasi whispered. "You are almost forty Circles old. Do you not think perhaps we are beyond the age of having children?" She softly grabbed his hand and caressed it gently with her lips. "I love you dearly, my love. Have you considered another to whom you may give the throne?"

Lanfeld stared at Miasi in disbelief before shaking his head. "I can not," he said. "Have you any idea how many Circles have passed since King Arlyon first established this ruling? Should I shame myself and my line by having no offspring?"

"Then come," Miasi said, pulling him to the hallway and their chamber. "Perhaps tonight will be fruitful. May the gods smile on us tonight and all your worries and troubles will be answered." She tugged on his hand, pulling him toward the bed. "Love me tonight," she whispered into his ear. "Tomorrow is a new day."

Lanfeld paced the hallway outside his bed chamber. Once more Miasi screamed from the other side of the door. He had watched her over the Moons as the child within her grew. They were happy for the baby would be born in the Moon of No'Dva, a full Moon before Nos'Nevel. They would have the child's presentation during the Nos'Nevel celebration. Lanfeld was ecstatic until he heard Miasi scream, again. He didn't realize childbirth would be this difficult for her.

"You have a son," the maiden said as she opened the door. She bowed and scurried down the hall away from the king.

Lanfeld frowned with concern as he thought she had too much blood on her. Suddenly, the maiden was back and hustled into the room, quickly shutting the door behind her.

Miasi screamed. Lanfeld turned back to the door. Miasi screamed again, but it ended abruptly. He could no longer take the mystery. He approached the door and was about to demand entrance when it opened and the physician came out.

"Miasi is weak, my lord. The births were hard on her." He wiped his hands on a towel and seemed unconcerned.

"And my son?" Lanfeld asked then paused. A frown crossed his face. "Births? Does he live?"

"Yes, sire," the physician replied. "Both of your sons are alive. I have never heard such a thing before. Never has a woman delivered multiple children. It is so uncanny; they are almost exactly alike." He leaned back against the wall and rapped on the door.

A maiden came out with a boy wrapped in towels.

"This is your first-born, King Lanfeld," the physician said. "Note the small birthmark above the right eyebrow. It will probably go away as the child grows older, maybe by the time six or seven Circles have passed. Have you a name, my lord?"

"His name is Raliton," Lanfeld said as he examined the cat-like birthmark.

Another maiden came out with the second baby.

"This is your other son, my lord," the physician said. "Raliton's twin brother. What shall his name be?"

Lanfeld shrugged. "I've not considered a second name." He waved his hand absently in the air. "Call him Lornear," Lanfeld replied. "Is there a birthmark on him?"

"No, my lord," the physician said. "Only Raliton has the birthmark. Call it an indication of his birthright."

A movement caught Lanfeld's eye and he watched a strange man, almost a shadow, dance down the hallway. He could hear giggling. Whispered words caught his ear... *when the sun is double.*

CHAPTER 6: Siblings

The sons are two as prophesy foretold
One is gentle, kind; the other mean, bold.
Raliton smiles, his eyes so blue
Lornear fumes, eyes a darker hue

from The Ballad of the Fire

Lanfeld stepped forward and gathered his two sons to him, holding them close, one in the crook of each arm. He stared down at the two babies and a tear welled in his eye, happy that he not only had one heir, but two.

"The great Cat King, Arlyon has smiled upon his descendant." Lanfeld swayed about the chamber, moving with glee. "Not only do I have one son, but I have two. Two identical sons, how fortuitous." Lanfeld smiled at Raliton, proud of his first-born who would reign when the time came. He turned his gaze to Lornear with concern, but shrugged off the thought.

"Please," one maiden pleaded. "I must return the babies so they suckle."

"Yes, yes," Lanfeld said. "Here, take them both." He handed the boys to the two maidens and looked at his physician. "Is my wife okay?"

"She rests," the elder doctor replied. "It was a very difficult birthing and she will need to rest for many days to gain her strength back. Obviously, you have a nurse to suckle Raliton, have you another nurse for the second son?"

Lanfeld frowned.

"I will have one sought out immediately," the physician said.

"Yes, yes," Lanfeld said absently as something niggled at his memory. "Do take care of that." Lanfeld motioned everyone from the room, placed a finger to lips in thought, turned and ambled the hallway to Innead's chamber.

"Are you sure you're up to this, my dear?" Lanfeld gazed at his wife who still failed to have color to her cheeks. He carried Raliton while a nurse followed with Lornear.

"Yes," Miasi sighed. "I am quite capable of moving about now. You mustn't worry about me as you do. The nurses have been very helpful."

"I realize that," he said. "It is just... there is the celebration of Nos'Nevel and the presentation of our son."

"I do not intend to participate by joining the crowd in the streets during Nos'Nevel." Miasi stood, her arm stretched out to the corridor wall, holding herself upright. "Standing on a balcony for a few minutes as the populace view our sons — that I can endure."

Lanfeld smiled at Miasi and reached out to clutch her free hand close to his heart. "A better wife or queen I could not have chosen." He kissed the back of her hand and smiled at the babe in his arms. "And with Raliton, my son, the crown prince, my life is complete."

"Don't forget Lornear," Miasi lightly scolded. "You have two sons, not one."

"True, my dear, but only one will follow in my footsteps to rule Adavinya and that will be Raliton, the first born."

Miasi frowned. "Will you not have Lornear taught in the ways of leadership? Will he be cast to the side?"

Lanfeld stopped and stared at his wife. "Lornear will be trained just as Raliton," he said. "They are both my sons and will share equally my rule." He hesitated. "But it must be understood, Raliton will be king. He is first born, and it is therefore his birthright."

"My lord is a wise man," Miasi said. She gazed at the floor with trepidation. "I fear this will not fare well as the boys mature."

They stood in front of the curtains leading to the balcony. Lanfeld nodded and the drapes were drawn and they stepped into the sunlight of the balcony. The populace below exploded into a roar of cheering.

Lanfeld stood beside Miasi watching the crowd then raised his hand for silence. The noise subsided to a murmur. He stepped forward from Miasi.

"I present to you, Raliton, Heir Apparent, the Crown Prince of Adavinya," Lanfeld shouted aloud and held the young babe above his head for all to see.

Lanfeld lowered the child and held him close. He turned to Miasi. She took Lornear from the nurse and held the child close to her bosom.

"I present to you, Lornear, Prince of Adavinya," Lanfeld said loudly and with a graceful sway of his arm and hand, acknowledged Miasi who held Lornear.

Miasi smiled but was troubled by the presentation of Lornear — Lanfeld had not held him to accept the younger child as his son or royalty.

"This afternoon," Lanfeld said. "I will join in the opening celebration of Nos'Nevel and my sons will join me."

"It is mandatory I ride my stallion to the opening ceremony," Lanfeld yelled. "Exactly how am I to carry two babies?"

"Perhaps the young princes could be carried in a litter behind you, my lord," an advisor suggested.

"My father carried me on his horse until time I could ride my own," Lanfeld said. "I expect no less of me. I shall carry Raliton with me. Take Lornear back to his mother."

"My lord, perhaps if we..."

Lanfeld glared down at the advisor and the words ceased. "I have spoken," Lanfeld said. "Raliton will ride with me. He is the Heir Apparent. There are no other choices."

Lanfeld snapped the reigns and the white stallion trotted off. The rest of the staff hustled about to join him: litters, horses and wagons quickly followed. They wound themselves through the narrow avenues to the Picnic Courtyard, a large expanse of lawn set aside by Princess Obera many Circles ago where legend claimed King Arlyon first appeared. King Lanfeld rode his horse to the large obelisk and watched as the rest of the entourage slowly joined him

"Today is the first day of Nos'Nevel. I, with my son, Raliton, now officially open the celebration. Let planting be done as we prepare for the Growing Time."

A wind blew casually across the low knoll Lanfeld was on. He shivered and immediately brought his robe up and around Raliton to ward off any chills the baby may have.

Lanfeld looked and a chair had been set up for him. He dismounted the horse with Raliton in his arms and walked over to the chair. Lanfeld sat, holding Raliton proudly in his lap.

Immediately an older woman approached with a small box. "A gift for the young princes, my lord. I hope it pleases Raliton and Lornear."

Lanfeld nodded and politely dismissed her. Others followed and the gifts piled. Lanfeld leaned down to Raliton. "Look, son, so many gifts for you."

"You dare to snub my youngest son?" Miasi screamed. "Today was his presentation also and yet you only saw fit to take Raliton."

"What do you expect of me," Lanfeld replied. "I could only carry one on the horse."

"Horse, bah," she sneered. "You only care about Raliton. If we were to have twenty more children you would care naught for them, only Raliton."

"Raliton is my first born. It is his right."

"Lornear is only moments younger. He is your son, also."

"Only one will rule," Lanfeld snapped. "Enough of this. I'll hear no more."

Lanfeld stormed from the room leaving Miasi to weep alone. The nurses waited patiently until they thought it the best time to enter Miasi's chambers. Both Raliton and Lornear were brought to her. She grabbed Lornear and held him close.

"I fear your life with will be one with strife, dear Lornear," she whispered. "Raliton is first born and although you are almost his equal, you will never be him."

Miasi broke down and cried some more. The nurses took the babies and left the room. They realized now was not the time.

"Bring me my sons," Lanfeld demanded. "If I am to sit in judgment, I wish my sons to be brought up with the full understanding of their duties." He sighed and grimaced. "It is the least I can do to appease Miasi."

His advisor bowed and while he held his head down, he frowned, wondering at the words spoken. "As you wish," he said and motioned for the king's wishes to be executed.

Nurses hustled in with the babies. Lanfeld took the two boys and held one on each side of his lap, letting them watch the proceedings of judgment. The nurse stepped back and lingered in the shadowed recesses, waiting.

"Now bring me the first case to hear," Lanfeld said loudly.

Lornear whimpered and Lanfeld nervously jiggled his leg under the baby in an attempt to appease it. Lornear seemed to be nodding off to sleep.

"My lord," the man said. He stood at the bottom of the steps, a tattered hat in hand and head bowed. "I beg your kindness and forgiveness. I have taken a partridge from your woods."

"Can you return said bird?" Lanfeld asked.

"No, my lord. My family feasted for two days on it."

"Two days? One small partridge? How can this be?"

The man dropped to one knee. "I have a small family, my lord. My wife and two children. We ate one meal of it, my wife made a porridge with a part of the leftover and the remainder she made a broth to serve over bread."

"Three meals? Perhaps I should have your wife serve in my kitchen to show them how to fix such meals with so little. Have her attend the cook tomorrow and I will forgive your transgression."

"Thank you, my lord." The man stood up and Lanfeld could see the tears in his eyes.

"Tell me," Lanfeld said. "Why do you cry. You have not been harmed."

"They are tears of joy, sire. I was told you would probably have one of my hands removed so I could never poach another partridge from your woods."

"Why, pray tell, would I condemn such a thing upon a subject?"

Lornear awoke and cried. The wail echoed within the hall.

"No!" Lanfeld yelled, grabbing the babies and standing up. "Lornear!"

The nurses fluttered forward and grabbed the babies and Lanfeld stood there, a wet spot spreading on his left lap side where Lornear had been cradled.

"Judgment is canceled today." Lanfeld yelled. He glared at the man cowering at the foot of the dais. "Your wife — to the cook, tomorrow."

Lanfeld stormed down the steps and to the back of the hall. He turned to the crowd.

"No children allowed in this hall from this date forward unless they can walk and control themselves. *That* is my final judgment of this day. I have spoken."

Lanfeld's robes billowed in the air as he whipped around and stomped out of the chamber.

From a corner near the top of the dais, a shadow moved and formed. A dark man danced merrily. "It is the start..." he sang, then giggled.

CHAPTER 7: The Rivalry Begins

The Other speaks and Lornear learns
The heart it darkens as it burns
Riddled words to a mind so young
Uncontrolled rage, the meaning stung
Raliton to rule, Lornear will not
A chance a fate, the second's lot

from The Ballad of the Fire

Lanfeld watched from a window above the open area where two young men worked through their sword lessons. Raliton regarded the opponent and parried accordingly. Lornear pushed, forcing his action with abandon upon his opponent, Raliton.

"Lornear," the instructor yelled. "Study your opponent. Move slowly. Learn their weaknesses and use that to your advantage. Why must you continue with brute force? Raliton studies his opponent, thinking through his actions."

"Fine," Lornear screamed and threw the sword to the ground. "Ral can learn what he needs to rule. Allow him to train with one of the puny peasants whom he will rule. I will rule as I see fit if, and when the time comes."

The eldest twin, Raliton; thoughtful.

Lornear, the younger twin. Always slighted.

"Lor," Raliton called. "Bamear only meant you need to step back and watch my moves to use against me."

"If I wanted," Lornear said. "Trust me, dear brother, I could have harmed you at any moment."

Lornear stormed across the courtyard to the archway.

"And father," he screamed up to the window. "I know you are watching. You always watch and it matters not what I do, I will never please you." He thrust a fist at the window. "Twenty Circles have taught me that."

"Lor," Raliton called again. "Please stay."

"I have better things to do with my life than be your teaching aid on how to be a king," Lornear spat, turned and entered the darkened archway leading to the stables.

"My prince," the stableboy said. "I did not know you would be riding today."

"I ride every day, idiot," Lornear said. "If my horse, Nightfire, is not ready, then make it so — and quickly." He waggled his hand to dismiss the boy.

The stable boy hastened about getting the tack, bridle, reins, saddle and other gear necessary.

"Are you napping?" Lornear asked, leaning into the stable and wrinkling his nose. "I need to ride, now." Lornear pulled back into the light, wrinkling his nose while turning his head away. "Ugh! The stench."

"I am doing this as fast as possible, my lord." A few moments of silence ensued. "Here is Nightfire." The stable boy lead the dark stallion out of the stable.

Lornear mounted his steed and looked down at the boy. "Two items. First, clean this stable immediately after my departure. It reeks." He wrinkled his nose again and then tapped it twice to reinforce his words. He sat there a few seconds viewing the open area. "And tomorrow, I want my horse ready when I get here. Is that understood?" He looked down at the young boy again with as much disdain as he could muster.

"Yes, my lord," the stable boy said and hung his head. "As you command."

"Fine." Lornear held the reins in one hand and swatted the stallion to bolt forward. Pushing the spurs into the sides, the horse gained more momentum and soon Lornear was galloping through the narrow avenues of the village, startling the peasants.

"Out of my way," he yelled and continued until he finally was in the open field beyond the walls.

He pulled the horse up to a stop and glanced around, deciding which way to go. He spied Obera's Obelisk and saw his friend, the dark man, dancing wildly around it.

"Well, Nightfire, it would appear our decision of where to go has been made."

He nudged the horse forward toward the obelisk.

"You there," Lornear said, motioning to the dark man. "Why must you always be dancing?"

"Ah, my dear prince." The Other turned and bowed to the prince. "I dance because I am happy."

"And why, pray tell, are you happy?"

The Other danced a little jig and once more bowed. "I do what I wish to do." He cocked his head and gazed at the prince. A smile slowly crept to his lips. "I know what I know." The Other once more began to dance.

"Oh?" Prince Lornear leaned in conspiratorially. "What do you know?"

The Other stopped dancing and appraised Lornear. He leaned against Obera's Obelisk, folding his arms in front of his chest.

"We have discussed so much over the passing Circles, my dear prince. Did you not listen to what I said?" He cocked an eyebrow and smiled. He placed an index finger to his lips. "What do I know? I know you will follow me."

"And if I don't?"

"But you will, Prince Lornear," The Other replied and started a two-step skip away from the obelisk and toward the forest. "You *will* follow me."

Lornear shook his head and snickered aloud. "Silly man," he said.

He watched the dark man continue toward the forest when suddenly he realized he had spurred Nightfire into action and was, indeed, following.

"Why are we going into the forest?" Lornear asked.

"Because I want to," The Other replied. "Also to show you something." Once more he held a single finger to his lips. "I know the secret."

"You intrigue me, funny man," Lornear said. "I will follow only to appease my curiosity. What secret do you know?"

"You will follow because I said you will," The Other countered and moved into the shadows of the trees. "Listen to my voice and follow."

"Why can't I see you? Where did you go?" Lornear and Nightfire entered the shadowy trees of the forest without hesitation.

"Listen to my voice."

Lornear could hear the man, he had to be directly in front of him, no less than twenty strides.

"Show yourself, immediately!" Lornear scanned the darkened woods.

"Tut, tut, my dear prince," The Other said. "Now, follow my voice."

Lornear looked to the right, that was where the voice had come from. He pulled the reins and Nightfire shifted right.

"Where are you now?"

Lornear pushed a branch away then turned in the saddle to look behind. He couldn't see the forest's edge. He had entered much deeper than he realized.

"Not much further. I am waiting," The Other taunted.

Lornear realized the voice was distant and had to be nearly fifty strides ahead of him.

"Are we there?" he asked.

"You are almost there, Prince Lornear," the voice replied, mocking him. "Do you see the opening in front of you?" There was a pause. "You can't miss it."

"Yes, I see it." Lornear spurred Nightfire to a fast trot.

Lornear and Nightfire stepped between the trees into the open area. Sunlight flooded the glade. In the middle was a sparkling pool of water.

"There you are," Lornear said, noting the dark man sitting by the pool. "Why did you hide from me?"

The Other giggled. "A simple question. A simple answer. Shadows only exist where there is light."

"Another riddle for me?" Lornear asked.

"No," The Other replied while shrugging. "You wanted an answer."

"Why are we here? What is this pool?"

Lornear dismounted and let the reins of Nightfire drop to the ground. The pool called to him with its shimmering highlights. He walked to its edge.

"This is the Pool of Truth," The Other said. "What do you see?"

Lornear stared down into the clear waters, into the blue depths. There was something beyond the sparkling shimmer of waves. A spark, then it wavered. The waves settled and the pool was like a mirror. Suddenly he saw an image in the reflection — a young maiden.

"She is beautiful," Lornear whispered. "Who is she?"

The Other giggled. "That is Enyra. She will find your looks to her liking."

"She will be my mate." It was not question but a statement. "Where does she live?"

"In Adavin, my prince. In Adavin."

"Why have I never seen her?" Lornear demanded and glared at The Other. "I have seen all the maidens of Adavin." He frowned. "Have I not?"

The Other giggled and curled in on himself, lowering his eyes.

"You do not treat a precious rose as you would pluck a common daisy." The Other whispered conspiratorially. "Now would you?"

Lornear's eyes flared. "You mock me?"

"Not I," said The Other. "This is the pool's image." The Other nodded to the reflection. "The pool's truth to you. Ask it a question."

Lornear stared down at the waters. They swirled, the image disappearing and then it was once more a pool, shimmering in the sunlight.

"Show me where she lives," he demanded loudly.

Once more the waters swirled, settled and became mirror-like. Lornear stared at his reflection in the water. He frowned but the reflection did not.

"The pool shows what it wants to show — not what you ask." The Other tittered. "But I know. Remember? I told you I know. I know the secret."

"Ah, the secret," Lornear said. "What is the secret?"

"Enyra's father is a jeweler."

"A jeweler?" Lornear stared The Other. "Where?"

"In Adavin, of course. You passed by it on your way out today."

Lornear turned from the pool, raced to his horse and mounted.

"Why must you riddle me. Are you not my friend?"

"With you, Lornear, longer than most." The Other giggled again, this time his voice carried a tone Lornear had not heard before. A tone which made Lornear nervous.

"Silly man," Lornear said and turned his horse to race out of the forest. "Fifty strides then left." he thought. "There was a stone, then maybe one hundred strides and another left."

Lornear looked about. There was no opening, only the dark of the forest.

"Silly man, am I?" The Other tittered. "Find your way out, if you can."

CHAPTER 8: Enyra

She finds his looks to her appeal
A pool has spoken, a done deal.
The appearance is twice, with twins
The Other has spoken and grins
A lie and a truth are entwined
Within the dual lives combined

from The Ballad of the Fire

Raliton paced the parapet until sunset's final light was gone. Lornear had not returned. He quickly hastened to Lanfeld's quarters where he discovered his father sitting at the edge of the window, staring blankly into the night sky.

"Father," he pleaded. "My brother has not returned and I fear for his life. He was angry with me when he left."

"Lornear is a grown man, Raliton," Lanfeld replied. "He has probably found himself a plaything and drunken himself into a stupor. With his actions, I am still amazed none have come forward to claim a royal lineage."

"Father, I fear although you believe him to be sitting in a tavern, I do not. He rode his horse out of the castle and village." He hung his head. "I have asked guards to keep an eye on him. He rode to Obera's Obelisk then into the forest."

"You set a guard to spy on your brother? Do you have one on your father and mother, also?"

"No, father. I set a guard to watch over my brother only. He lingered near the village, watching Lornear at the obelisk until my brother entered the forest. He then hastened to catch up to him but found no path to follow in the forest. *That* is what my guard informed me."

"Interesting, Raliton," Lanfeld said while tapping his lower lip and noticed a shadow waver in the corner. He hesitated. "You were wise to watch over your twin. You have learned your lessons better than I had hoped. Keep your friends and family close, your enemies closer."

"Lornear is family, father. He is not my enemy." He walked to the window and glanced out at the darkness of the courtyard below. Only a lone torch flickered near the stable archway.

Lanfeld cocked an eye to his son. "Do you think Lornear is not your enemy?"

"He is my brother. I trust him with my life, father."

"Then you haven't learned a thing, Raliton," Lanfeld said. "Lornear is your twin brother, your younger brother by birth — not in Circles, but in heartbeats. He desires the rule. Did you not hear what he told you? That is a threat."

"Lornear was angry," Raliton replied then heard the clatter of hooves on stones from the courtyard below. He watched out the window.

A stable boy came quickly with a torch and grabbed the reins of Nightfire. He placed the torch on the opposite side of the stable archway and glanced up at the window where Raliton stood. Raliton nodded.

Lornear stomped toward the castle then stopped and turned to the stable boy.

"Remember, tomorrow I ride and I want my horse ready. I do not expect to wait. Am I understood?"

The stable boy nodded his head in silence.

"Idiot," Lornear mumbled and stomped into the castle.

Raliton turned to his father. "Lornear is now back. I want no further discussions like we have had this night." He glanced at his father. "Understood?"

"As you wish, my son," Lanfeld replied.

Raliton strode to the door and left.

The shadow moved and dissipated, but didn't leave.

"Today is a good day," The Other whispered in Lanfeld's ear. "I have put brother against brother and now son against father." He giggled. "It is too easy."

"Lornear," Raliton called. "Where have you been all day? I was worried."

The younger twin stopped then glared at his older brother. "Sorry." Turning away, he stomped a few steps then stopped again. "You want to know where I have been? I'll share a secret with you. I have seen my future, my true love. She is the jeweler's daughter."

"Enyra?" Raliton asked.

"How do you know her name?" Lornear asked, stepping closer with a clenched fist. "Have you met her?"

"Of course, Lornear," Raliton said. "I followed you shortly after you left. Your departure was not that difficult to trail. You destroyed the jeweler's one table he had set up when you kicked it with your foot as you left the city."

"I will go and apologize tomorrow," Lornear said with a guilty look, head slightly down.

"There is no need. I've already made amends for you."

Lornear eyes flared wide and his head snapped up. "I said I would. You don't need to do anything for me. I am quite capable of handling issues myself."

"It is just..."

"No," Lornear yelled, his voice echoing in the hall. He turned and headed to his quarters.

Lornear left the castle early, the stable boy having his horse ready for him. He rode slowly and carefully down the narrow streets of Adavin. He knew where the jeweler lived. He'd had a necklace made for his mother's birthday a few Circles back. Nightfire slowly clopped his way through the streets, all the while, Lornear gently shifted back and forth to the rhythm, watching the peasants as he passed them.

"Good morning, Prince..." they would stare a moment before continuing. "Lornear." He was sure they were using the horse as a guide since it was common knowledge Prince Raliton Road a red roan and Lornear the black.

He spotted the sign: Aldiar's Stones and Gems. Below it, an elderly man was tinkering with a small table.

"Jeweler," Lornear called. "I have come to make amends for my transgression yesterday."

The old man turned to face the prince and upon seeing him, immediately lifted his hands to protect himself as the horse was almost upon him.

"Nightfire," Lornear chastised. "Be good."

The old man bent his head and bowed. "My lord," he said. "I am Aldiar, at your service." Straightening up, Aldiar placed a steadying hand on the table.

"I am told my anger of yesterday destroyed your table," Lornear said and walked to the new table with necklaces, bracelets and other polished stone items. He picked up a necklace of red granite with a delicate leather strapping. "Did I damage any of your goods?"

"No, my lord," Aldiar replied. "Your brother replaced the broken table. All is fine."

Lornear could hear the waver in the old man's voice. It was fear, not age. Suddenly, a movement in the window caught his eye, and there she was, Enyra. He looked directly at her and she smiled. She smiled then lowered her head but not before Lornear had returned the smile.

**Enyra, chosen of both Raliton and Lornear.
Daughter of the jeweler, Aldiar.**

"Prince Raliton," Enyra said, coming through the doorway. "You visit us again."

Lornear's eyes flared wide and his face darkened in temper. Aldiar grabbed his daughter's hand to stop her. Lornear controlled himself.

"I am Prince Lornear," he said. "Raliton is my older brother."

"I beg forgiveness, my lord prince," Enyra said. "I have mis-spoken your name." She hung her head in shame.

Lornear reached out and cupped her chin gently and lifted her face to look at him again.

"With one as beautiful," he said. "You never need beg my forgiveness. To be in your presence is my blessing."

Enyra blushed, pulling away from Lornear's grip to hide it. "You are very kind, Prince Lornear," she said then gazed at him, searching for anything to mark him different from Raliton. She found none.

The silence continued until Aldiar coughed to clear his throat. "You have a lovely choice in your hand, my prince. Do you wish to keep it?"

"It pales to Enyra's beauty," Lornear said, holding the necklace up to her pale skinned neck and auburn hair. "I will, indeed, take it." He snapped the necklace into his palm's grasp. "Will three gold marnas cover the expense?"

"My lord," Aldiar replied. "One marnas and a silver han will be more than sufficient."

"Three gold marnas it is then," Lornear said and dropped the coins in the old man's hands. "One other request I have, jeweler." He strode to Nightfire and mounted, noting the other peasants who now watched the discussion between him and the jeweler.

"Anything, my prince," Aldiar said.

"May I have your lovely daughter, Enyra, go riding with me this afternoon? We will go to Obera's Obelisk, no further." He looked to Enyra. "You do ride a horse?"

"I do not, my lord prince," Enyra replied. She hung her head, searching the cobble stones of the street.

"I will have a litter brought for you," Lornear offered. "Will that be satisfactory?"

Enyra nodded.

"Begging the prince's pardon," Aldiar said. "She has another obligation and cannot go today."

Lornear sat up in his saddle and frowned. He was amazed one would deny his request. He studied the old man. The two of them, father and daughter, stood there gazing at the street.

"Perhaps tomorrow?" Lornear asked. He was not about to be put off. He had seen her face in the Pool of Truth and knew she found his features appealing.

"She will be waiting, my lord prince," Aldiar said and scurried her into the building. "An honor, sire."

Enyra, with head bowed ever so slightly, peeked through the doorway at the young man on the black horse and smiled.

"Ask her," the voice whispered in his ear.

Lornear shook his head to dismiss The Other. He was with Enyra, the sun was shining and the late afternoon snack had been pleasant. They had laughed and run about the park, finally to rest under a big tree, leaning against its rough bark and enjoying the cool breeze flowing about them.

"I love Ge'Dva," Enyra said. "Next Moon will be Ge'Nom and then Nos'Hanlah will be celebrated. The fields are growing fine and Nos'Hanlah will be a wonderful celebration this Circle."

Lornear frowned. He had wanted to bring up the subject of Nos'Hanlah but was unsure.

"Ask her," the voice whispered then tittered. "Ask her about yesterday. You want to know. Remember — I know."

Lornear waved a hand past his ear.

"Do you have an ear ache, Prince Lornear?" Enyra asked. "You have fiddled with that ear a lot today." She watched him. "And shaken your head, too."

"It is nothing," Lornear said. "May I ask permission from your father for you to attend Nos'Rovlah with me?"

It was ever so slight but Lornear caught it. Enyra froze.

"I have been asked by another," she whispered. "I am sorry."

"Ask her about yesterday," The Other whispered once more in his ear then appeared suddenly in front of them.

Lornear quickly glanced at Enyra, but she didn't seem to see him. The dark man danced about them and then tip-toed near to Enyra and put his face directly in front of hers.

"She is a lovely one, is she not, my sweet prince?"

"Go away," Lornear blurted.

Enyra stared at him in total shock. "If you wish, my lord," she said and got up. Her hand went to her face and Lornear was sure she was brushing a tear from her eye.

"Not you, Enyra," he yelled after her. Finally, he got up and ran behind her when he realized she was not coming back.

Enyra climbed into the litter. "Take me home," she shouted. The attendants lifted the litter from the ground where it rested.

"Enyra, wait." Lornear called. "Halt!" he demanded and the bearers stopped immediately. "I was not speaking to you," he said to her as he sat on the litter's edge. "My outburst was for another."

"But, Lornear," she said. "We were alone, just you and I. Are you mad at me for having another escort me to Nos'Hanlah?"

"No," Lornear said. "I was surprised. I didn't realize others were already courting you."

Enyra closed her eyes and lowered her head. "I shouldn't say this but I have five other gentlemen courting me."

"Are they more attractive than I?" Lornear asked.

Enyra edged beside Lornear and dangled her feet over the litter's edge. She smiled at the prince.

"There is one who might be," she giggled. "But I must wait and see what comes of it. I have only just been allowed to court by my father. He has been very strict."

"A wise man, indeed," Lornear said and leaned in to her.

"No," she said pulling away. "I must not. I think we should call today finished. I have another obligation this evening."

"Ignore it. If you want," Lornear sighed. "There are still a few berries and pastries we could nibble on."

"I know." The Other danced about, clapping his hands. "I know. Ask her."

Lornear sighed deeply then filled his chest with air as he breathed in a long breath. "Yesterday," he started. "I asked you to ride and your father declined. Why?"

"Yesterday afternoon I was with another suitor," she replied.

"So, I have my competition already set," he said. "Tell me his name so I might know my adversary."

"Yesterday was..." she hesitated. "Tonight, I dine with Under-lord Bartush's son, Methiol."

"And yesterday?" Lornear queried with a smile. "You avoid my question."

"Yesterday," she said. "Yesterday, I was courted by your brother, Prince Raliton. We spent the afternoon with my father, eating dates and nuts while we played varied dice games."

"My brother?" Lornear yelled and jumped from the litter. "You were with Raliton? What game do you and your family play with the royal family?"

"None, Prince Lornear," Enyra said and glared at the young prince. "Take me home," she said to the bearers. She glared at

Lornear. "Your manners need work, my prince. You were very rude, but I thank you for an otherwise pleasant afternoon. Good day, Prince Lornear."

Lornear watched the litter move back to the village. He seethed in anger, all the while The Other jumped and danced about in glee.

CHAPTER 9: Nos'Hanlah

To celebrate the summer's end
A festival, near forest glen
The Other moves, his plot thickens
True love shows it is ill-stricken
Beneath the guise of what appears
The truth unknown until it clears

from The Ballad of the Fire

Lornear stormed into the chamber, stopping when he was less than one stride from Raliton. The older brother held his ground.

"You are my brother, my blood, yet you deceived me," Lornear said.

"Regarding what, Lornear?"

"Upon my return the other night I told you of Enyra. Today I find you courted her yesterday afternoon."

Raliton stepped back to appraise his brother's anger.

"It is true," he said. "I don't deny the fact, but you wouldn't let me explain the other night when you returned. I'd met Enyra the morning you destroyed her father's table and asked her then. At that moment, you did not know she even existed."

Lornear clenched his jaw and flexed his fists. He narrowed his eyes and glared at his elder brother. The truth was obvious. It hurt.

"You only need know I am her chosen love," Lornear said. "She finds my appearance appealing. It is a truth; I was told such at the Pool of Truth."

"Interesting, my dear brother. She finds your appearance to her liking." He hesitated and placed a finger to his lips, contemplating. "Then would she not also find my appearance appealing? Are we not a mirror?"

Lornear glared at Raliton, remembering the words of the dark man at the pool's edge. Now Lornear questioned if he had been tricked.

"Listen, my dear brother," Raliton said. "If you stand before one mirror and say 'You are the most handsome man' and then stand in front of another to say 'You are the ugliest person' it makes no sense. You look like me and I look like you."

Lornear shook his head silently.

"Enyra cannot stand before us and say you are handsome and I am ugly. We are identical in appearance, Lornear. You must be logical in this matter."

"So that is how it will be," Lornear said. "So be it."

King Lanfeld led the procession to Obera's Obelisk where the tents and stands stood ready for the great celebration of Nos'Hanlah on the open field. The forest stretched a distance to encircle a part of the glen. Lanfeld made his speech and soon the population of Adavinya started the week-long party with wild abandon. Children raced among the man-made corridors of stands where vendors hawked foodstuffs and items to fill almost every whim. Some vendors offered games of chance, skill or just simple brawn.

Raliton and Enyra walked among the participants, checking that which the various vendors offered. Enyra felt comfortable with the young prince and he walked proudly with the young lady on his arm. They stopped at the popcorn vendor when Lornear happened upon them.

"Enyra," Lornear said. "You look lovely today." He bowed politely and upon standing, acknowledged Raliton. "Brother."

"Prince Lornear," she said and smiled at him. "Will you not join us today?"

Lornear narrowed his eyes at Raliton to watch his actions. The elder brother was stoic. "Perhaps later," Lornear replied. "I have other items to attend to and will be busy most of the afternoon."

"What are your plans, my brother," Raliton asked.

Lornear hesitated. He had no other plans; he just didn't want to be a pity case. She was with Raliton, not him. He had no need of sympathy.

"I need to find a particular item for a special occasion," he said with an air of indifference. "I will find you two later and perhaps we can enjoy a meal together."

"That would be wonderful," Enyra said. "Don't you agree, Prince Raliton?"

"Yes, that would be fine," Raliton said then flicked a popped kernel of corn into his mouth.

"Until later," Lornear said and ambled away, finding himself in a cluster of revelers who had already drank more than they should. He glanced back over his shoulder and watched Enyra and Raliton moving on from the vendor. Raliton had his arm about Enyra's waist. Lornear stopped and stood there, watching, his nostrils flaring from the anger-induced heavy breathing. "She is suppose to be with me," he gritted in low tones. "With me!"

"Young prince," a voice called. "Test your strength. Win a prize for your loved one." The rotund man laughed jovially, motioning for Lornear to come closer.

"Do you see a loved one with me? Is there a young lady on my arm?" Lornear spat and flung his arm with a tight fist at the end of it in the direction of the fat man talking, barely missing him. "Do you mock me?"

"My error," the man said. "I only wanted you to join in the festivities, Prince Lornear." The man had stepped back and held his hat between his hands at chest height. He had no doubt the correct name since Prince Lornear's temper was well known in the village.

"Lornear!" Enyra called, her voice sharp. She tapped him on the shoulder.

He turned to face her and could see his brother in the distance, munching and slowly walking to join them. "What do you want?" he snapped and looked away.

"First," she said. "I want you to apologize to this man. You were very rude. This is a side of you I don't like." She folded her arms in front of her. "Are you listening to me?"

Lornear frowned and cocked his head at Enyra. He could not believe she was chastising him in public. Him — a prince. He stood there momentarily stunned. Not one person had ever spoken to him as such, except possibly his mother. It was a new sensation. He smiled.

"Most definitely, Enyra," he said, quickly stepping to her and grasping her hand to kiss the back of it while stooping to one knee. "It was my error."

He turned to the rotund man. "Sir, I pray I have not offended you in any manner with my sharp tongue. You are most certainly correct; I should attempt to gain my love a gift."

"Uh, why… yes," the man stumbled on his words. "Prince Lornear, if you will." He handed the prince a thick rope, such as those used on the wharves at the river to tie up ships. "The name of this game is Pull Tug. Now pull this as hard and long as you can. The more rope you pull out, the stronger your love. If you are truly strong enough, you will ring the bell at the top." He pointed at a tall board with markings and a large bell on top. "If not, you will be tugged to this, the loser's line." He pointed at a pink ribbon and tapped the top of one of the black poles to which the ribbon was tied.

"I see no problem here," Lornear said. He grabbed the rope and wrapped it about his arms to get a good grip. "I am ready."

He was suddenly jerked forward, his eyes wide in surprise. He dug his boots into the dirt and leaned back to hold his ground. People started to cheer. Lornear grimaced and although he was fighting, his boots scraped closer and closer to the loser's line. Some of the crowd started to laugh, yet there was many of them cheering. He knew he was losing. Lornear turned and snapped the rope over his shoulder, leaned and pulled the rope. He moved forward. He watched the ground. All the while, sweat formed on his brow. A step. He knew he was being made a fool of and he was mad. He knew he should never have accepted a sucker's chance. Suddenly the rope gave and he lurched forward then it snapped taunt. A full stride gained. The boot scrape line disappeared beneath his boot. He was gaining. He trudged slowly, laboring in deep breaths. He jerked the rope. The rope gave and he heard the bell.

"You win," the man yelled. "Here you go."

Lornear stared at the prize and frowned. Sweat drizzled down his brow and he wiped it away. The man waved the mug at him, again. "For your lady love." *A mug?* Lornear reached out and grabbed it. His arms ached and the mug felt it weighed as much as a horse.

"For you, Enyra," he said and offered her the garishly colored cup.

"Thank you, Lornear," she said. She stepped on tip-toe and kissed him politely on the cheek.

He wanted to take her in his arms, the hold her tight, to kiss her, to pick her up and whirl her around. Instead, he feebly smiled, turned and walked away.

"Brother, perhaps I should try," Raliton called out.

Enyra ran to catch up with him. "Lornear," she called. "Wait."

He turned to see her running toward him. He smiled and thought perhaps she realized his true love for her and she was leaving Raliton.

"I wanted to tell you." She paused to catch her breath. She reached out and grabbed Lornear's hands and held them. "Raliton agrees it would be best for us to dine tonight at the "Inn of Mother Bear." The owner is my mother's sister's husband and the cooking is very good. It will be a feast to enjoy."

"Ask her to join you now for a meal, alone," the voice whispered in his ear.

Lornear brushed his ear then feigned a headache, rubbing his brow. "I won't be able to make it," he said. "I fear the Pull Tug game has worn me and I have a headache."

"Oh," Enyra said, appearing let down. "It would have been so much fun."

He let her hand slip from his as he stepped back away from her. "Not really," Lornear whispered to the wind as he turned and left her to find Nightfire so he could return to the castle.

CHAPTER 10: A Twin Split

Beware to all when the son is double
It is the start, both the fire, the trouble
The Moon of love can touch but one
And cause all plans to be undone

from The Ballad of the Fire

The summer soon passed and harvest began. Raliton and Lornear were among the many young suitors to court Enyra. The other suitors waned when they realized Princes Raliton and Lornear were also knocking at her father's door.

To most it was obvious Enyra was enamored with Raliton, but Lornear knew the truth, he had the prophesy from the Pool of Truth. Lornear was not about to be pushed aside.

It was on the night of full moon in Ha'Dva, the month before Nos'Rovlah, that Lornear was with Enyra. He was prepared to ask her hand in marriage.

"Next Moon, Ha'Nom, will be Nos'Rovlah," Lornear said.

"I have..." Enyra started.

"Hush, my love," he whispered, putting a finger to her lips to silence her. "Allow a prince a moment."

"But, Lornear," Enyra said. "I must tell you—"

"It can wait," he said, holding his index finger to her lips. "You know I love you dearly."

"Lornear, no," she said and grabbed his hand from her face and held it in hers. "Allow a silly girl her moment, first, please. I wish not to hurt you."

He pulled back, questioning her actions. He stared into her eyes, a smokey blue, searching for an answer. He smiled. She dropped her eyes and he followed the gaze to their hands. He frowned.

"Lornear," she said. "I care for you deeply. You are a special person in my life, but I love another and he has asked my hand in marriage. I need you..."

Lornear pulled away and glared at Enyra.

"This cannot be," he said. "The Pool of Truth said you would find my appearance—"

"Lornear, this has nothing to do with looks," Enyra said. "Both you and Raliton look the same. It is here." She placed a hand to his chest, over his heart. "This is what I love in your brother, Raliton. He is a kind and gentle man. That is why I accepted his proposal."

"But, the pool," he sputtered. Enyra's hand still touched his chest.

Lornear heard the giggling. He'd heard it before.

"That's correct. The pool said she would find your appearance appealing, Prince Lornear," The Other whispered into his ear.

Lornear's brows furrowed, his eyes narrowed and he shoved her hand away.

"No!" Lornear yelled.

Enyra reared back, totally surprised by the outburst.

"Did the pool reveal the name of the face?" The Other asked and skipped about the two, unseen by one.

Enyra watched as Lornear followed some invisible point, his head moving left then right.

"Are you well?" Enyra asked and reached for his forehead.

Lornear pulled back and brushed her hand aside.

"It was the Pool of Truth," Lornear hissed. "It lied."

"Nonsense," The Other said. "The pool showed you a face — it was the face of Raliton. Do you not appear the same?"

Lornear stood, flailing his arms in the air to hit the image to which he listened. "Begone, foul spirit," he screamed to the night air, chasing The Other, flailing the wind with his fists.

"Lornear?" Enyra called. "Are you truly ill?"

Lornear stopped, turned and faced Enyra.

"And you," he said, pointing at her. "You are a... a..." He held his tongue and watched her.

"Lornear," she said softly. "Your temper scares me. I wish you to take me home, immediately."

"I know what I know," The Other chanted. "Now, you know the truth. Raliton is Enyra's true love."

"I said begone," Lornear screamed, his arm outstretched, pushing an unseen assailant away.

"Lornear!" Enyra cried and ran from him.

Lornear stormed through the castle, slamming doors in his search, pushing servants, screaming and demanding of them, "Where is he?"

"With your father," a young servant said, cowering on the floor after being knocked down. "Prince Raliton is with your father. Your father is..."

"I care not about my father," Lornear screamed and rushed to the king's chambers.

"You!" He slammed the door open, startling those inside. "Raliton, my dear brother." The words were slurred and spoken snidely. The door banged shut.

Raliton stood. He'd been kneeling beside the bed, holding Lanfeld's hand. Queen Miasi sat in a nearby chair.

"My brother, Lornear," Raliton started. "Our father..."

"May go to Bre's reward," Lornear spat. "You have deceived me a final time." He stood, every muscle pulled to full tautness, glaring at Raliton.

"Lornear," Raliton said. "Our father may be dying." He cast a look at the bed.

The young prince approached the bed, stood at its end, looked down at his father, then shrugged his shoulders. He looked up and glared once more at his brother.

"If he dies, you will become king," Lornear sneered. "It makes no difference to me. All remains the same for my life. I am still the second son, the second choice." He paused. "Second."

"Lornear," Queen Miasi said. "You are a cold, hurtful son. You care for none but yourself. I am ashamed to call you son."

"Brother," Raliton called. "Do you wish to speak with father?"

Lornear stood still. "I wish to speak with none of you but I will say my piece." He turned and faced Miasi. "Mother, you have always treated me as a losing son, one who will never aspire beyond. To you I say, you need not call me son anymore." He placed his hands on the bed's footboard. "My dearest father. To you I have been but a thorn, never a son but a duty for you to bear. Your obligation is done." Lornear paced the distance between him and Raliton. "And you, my brother. You have cheated me of all during my life since birth. *You* will be king. *You* will marry Enyra. It is always about you. No more will I be your shadow, your problem." He turned and strode to the doorway. "Whether father dies or lives makes no matter to me. I no longer exist in your lives. I never did, now I make it so."

"Lornear," Raliton called.

"No more, my brother," Lornear said. "Tonight I was to ask for Enyra's hand. As in birth, you were first. No more will I be second." He turned and left the room.

Lornear mounted Nightfire, stared down with eyes of piercing anger at the stable boy who had just arrived. He kicked him in the chest. The boy stumbled back and fell against the door of the stable, hitting his head.

"Learn your station and watch your manners," Lornear shouted. "I told you to have my steed ready for the next ride. I did not say tomorrow."

He spurred Nightfire, galloping out of the castle and down the narrow avenues of Adavin.

Any within range of his foot he would kick, those within striking distance of his whip received a lashing. Everything in his way as he charged through the streets was destroyed in some manner. Lornear's acidic tongue screamed obscenities into the night air and curses on the inhabitants of Adavinya.

He stopped in front of the jeweler's door, leaned in and beat his fist on the door to awake those within. Lornear didn't wait.

"You reject my love, Enyra," he screamed. "So be it. I have no need of Adavinya. If I return, it will be with a curse to the realm."

Lornear again spurred Nightfire and soon distanced himself from the city and into the dark forest. He knew not where he would go but he knew where he didn't want to be.

A shadow shifted from the corner of the jeweler's door where it had been sitting. The Other tittered nervously then giggled maniacally.

"It has been a long time, my dear friend, Arlyon, but it is happening. The end is coming." The Other stood and lightly wove a path in and out of the Adavin night shadows.

CHAPTER 11: Penance

To the one left behind it falls
Decisions' final judgment calls
Penance by one, deed another
A test by love of a brother

from The Ballad of the Fire

The morning sun hung in the sky, detailing a beautiful day which hid the night's prior affairs too well. Raliton, the ever-faithful son and brother, assembled a search group to find Lornear and bring him back to the castle. He sent forth messengers to the three over-lords asking their assistance through their under-lords. The servants' tongues waggled. Word traveled fast of Lornear offending Raliton, their mother, and caused their father's health to wane even more. Even worse, Lornear's anger and his hasty departure during the night also caused many casualties. Prince Raliton needed to reimburse the villagers for the damages Lornear had caused. There had to be accountability.

Prince Raliton fretted over his father's health, but knew he must lead the search, at least on the first day. He rode his steed, Shadowfeet, and rallied the group to follow him as he went forward, beyond Obera's Obelisk. He watched as the three messengers broke away to gallop their separate ways toward the over-lords of Adavinya.

"Forest, Fire and Water," Raliton said. "By the three, Prince Lornear will be found and returned to confront me. He cannot hide in Adavinya."

Ten days later he trotted Shadowfeet into the courtyard and the stable boy took the reigns as he dismounted. He cast a glance up to the window of his father's chambers. Queen Miasi waved. He shook his head; he had not found his brother. He strode into the castle and to his father's chambers.

Surprised, Raliton found his father sitting in the chair his mother occupied the fateful night Lornear left.

"Father," he said. "You have gained good health. The holy gods of The Four be blessed."

"The gods have been very kind, indeed," Lanfeld said. "Did you find your brother?"

"No, father," Raliton replied. "Still, the search parties continue and all the lords are assisting. Lornear cannot hide forever."

"Within the realm of Adavinya there are paths that lead out," Lanfeld said softly. "We speak not of them." He paused and gazed at his son. "Unless we must. Innead knows of them." He absently shook his head. "I fear he may have absently mentioned their existence to Lornear."

"Paths? Out of Adavinya?" Raliton echoed. "Why have I not been told?"

"Think no more of it, my son," Lanfeld said. "If your brother has chosen to use one of those paths, there is little hope of his return. Instead, we must consider the next course of action."

Raliton looked sheepishly at his father. "Then mother has told you?"

Lanfeld stood, strode to his eldest son and placed a loving arm about his shoulder. "She has told me only you wish to marry this beauty of the jeweler. A rare gem, indeed, I've been told."

"Enyra has agreed to be my wife," Raliton said proudly. "I fear it is what caused Lornear to be angry. He was upset by the news."

"Unfortunately, we must postpone any nuptials until a prudent amount of time has passed. For lack of an offender, I must indulge you do penance for your brother's actions. Are you man enough to accept this charge?"

"Father, I realize Lornear has caused much damage and I will accept his guilt as my own for the people of Adavin. Enyra and I planned to announce our betrothal during Nos'Rovlah, but instead, I will announce my penance if Lornear is not found. Do you feel a full Circle to be of sufficient time?"

King Lanfeld closed his eyes and nodded his head. "Most generous," he whispered.

King Lanfeld led the procession to Obera's Obelisk and performed the opening ceremony of Nos'Rovlah.

"Before I commit the words to begin Nos'Rovlah," Lanfeld said. "Prince Raliton wishes to speak to the people of not only Adavin, but to all of Adavinya."

Prince Raliton moved to where his father stood.

"People of Adavinya," he said. "My brother, Prince Lornear, left us less than one Moon ago. In his departure he caused harm and destruction." Raliton took a deep breath. "To those whose property was damaged, restitution has been made. If not, please attend Judgment in the morning." He hesitated, slowly reviewing those in attendance. "For those of you who were injured in my brother's angry departure, I beg your forgiveness. In that regard, I will now perform a year of penance. Please attend Judgment tomorrow morning so a proper atonement deed may be decided." Raliton stood there momentarily watching those closest to see their reactions. "I have forgiven my brother. I hope you will also."

Raliton stepped back and let his father come forward.

"Good people of Adavinya," Lanfeld said. "Let Nos'Rovlah commence. Celebrate the harvest." He moved back to Queen Miasi and pulled his cloak closer to him. "Is it me, or is it chilly today?" He smiled at his wife. "Perhaps, it is only me."

The Other danced a silly footstep around the royal family, but none saw him.

The morning sun shone brightly and carts moved between the city and the stands of Nos'Rovlah's celebration. Raliton stood in the Hall of Judgment watching the villagers wishing a fair judgment from King Lanfeld.

"My name is Basall," the man said. "Your son, Prince Lornear, attacked me the night he left. My wife, who is with child and I were walking near Baker's Pan when he rode by. I was able to protect my wife but he struck me with his whip, cutting my ear and kicking me in rib." He pulled up his shirt to reveal cloth wrapped tightly about his chest. "Your physician has helped to heal me but I have not been able to harvest my crops in a timely manner.I beg assistance."

Raliton stepped forward. "I will help you, Basall," he said. "I will arrive in early morning and work until mid-day meal. Is that fair?"

Basall bowed. "More than desired, lord prince. I thank you."

"So it shall be," King Lanfeld said.

Basall backed from the dais and left the room. Another man took his place.

"My name is Zanez," he said. "I, too, cannot perform my duties. I assist the tailor and, on that night, Prince Lornear's Nightfire, reared up and his hoof caught my forehead. I still get dizzy lifting the spools of thread for the master tailor."

Raliton scrutinized the man and moved closer to view the wound.

"It is a nasty wound, indeed," Raliton said. "Perhaps our physician should attend to it first and then we can make the proper judgment. Father?" Raliton looked askance to his father. "This wound seems not to heal properly."

"Our physician will attend to your needs immediately, Zanez."

"Thank you, my lords," the peasant said. "And my work?"

"Let us hear what the royal physician says, then we will make judgment. We would not want to be hasty and slight you," King Lanfeld said. "This may be very serious, indeed."

The royal physician was called and he escorted Zanez out with two guards. Another stepped forward for judgment.

"My name is..."

King Lanfeld held up a hand to silence the new petitioner. The hall doors slammed closed.

"If any others wish to make a false judgment request, please step forward now. I will not play games, nor be made a fool. My son will perform penance for the worthy. If a horse truly did scar his forehead, there would be a healing process by now. Zanez's wounds were fresh. I feel he stumbled and cut his forehead last night with too much wine and revelry. The Hall of Judgment will not be made a mockery."

There was silence.

"Fine," King Lanfeld said. "Now, those who truly wish a judgment, please step to the right wall and make a line. All others remain or move to the left."

Five people moved to the right leaving two men standing alone in the hall.

"You there," Raliton said, pointing to one. "Why are you in judgment?"

"To thank you, my lord," he stammered. "My wife's bowl was broken that night. It has been replaced and I personally wanted to thank you."

"You have thanked me," Raliton said. "And why are you here?" he asked of the other.

"I am his brother," the man said, his face ashen and eyes wide with fear. "I only wished to see the Hall of Judgment."

Raliton saw him shaking in fear. "You have seen the hall," he said. "Now, both of you leave the premises immediately and never again attempt to mock judgment. Am I understood?"

"Yes, my lord," they replied in unison.

"Begone," King Lanfeld said and waved his hand to dismiss them.

Both men quickly bowed and backed from the room.

"Father," Raliton said. "I beg, let me negotiate with these men to set my penance." He looked to the group of five for approval. "If that is acceptable with you."

They nodded their heads.

"Please, father," he continued. "I ask you go and rest, gain your health."

Lanfeld scanned the men's faces and saw they appeared an honest lot.

"So it shall be," he said performing the final pronouncement of judgment.

He stepped slowly and feebly down the stairs of the raised dais to the waiting arms of Raliton.

"Go, father. Rest," Raliton whispered and hugged the old man.

"You will be a wise king," Lanfeld said. "Some day, my son." He placed a loving hand on Raliton's shoulder. "Perhaps sooner than expected." He hobbled away.

Raliton spoke with the five men, listening to the injuries sustained in Lornear's angry departure. He realized he would be required to perform some severely difficult labor, but the people of Adavinya would know him to be just.

CHAPTER 12: Betrothal

Wind blows and a scent is taken
The Dark One now does awaken
Plots and plans, a young prince doth make
For future, past, present to shake.
Ignore The Other one does not
When he shows and speaks your lot.

from The Ballad of the Fire

The morning sun shone in Raliton's room and he yawned, carefully stretching the muscles he had used the day before. Old widow Marnona had lost her husband during the Quiet Time and usually needed a body to help her with the garden. Raliton found he could usually be there at least once or twice each month. The last required penance had been brought to Judgment and completed very quickly back in Ge'Adin. Yesterday, at Judgment, none came forward and his penance was finished. Almost a Full Moon without a required penance to do. If there were none today, he would go out into the city and realm to find a person in need of assistance. Today was the first day of Nos'Rovlah. One Circle, one Full Circle of Moons, Raliton had performed a penance for his brother's actions. He sat on the edge of the bed, smiling, remembering the tasks he did during that time. He harvested corn and wheat, slopped hogs, butchered and even worked as a woodsman with a double-edged ax in hand, cutting timbers. Raliton felt he knew his subjects better than most of his forefathers when they became king, except with possibility of King Arlyon. The great Cat-King had helped the humans and built Adavin into the realm of Adavinya. He worked with them, cutting wood, moving stones and even performing petty work. Raliton nodded his head. *I have performed well during the Circle.*, Raliton thought. *I know my people probably better than my father*

He strode to the window and looked down at the courtyard. A scent caught his attention, yet he could not define nor fine its source. A few servants moved about, performing their assigned duties. In the arch of the entrance to the water gardens, Raliton noticed a shadow move. It floated about and he looked to the sky for a source, perhaps a bird. There was none, not even a cloud. The threads of the shadow gained substance and a man with a strange double horned hat stood there gazing back at him. Raliton frowned. There was a familiarity to him. Eyes of red and gold gleamed when the dark man smiled at him. Suddenly, and with a full flourish, he bowed, acknowledging Raliton's presence. The prince's muscles tightened and he continued to watch the dark man. The Other slowly stepped, very precisely and deliberately, toward the stable, bowed again and reached his arms toward the stable door. The Other cocked his head to gaze up at Raliton and smiled — an evil smile. Raliton watched as the servants walked about the courtyard totally ignorant of the man. He was amazed.

The Other stood near the stable then motioned to Raliton to wait. The Other became somewhat smaller, all the while a stream of shadow raced a twisted path into the stable. A miniature version of the man remained there. The duplicate man walked from the stable and stood beside the first one.

Raliton was disturbed by the image, especially when the two men locked arms over each other's shoulders. He stepped back from the window.

"The future is the past," a voice said, startling Raliton. The voice was beside him.

He turned to see the dark man in his room. A quick lean toward the window and Raliton assured himself the strange man was no longer in the courtyard. Again, there was the familiar scent to befuddle him.

"How did you get in here?" Raliton asked.

"Listen well, my prince," The Other said. "The future is the past. Now exists only momentarily as the present. Still, the three are connected."

Raliton frowned. "You make no sense, but state the obvious."

The Other danced about the room. "Do you like riddles? I do." He stopped near the window and looked out at the distant horizon. "Your future is your past," The Other said. "When your past collides with your future, your present ceases to exist." He held up a finger. "But your future will continue without you." He danced merrily to the door. "This much I promise you, Prince Raliton. This much I give you, great grandson of King Arlyon." He winked at the prince. "But no more."

The shadow dissipated. Raliton was alone with his thoughts.

Raliton followed his father in the procession. He watched the old man, wondering how many more Celebrations of the Circle the king would see. Raliton turned to the one riding beside him, Enyra, his bride to be. He smiled at her and she beamed back him. Raliton let his mind wander back to the morning's scenario.

Before he realized it, they were on the platform and his father was getting ready to pronounce Nos'Rovlah officially open. His father's words blurred as his mind wandered to the words of the dark man.

"Raliton!" Lanfeld called and Enyra nudged him, waking him from his day dreams.

"Sorry, father," he whispered and moved forward.

He gazed at the gathered people. Was the strange man there? He noticed a few he personally knew from doing penance and in visiting the city to court Enyra.

"Today," he started, then hesitated. "Today I stand before you, your prince and free of penance for my brother, Prince Lornear."

"Lornear is not a prince. A prince would never desert his people," a deep voice called out.

"A proper prince would never hurt his people," a woman cried.

"Please," Raliton said, raising his hands to stop the jeering and murmuring. "My brother has been absent over one Full Circle. I have done his penance and he is to be forgiven his transgressions. If any think otherwise, please attend judgment today and I personally shall discuss it with you." He scanned the faces trying to read the true feelings of the people.

"Furthermore," he said. "I wish now to make a happy announcement." He turned and held out his hand to Enyra. She moved forward to take his hand. "Today I wish to announce our betrothal. I have asked the jeweler, Aldiar, for his daughter's hand in marriage." He paused a moment to gaze into Enyra's eyes before turning once more to the crowd. "Enyra has agreed to be my bride."

A cheer erupted in the crowd and Enyra blushed while leaning against Raliton's shoulder for support. He leaned his head down and whispered. "Get accustomed to this, my love, for when I am king, you will be queen and will need to greet the people." She squeezed his arm.

Raliton held up his hand to quiet the crowd. "I further wish to notify the Adavinyan people of our plans to wed in the next Circle of Planting Time, the day of full moon in Po'Chi; a month after Nos'Nevel. There will be three days of celebration." He looked to his father who was frowning.

"I beg my father's indulgence," Raliton said. "King Lanfeld wished our wedding to immediately follow Nos'Nevel. Having performed penance, I know the farmers will be exhausted with the planting and then the celebration of Nos'Nevel. I am giving the people a full month to rest in preparation of the wedding. I wish all of Adavinya to celebrate my happiness."

Again, the crowd began to cheer the young prince. Raliton again looked to his father who was now smiling. The old man moved forward and put an arm about his son's shoulder.

"He will make a wise king when I go to the Isle of Forgotten Sleep," he said to the crowd which continued to cheer. "I now pronounce Nos'Rovlah begun."

Horns and trumpets blared and the people cheered even louder.

Raliton searched the crowd but never saw the one he sought — the dark man. All the while, unseen by anyone, The Other danced on the platform behind the king and prince, his plans were coming together.

CHAPTER 13: A Wedding Return

The wedding performed, a foul wind blows
Three day's celebration he has chose
Three day's judgment is the call
For King Lanfeld within the hall
Prince Raliton to each word hear
A return, come see Prince Lornear

from The Ballad of the Fire

Queen Miasi adjusted the sash on Raliton's chest. "I had hoped for a double wedding," she mumbled. "To see my two sons proceed down the aisle to share the dais for the marriage vows. Imagine," she said. "Never once in the history of Adavinya has there been twin sons. It would have been the first." A tear coursed down her cheek. "But... well, that will never be." She grabbed a hanky to dab at her eyes. Queen Miasi patted Raliton on the chest. "There," she said, as if she had just adjusted something to perfection. "You are one handsome young man."

Innead strolled into the chamber. "My prince," he said. "Time is getting short. It is necessary for you to be there in plenty of time." He stroked the prince's shoulders, brushing away imaginary lint. "Your father is already at the throne." He looked Raliton in the eyes. "Very impatiently, I might add. Shall we go?"

"Proceed," Raliton said and waved his arm to let Innead take the lead.

They moved through the hallways of the castle, always heading for the Judgment Hall which housed the throne and where all royal weddings, including King Arlyon's, was held. They were met by staff who wished Raliton the traditional phrase 'A marriage well in the Circle of Time' or some other greeting.

The huge corridor before the hall was decorated in boughs of flowers and ribbons. Innead stood before the great wooden doors, opened them and sauntered to the front of the hall to stand at the bottom step leading up to the throne and King Lanfeld. He thumped his staff three times on the floor. "Her majesty, Queen Miasi of Adavinya," he said.

Miasi slowly and majestically walked the aisle, nodding to different lords and ladies as she did so. She made sure to acknowledge the three over-lords and their wives. When she arrived at the foot of the steps, she daintily lifted the front of her gown and walked up the steps to join her husband at the top. She greeted him, curtsied then stood in front of the chair to the right where she would sit.

Innead stood motionless, watching Queen Miasi's ascent. When she nodded to him, he turned to face the hall and thumped his staff again three times. "Presenting his majesty, Crown Prince Raliton of Adavinya."

Raliton strode into the chamber wearing the boots made of cat fur in honor of King Arlyon's transformation and to designate his leonid lineage. He walked with confidence while being sure to make eye contact with different lords and most definitely, the over-lords. When he approached the bottom of the steps, he stopped, sharply and snappily turned ninety degrees and took two strides before committing himself to an about-face. He stared at Innead, keeping his face as stoic as possible.

Innead waited then heard the trumpets blare. Again he struck the floor three times. Musicians struck up a song. Raliton listened, it was a tune he remembered Enyra enjoyed. The lutes, fiddles and other instruments blended well.

"I present Enyra," Innead said solidly. "The Crown Princess Chosen."

Enyra entered the chamber, her gown of the finest material and flowing as she slowly and delicately walked toward the steps of the dais. The bodice, encrusted with semi-precious clear stones which glittered in the sunlight. Rainbow hues covered her when Enyra stepped under the stained-glass window reflecting on the floor. She was radiant and the gathered guests murmured among themselves at that moment. Enyra's father, blinking to fight back tears, walked beside her, her arm wrapped in his. Together they carried the traditional cat pelt offering.

Enyra and Aldiar stopped at the steps. Raliton stepped forward. Aldiar and Raliton pulled ceremonial swords and performed a mock fight. The clang of metal filled the chamber as each positioned their swords to touching. Four quick strikes of metal and Aldiar stepped back, sheathed his sword. Aldiar grabbed Enyra's hand, bowed to Raliton while offering Enyra's hand to the prince. Raliton took Enyra's hand and bowed to Aldiar. Aldiar stepped back even further to stand with the other guests. Raliton and Enyra proceed up the steps of the dais to the king. Innead followed.

Raliton led Enyra to Queen Miasi who stood to kiss Enyra in acceptance. He then led her to his father. Enyra lifted the pelt into the air.

"Last night I stayed in the den of the cats to prove my worthiness of the lineage. King Arlyon has smiled on me. I have the sacred pelt and I now offer it to my future husband." She turned and gave Raliton the pelt.

"Father," Raliton said facing Lanfeld. "Enyra has passed the test of lineage. I return to you the sacred pelt of the cat."

Lanfeld reached down, retrieved the pelt and placed it over his shoulders. Raliton stepped back. Lanfeld moved to Enyra, embraced her in his arms and then kissed her.

Innead faced the gathered guests. "Be there any who denies this couple a marriage? If so, let him come forward to contest this union." He waited before turning to King Lanfeld and the wedding couple. The king took Enyra's right hand and put it in Raliton's right hand. He then took two rings, lifted them for all to see and placed them on Raliton's and Enyra's left hand index finger. He then turned them to the assembled guests.

"This is my son, Raliton. I am well pleased. This is his wife, Enyra. I am well pleased. The cats of our lineage have spoken. They are man and wife." He turned to Queen Miasi and she joined Lanfeld. He lifted his arm and pointed to Aldiar. "Are you pleased," he asked.

"I am pleased, my lord," Aldiar said.

Raliton and Enyra kissed then faced the lords and ladies once more. "We are pleased," they said in unison to the guests.

"We are pleased," the assembled group yelled in unison.

"Let the three-day feast begin," King Lanfeld said.

The guests applauded. Music echoed in the chamber.

Prince Raliton and Princess Enyra walked among the revelers each day. They held hands and greeted friends and total strangers alike. Sometimes a small group of revelers would grab hands to encircle the couple and they would be forced to kiss to be set free from Love's Ring.

Raliton grabbed Enyra, swung her around and continued to hold his arms about her waist while leaning against Obera's Obelisk.

"Did you think this day would ever come?" he asked.

"I love you and it mattered not how long the wait," Enyra replied. "It was necessary to clear the air and purge the ugly issues of your brother's departure."

Raliton frowned.

"I am sorry, Raliton," Enyra said. "I have spoken beyond my boundaries."

"No, my love," he replied. "We are wed and there are no boundaries of our talk. It just pains me my brother, Lornear, was not here to participate in our happiness."

"It is our happiness that causes him the anger," Enyra said. "I tried to lessen the pain, hoping in time he would realize it was you and I destined to wed, not him and I. He didn't understand." She stepped away from Raliton and watched her husband.

He stared into the air, watching the clouds. It was a warm day.

"Since the day he left the castle in anger," Raliton said. "There has been no word of him anywhere within the realm of Adavinya. It seems he rode Nightfire into oblivion."

"I am sure he will return some day," Enyra said. "It may be many Circles before he can be happy with his life, but I feel he will return when the time is proper. You are his family."

A wind blew and Enyra wrinkled her nose. The smell was unpleasant, foul.

"You are an optimist," Raliton said pulling her to him. He kissed her. "I love you," he whispered into her ear.

It was the third day after the celebration of his wedding had ended which found Raliton sitting in his mother's chair at the top of the dais with his father. Some did not involve him but most were complaints regarding a celebratory fracas demanding a judgment, a judgment to involve him doing penance.

"I did not realize my marriage would cause so much to need judgment," Raliton whispered to his father.

Lanfeld sat on the throne, leaned forward with one elbow on a knee, his index and thumb slowly rubbing the area below his lip. He scanned the group before him.

"Next," he said.

"I am Azon," the man said. "I was a vendor at the wedding celebration. During a disturbance—"

"King Lanfeld! Prince Raliton!" Innead yelled, thumping his staff on the floor while charging forward to the bottom of the dais. "Forgiveness, my lords. Come, please. I have just been notified. You must see who is coming."

"What is this?" Lanfeld yelled. "Innead! This is my court."

Raliton frowned and watched Innead turn and rush to the back of the chamber. He stopped at the door, looked back at the dais. "Come!" he demanded and disappeared behind the closing door.

"I think we should follow, father," Raliton said and started down the steps of the dais.

"Judgment for today is ended," Lanfeld said. "Attend tomorrow for judgment." He followed Raliton down the steps, but not as quickly.

Raliton found Innead standing by a window, scrutinizing the courtyard.

"There! There!" he screamed and hustled to the stairway leading down.

Raliton peered out the window and saw the three horses entering the courtyard. His father joined him and he pointed to the strangers below.

"If I am not wrong," Raliton said. "That is Nightfire and on him... Is that my brother, Lornear?" He grabbed his father and hugged him. "Lornear has returned, father."

"Who is that strange woman with him?" Lanfeld asked. "She is not of Adavinya." He wrinkled his brows and glared at the group below. "If you say that is Lornear, so be it, but I do not recognize him. He does not appear as you."

"Come, father," Raliton said. "Let us welcome my brother back." He raced away to the stairs leading to the courtyard.

Enyra and Miasi joined him just before he went through the arch into the courtyard. He grabbed Enyra and hugged her.

"You were right," he cried. "You said Lornear would return when he felt it proper. My brother has returned."

"Where is your father," Miasi asked and looked up the stairs where Raliton had come.

"He is coming, mother," he replied. "Father is slow, but one of the servants will help him here."

Raliton broke into the courtyard and bright sunlight. The stable boy held the reins of Nightfire, his head bowed but guardedly watching Lornear.

CHAPTER 14: Lornear's Tale

The prodigal son does return
To some 'tis a major concern
Has he changed or remains the same
The Other knows, he plays the game
To Raliton, a brother found
Friend and comrade, with neither crowned

from The Ballad of the Fire

Prince Raliton raced excitedly through the castle at Prince Lornear's return. His brother had barely dismounted when Raliton slapped him on the back, grabbed his arm in a welcoming clasp and pulled his younger brother close in a hug.

Raliton stepped back to inspect the changes of his younger brother. The skin was a dark ebony, but still his eyes were blue. A golden emblem pierced the center of Lornear's forehead and deep gouged scratches were on the left cheek. Raliton smiled, reached up, and stroked the mustache under Lornear's nose.

"Interesting," Raliton murmured. "Perhaps I should consider one." He grinned. "Brother, I have missed you," Raliton said, tears welling in his eyes. "Where have you been Lornear?"

"My name is Namo-Lor. If you wish to call me Lornear, so be it," Lornear replied, standing stiffly with a formal demure.

The young prince remained aloof, warily watching those gathered around him. His eyes fell on Enyra and he noted the ring on her index finger.

"Lornear!" his father called from the arch. "You have returned, my son."

Lornear slowly turned and faced his father. "You still call me son, my father?" he asked. "Even after my departure almost two Circles ago when I denied you as family?"

Raliton eased up beside his brother. "You are family. You are my brother. I have performed the penance necessary. You have been forgiven."

"Enough of this," Miasi said. "Tell me, my son, who is the young woman on the horse."

"My name is Namo-Ke," she said, not waiting for Lornear to respond. "I am Lornear's chosen."

Lornear quickly moved to her side and helped her down from the steed she rode. "This is my bride," he said. "And I have a son."

Namo-Lor, the change he took to become
one with Namo-Ke

Namo-Ke pulled back a fold of the robe she wore and revealed a small child in her arm. Lornear reached out and gently pulled the young boy from his mother's arm.

"This is Namo-Hoj," he said. "My first born." The words were cold and deliberate — the meaning not lost on those in attendance.

"Tell me, what is this?" Raliton reached up to touch the strange markings on Lornear's cheeks and forehead.

"In my wife's lands, there are trials a man must perform to be considered worthy of marriage," Lornear said. "This are my rites of passage," he touched his forehead. "This is my family markings. You can see identical markings on my son and wife." He reached up and touched the gold emblem on his forehead. "This is my family clan, Namo."

"Enough of this charade," Namo-Ke said as she slid from the horse, threw back her hood, allowing the robe to drop from her shoulders.

There was a gasp from a couple of the servants. Namo-Ke stood there, tall, dark, regal and very unabashedly, scantily clothed. A small gathering of fabric wrapped from her back to her front, covering each breast, the fabric crossing above them to be tied in a knot behind her neck. A tattoo of a serpent coiled from her left shoulder and down her left arm. Strange tattoo markings were on her face and another larger serpent was tattooed on her right leg, coiling about it from ankle to upper thigh. Her lower garment was cinched at the waist and flowed open and loosely about her legs to gather at the ankles.

She grabbed Namo-Hoj from Lornear's grasp and pointed at a servant. "You. Show me to my room." She took three long strides, with which her long legs bared to reveal the serpent. She stopped at the arch where King Lanfeld stood. "You are my husband's father," she said with a sneer and downward glance. "Barely acceptable, but it matters not." She turned back to find the servant she had selected standing still, staring at her. "Do they not perform as requested?" Namo-Ke inquired of her husband with a glance.

Namo-Ke revealing her markings.

Miasi nodded and the servant moved to the arch to assist the newcomer.

"Namo-Ke? Let me show you to your room." Miasi joined her at the arch. "We can talk. Having another daughter-in-law is a pleasant surprise."

Namo-Ke shrugged. "If it so pleases you."

King Lanfeld hobbled toward the two princes. The servant hurried to the arch, bowed to both women and led the way to the chambers.

"My two sons, together, again," Lanfeld said. He clapped his hands together. "There is no mistake to be made as to who is who. Let us go to the council chamber. There is much to talk about."

The three walked through the castle hallways to the council chamber, all the while meeting servants who happily greeted Lornear, welcoming him home.

Lanfeld motioned to the chairs. "Sit," he said. "Tell me, Lornear. What has transpired since your departure." He smiled at his son. "I know you have married and changed your appearance."

Servants quickly followed with refreshments and placed them on the large table.

"You have a son," Raliton said. "How wonderful."

"I have a son, indeed," Lornear said and sat in his chair carefully watching the other two.

"Where were you?" Raliton asked. "We searched for you and even the over-lords assisted. You disappeared." He reached over and took a goblet and drank.

Lornear leaned back in the chair and observed his brother, then let his eyes narrow and glance at his father. Sitting there, he raised a hand to his chin, allowing a finger to tap his upper lip. Lornear analyzed the situation.

"There is a change in you, my son," Lanfeld said, breaking the silence. "Your rashness seems less. You take the time to study and think your thoughts. Are you not analyzing us at this very moment?"

Lornear nodded. "Namo-Ke has provided me a training and in doing so, I have learned to evaluate slowly to make a decision." He raised his hands to his brother and father. "Not that I must evaluate my words to you. I am selecting the proper approach of my tale."

"Start when you left me," Raliton said. "I know you were very angry as you left the castle and the city."

Lornear's eyes flared.

"Please, dear brother, worry not about that. I have performed a one Full Circle of penance in your name. You are totally forgiven and I bear you no ill-will. Now, please, the tale."

"Yes, I was angry. I had been made a fool of by the Pool of Truth and—"

"Again, you mention this place, yet I don't recognize it," Raliton said. "Where is this Pool of Truth?"

"I followed the dark man into the forest and he showed it to me."

Lanfeld spread his hands on the table before him. "The dark man? I fear that to be an ill-omen."

"Enough of this dark man," Raliton said. "Continue your story. This person showed you the pool. Where did you go?"

"I left the city and I rode beyond Obera's Obelisk to where the field narrows and the forest is thick on both sides. I guided Nightfire into the woods. It was dark, even with the Full Moon of Ha'Dva shining above. The brush was thick, but I continued in. Nothing... nothing was going to stop me."

"You went into the south forest?" Lanfeld asked. "There is nothing there, nothing but trees. As it is written."

"So it is, father" Lornear said. "Still, I went and I traveled for days. Time was lost — I don't remember. At times it was so dark I could not tell if it was night or just the giant trees blocking out the light. I came upon an opening. The sun shone bright and I rested there. I found berries to eat and finally a small rabbit came into the small glen. I killed it, started a fire and ate."

"You saw no one during this time?" Raliton asked.

"None," Lornear said. "I rested and during the night, in the light of the moon I saw fires, small, moving burning lights. At first, I was fearful, but they never approached me. On the second night I dared to follow the dancing fires, but I didn't want to leave Nightfire alone. I quickly returned to the glen for fear of losing myself in the dark. On the third night I followed again, but with Nightfire by my side. I did not ride him since I didn't want to get caught up in a low branch. The fires disappeared. I was alone with Nightfire in the dark, a dark so black I could barely see him. I rested against a large tree with Nightfire beside me. Imagine my surprise when I awoke the next morning to see a large outcropping of stone where the fires disappeared. There was also an opening and as I approached it, I could hear sounds, indistinct voices. It was a tunnel. I entered."

"You went in?" Raliton said. "Why?"

"Why not?" Lornear said. "I had nothing out here to keep me, except Nightfire. I tied Nightfire to a tree making sure there was plenty of food for him and I entered the tunnel, following the sounds I'd heard. I'd traveled only a short distance when something fell from above, striking me on the head, knocking me out. When I awoke, my first vision was Namo-Ke looking over me, tending to my wound. I fell in love with her."

"What is the name of this place?" Lanfeld asked. "Could you find it again."

"I could, father," Lornear replied. "But you needn't go there, so I won't bother to show you where it is."

Lanfeld cocked an inquisitive eye toward Lornear. For an instant he sounded like the boy who had left in anger.

"So why did you return now?" Lanfeld asked.

"If you don't want me father, just say so," Lornear said. "I can remove my family from this place if you so desire."

"No," Raliton said. "You will remain here. This is where you belong."

"Truly, brother?" Lornear asked. "I am your duplicate, but the younger. Except now I have this mark." He touched his facial tattoo, allowing his hand to stroke the grooves of the scar on his cheek. "Never in the history of Adavinya has there ever been a birth such as ours. I am the living proof of this strange aberration to nature. I am the mark which has been cast on the royal lineage of King Arlyon." Again, Lornear touched his tattoo.

"I do not consider either of you an aberration," Lanfeld said.

"The Other has explained to me the meaning of our birth," Lornear said.

"Who is The Other?" Raliton asked. "My brother, you continue to speak in riddles. You act as if things have changed. Things have not. You are my brother." He pointed to Lanfeld. "This is our father, not yours, not mine, but our father."

"Enough," Lanfeld said. "Lornear, let us join your wife, Namo-Ke. I would like to meet and visit with my grandson. Raliton, if you wish, may join us."

Lornear turned so Raliton wouldn't see his smile.

CHAPTER 15: Namo-Ke and Namo-Hoj

A beauty of ebony skin
With a son, both to be of kin
Tattoos of blue and deepest black
Seem alive to move on their back
Strange designs, unknown and obscure
Tales of a life lived unsure

from The Ballad of the Fire

Lornear placed a hand on his father's arm. "Before we leave, father," Lornear said. "Tell me what has transpired during my absence." He hung his head in shame. "I heard Raliton has done penance for my errors, but what else has happened?"

Lanfeld frowned in thought and tugged at his beard.

"Very little has changed," Lanfeld said. "I am older and perhaps Raliton is a bit wiser."

Raliton laughed.

"Yes, I did a year's penance," he said. "It was a learning time for me. I harvested corn, wheat and slopped hogs." He sat proud and straight in his chair. "I also did some lumber work with a couple of woodsmen. I was able to glean a better understanding of our people within the realm of Adavinya, especially in and surrounding Adavin."

"Is that all that has transpired?" Lornear asked.

"I married," Raliton said. "Enyra and I were wed but a few days ago."

Lornear narrowed his eyes and glanced over at Raliton.

"So, you have no children then, is that what I understand?"

"Not yet," Raliton replied.

The slightest of grins crossed Lornear's lips to curl the edges. He kept his emotions stoic.

"Well, then," Lornear said. "Let us go up and meet my wife and son." He slapped Raliton on his back and hugged him close. "Come, father. Do you need assistance?"

"Not yet, my son," Lanfeld said. "This walking stick suffices."

Raliton opened the door and there stood Enyra.

"I was coming to get you," she said. "I brought Namo-Hoj with me. Isn't he sweet?" She held the young boy in her arm.

Raliton looked at the markings on the small boy's cheeks which mimicked Lornear's. He tried to remember the tattoos on Namo-Ke and couldn't envision the same markings on her.

"Tell me," Raliton said turning to Lornear. "Does your wife bear your family markings?"

Lornear stiffened and stared at his older brother, then smiled.

"Each child is marked with the family insignia shortly after birth," he said. "Namo-Ke's are of her father's lineage."

"It is an intriguing design," Lanfeld said while staring at the three marks. "Does it signify anything?"

"I call it..." Lornear hesitated and glanced at the three standing before him. "I call it Scar of the Cat. Three claw marks."

"Interesting," Lanfeld said.

"It seems appropriate, brother," Raliton said. "It signifies our cat lineage."

"If you see it that way, fine," Lornear replied. He turned to Enyra. "Is Hoj too heavy to hold?" He reached out to take his son.

"Please, Lornear," Enyra said. "This little guy is just fine. I must learn to hold children." She smiled at Raliton.

Lornear gave his brother a puzzled look. Raliton shook his head.

"In time, Lornear," Raliton said. "A future we both look forward to." He approached Enyra and put an arm about her and hugged her close. "Someday soon, we hope."

"May I hold my grandson?" Lanfeld asked.

Enyra carefully handed Namo-Hoj to Lanfeld and he cradled the baby. He looked down on the child then carefully touched the cheek tattoo.

"Scar of the Cat," he whispered.

Namo-Hoj's eyes opened and he glared at the old man through dark eyes. He shook his hands before letting out a wail to echo in the hallway. Lanfeld was startled and stared at the others.

"Let me," Lornear said and grabbed the child from his father.

He immediately stuck his index finger into the child's mouth then winced in pain. The baby suckled on his finger.

"Let us take the child back to Namo-Ke," he said. "Are we in my old room?"

Lanfeld nodded and Lornear led the way to the room. When they arrived, Lornear noticed Namo-Ke was talking with Innead. There were no others were in the room.

"I thought my mother to be with you," Lornear said.

"We talked, she left," Namo-Ke said. "I am talking with this person. He says he is advisor to your father. He considers himself a magician."

"Innead?" Raliton said. "A magician?"

"He dabbles," Lanfeld said and shrugged his shoulders. "He makes potions and such. I thought he had given most of it up since your birth."

Enyra leaned up and whispered in Raliton's ear. "I will go to your mother."

Raliton nodded and watched her leave the room.

"Why our birth?" Lornear asked. "Why then?"

Lanfeld hobbled to a chair and collapsed into it. "It was so many Circles back," he said. "I asked Innead for a potion, one to assist us in having a child. Your mother and I attempted conception many times without success. Innead made a concoction we consumed. The rest is history."

Raliton and Lornear looked to each other then back at their father and finally at Innead.

"You are the reason for this aberration?" Lornear asked. "You caused this?"

"We are not an aberration, my brother," Raliton said. "We are a blessing from our great-grandfather, King Arlyon, himself."

"I only did as commanded," Innead whimpered. "I am at your father's call."

Raliton reared up and stared at Namo-Ke. He realized the two had been talking magic.

"Do you know magic?" Raliton asked Namo-Ke. "Are you a witch?"

"I am knowledgeable in the arts," Namo-Ke replied. "I do not consider myself a witch — they practice potions and chants. They are said to pray to demons." She looked slyly at the assembled group. "I pray to no demon," she added haughtily.

Innead bowed. "I pray not to demons," he said. "I have continued to practice my studies in the arts with potions and other such things." He waved his arms to dismiss the conversation.

Namo-Ke reached over and placed a hand on his arm. "If you wish to learn more," she said softly. "Perhaps you will allow me to join you in your potions chamber." She stood back and laughed. "But only if you wish, mortal."

"Mortal?" Raliton echoed. "Why do you say such to him? We are all mortal, are we not?"

"I am Namo-Ke," she said with authority. "I am—"

"You are my wife." Lornear cut her off. "The mother of my son." He glared at his dark-skinned wife. The silent glare finally ended with a cocked eye of questioning silence toward Namo-Ke.

Lanfeld and Raliton frowned at Lornear and his words. They could not see his face since he had his back to them.

"What was your wife about to say?" Raliton asked. "Exactly who is she?"

"I have spoken when I shouldn't," Namo-Ke said. She hung her head. "I ask my lord regent's forgiveness and pray I have not placed my husband in a position of shame with his father and brother."

Lanfeld went to Namo-Ke and embraced her. "You are my son's choice," he said. "We are all family here. You may speak freely with us when we are not in public." He turned to Lornear. "You have a strong-willed wife. I hoped you would marry such a woman and not some addle-brained follower."

Raliton listened to the words being spoken and fretted. Did he consider Enyra such?

"You have both chosen well," Lanfeld said placing an arm on a shoulder of each son. "I am very pleased with my new daughters and know I will have many grandchildren to spoil as I grow older."

Raliton blushed, missing the furtive looks between Lornear and Namo-Ke.

"I must find my wife," Lanfeld said and hobbled from the room.

CHAPTER 16: Innead and Namo-Ke

She haunts the hallways of boredom
To find a nook to give her calm
Within Innead's chamber walls
Doth the beginning secret falls
A hint of this, a dash of that
An unknown creature from the hat

from The Ballad of the Fire

Days turn into months and soon a full Circle has passed. Suddenly it is Quiet Time again and the snows fall upon the realm of Adavinya. Masia and Enyra spend their time with Namo-Hoj, playing and watching him grow. Masia enjoys her grandson and Enyra hopes soon she, too, will have a child. Lornear shadows Raliton constantly, learning as Raliton continues his education to kingship. Lornear, it appears, has indeed turned his temper, for rarely does he get angry.

Namo-Ke finds no peace in Adavin, especially now that Quiet Time has come and the snows cover the land. She wanders the hallways, searches the library, and scolds the servants for the simplest of causes. Namo-Hoj is old enough he no longer needs his mother's immediate care. The Queen and Crown Princess keep him occupied.

The snow flurried outside causing drafts in the hallways. Namo-Ke wandered the hallways when she spied Innead entering a chamber. She moved quickly and quietly pushed the door open. Namo-Ke surveys the chamber she had discovered locked during her earlier excursions. Namo-Ke wanted to ask Lornear what was behind the large oak doors but he was always in attendance with Raliton. He had very little time together alone with her. She stood, searching the chamber — this had to be Innead's study or workroom. She noted the vials and bottles which lined shelves on the wall. Namo-Ke stepped in.

"So, the advisor does fancy himself a magician, a student of the arts," she said.

Startled, Innead jumped back from the table, spilling liquid and dropping a flask.

"Nothing too important, I hope, " Namo-Ke said. "May I ask what you are doing?"

"An experiment," Innead replied.

Namo-Ke laughed with contempt while approaching him. She placed her hand gently on his arm. "They are always experiments, Innead."

"I only meant I dabble," he stammered.

Namo-Ke narrowed her eyes and looked directly into his. She now held both his hands in hers. She squeezed them.

"Would you like to learn? I mean truly learn?" she asked.

Innead trembled and Namo-Ke felt it.

"There is nothing to fear," she said. "I know a few tricks." She smiled slyly at him. "I'm sure you would a make an excellent apprentice."

"Apprentice?" Innead jerked his hands from hers. "I may have said I dabble, but in reality, I have been practicing for many Circles. I don't feel I should be considered somebody's apprentice."

"Fine," Namo-Ke said. "Let me show you this."

She quickly grabbed an empty flask and walked about the room, carefully smelling the contents of different bottles and vials, reading the labels.

"This is interesting," she said holding up a bottle of creamy powder. "Is this truly a powder made from ground Winter Bear bones?"

Innead shrugged. "I found it at a market. They claimed it be pure. I'm unsure of where to use it."

"The market?" Namo-Ke echoed. "Perhaps your market places are not as useless as I first thought. May I join you next time?"

Innead bowed his head. "If you wish."

"Now, how to use," she snickered. "Watch and learn." She sprinkled in a small amount of the powder. "We mustn't use too much."

"What are you doing?"

"Showing you my skills," she replied and smiled slyly. "Now watch."

She grabbed a bottle. "Perfect," she said and poured the blue liquid into the flask. A plume of light blue smoke wafted up, swirling into the room, taking a strange shape and form. The cloud thickened, red eyes burned and glared within the blue forming head.

Innead cowered down by the table, staring up at the thing. "What is it?"

"A pet," Namo-Ke said. "It is called a falgon."

The smoke continued to congeal and finally the creature existed in its entirety, hovering above Namo-Ke with a suspicious eye to Innead.

"Stand up, you idiot," Namo-Ke screamed. "If you continue to be scared, it will consider you food." She glared at Innead. "I won't be able to control it if you continue to hide."

"Get rid of it," Innead said. He stood nervously, keeping a wary eye on the creature.

"No," Namo-Ke purred. "I find the creature pleasing." She held out her arm and the hovering beast gingerly approached. "There, there," she cooed. "I will call you Namo-Jal. It is appropriate."

"Fine," Innead whispered. "Call it whatever you wish." He stared at the creature, tempted to reach out and touch it but considered it better to wait. "What is a falgon?"

"It is part falcon, part dragon," she said petting the feathers on the creature's back. "Look at the eyes. They are the eyes of a dragon within a head of a falcon." She pointed at the beak of the falcon." She gently pulled out a wing. "Don't you love the feathers and leather mixture — dark blue feathers, light blue leather." She glanced at

Innead and smiled. "Bat wings with feathers. And the tail — long, scaly and reminiscent of a great serpent. What a magnificent creature."

Innead leaned against the table, more comfortable with the creature. "It is an attractive beast, but to be truly magnificent, I would think it should be larger."

The falgon cocked its head at Innead's comment and fluttered it wings before it lifted into the air. It hovered, looking about. The falgon flew out the window.

"Namo-Jal," Namo-Ke yelled while running to the window. "Come back."

The beast hovered, lifted a little higher into the sky.

"It is all your fault," she screamed and slapped Innead's face who now stood with her at the window.

"My fault?" He slid the back of his hand across the cheek, feeling the heat of the slap.

"Watch and learn, silly human," Namo-Ke said, her reddish yellow eyes flaring.

"What will I see?" He considered the slap and her calling him a silly human.

Innead watched the flying falgon as it soared higher into the sky. There was a screech which ended in a loud roar.

There, in the sky above the castle, flew a huge beast of blue. No longer was there the head of a falcon but a gigantic lizard-like head with a huge beak. The body was covered in scales and the wings were completely covered in feathers. The wings each spanned at least eight to ten strides of a grown man. The falcon's head turned upward in a roar and smoky fire spewed forth from it. As the wings flapped, the ends of the leathery feathers appeared to be on fire. Flames!

"Namo-Jal doesn't mean to harm any," she said noticing the bowmen taking aim from the courtyard below. "It only desired to show you its true magnificence." She stretched out the window holding her arm out even further. "Namo-Jal," she called.

The falgon again roared and hurtled down toward them, allowing the on-coming arrows to hit the scales and fall back to the ground. The falgon changed in flight back to the small beast it had been originally. It landed on her arm and she carried it back into the room.

"Now do you agree Namo-Jal is, indeed, a magnificent creature?"

"I did not know," Innead said. He shook his head. "Namo-Jal is truly magnificent. May I hold it?" He offered his arm as a resting place.

The falgon hopped across the small space between them, landing on Innead's arm. The creature inched closer up the arm to near the shoulder then brought its head close to Innead's face. The falgon stared directly into Innead's right eye. Innead froze in fear. The falgon's beak opened and the upper beak scraped across Innead's cheek, drawing a line of blood. Innead felt the tongue lick at the wound, tasting the blood. It pulled away and flew back to Namo-Ke.

"You are a part of the falgon," Namo-Ke said. "She has tasted your blood and you are bound to her." She tittered. "And you are bound to me."

Innead stood there before reaching up to touch the wound. He gazed at the blood on his fingers, paused, lifted them to his lips and licked them clean.

"Will you teach me?" he whispered. "I want to learn. I wish to be your apprentice."

Namo-Ke sauntered to the corner where a perch appeared for Namo-Jal.

"Rest, my baby," she hissed. "Keep watch of the floor, if a morsel wanders in..." She left the sentence unfinished.

CHAPTER 17: **The King's Health**

Quiet Time with snow covered land
Missing, The Other plays his hand
The king is ill, the Dark Man gone
Who will giggle, and to dance on?
With bonds of truth and bonds of lie
Circles will pass to live and let die?

from The Ballad of the Fire

The celebration of Nos'Dovel was poorly attended since a storm blanketed the city with almost a foot of snow. King Lanfeld was adamant the celebration must be held and he led the small procession to Obera's Obelisk. The small group in attendance cheered when Lanfeld opened the celebration, but with only two vendors the festivities were lacking and soon the whole group worked together to tear down the stands and return to the warmth of the city and homes.

King Lanfeld wandered the hallways for the next two days fretting over the poor attendance and the lack of proper celebration of the holiday. The cold corridor echoed with his shuffling slippers and hobbled footsteps. Everyone felt King Lanfeld's mutterings were louder and longer.

"Father," Raliton called. "Please. Let us go to your chamber so you may rest." He put his arm about the old man. "You seem to be catching something, your cough sounds congested."

"It is nothing," the old man replied. "I will be fine."

Lanfeld collapsed. Raliton immediately fell to his knees beside him.

"Father!" Lornear yelled and joined Raliton on the floor to help the man up.

"Perhaps," Lanfeld stammered. "Perhaps I should go to my room."

Raliton and Lornear lifted the man between them. He was weak and staggered along as the two carried him to his chambers. King Lanfeld's words slurred and Raliton watched as his father's eyes rolled aimlessly, focus momentarily, only to stare absently into space.

"This is not good," Lornear said, shaking his head. He held tightly to Raliton's arm to help support the old man.

A servant stepped into the hallway and immediately slammed against the wall to allow the three to pass.

"Seek out Innead," Raliton shouted. "Tell him to attend the king's quarters, immediately."

The servant bowed, dropped the tray of foodstuffs on a nearby shelf and headed down the hallway toward Innead's work area.

"Only another ten strides, father, and we will be to your room," Raliton said.

"There you can rest and Innead will work his magics to make you better," Lornear added.

Raliton snapped to look at his brother. "There will be no magic performed. A potion of healing is all to be required."

Lornear turned a pained expression to his brother. "Perhaps you would allow Namo-Ke to offer her healing? She is learned in the arts of medicine."

"Innead is the advisor," Raliton said. "He will perform the necessary duties. There is no need to involve a member of the family in the process of healing."

"As you wish, brother," Lornear said and bowed away from the bed. He stood in the corner, taking in each movement.

"My king," Innead said, flowing into the room with his robes billowing around him. "What has caused this?" He felt Lanfeld's forehead. "You are burning at the temples," he said. "This is not a good sign." The old man hacked. "A cough," Innead announced and pulled open the eyelid. "The skin is cool and the eyes do not focus well."

Innead turned to Namo-Ke. "Please, Namo-Ke, I will need a leaf of mint, the blue vial on the left top shelf and the ingredients to make a poultice. Please hurry."

Namo-Ke, who stood in the shadows, raised her head, opened her eyes and stared at the novice magician. "You ask me to be your servant?" she queried. "Like a commoner?"

Innead stopped and turned to face her. "I do not ask you as I would a servant. Instead, I entreat you to use your skills to retrieve the proper items necessary for us to prepare the king's medication. He is weakening as we talk."

Namo-Ke stood tall, brushed her braids behind her back and strode to the doorway. "I will bring what I feel necessary."

"Don't forget the mint," Innead said.

"I will bring that which is needed and only that," Namo-Ke stated. She turned and sauntered out the doorway toward Innead's work laboratory.

"How is my father?" Raliton searched Innead's face for any tell-tale signs.

"He is weak," Innead replied. "He has the fever of Nos'Dovel. We will keep him warm with more blankets. I will make a poultice to place on his chest. He should be up and moving within a moon with no difficulties." He smiled at Raliton.

"Perhaps father should begin the process to step down and allow Raliton to ascend to the throne," Lornear whispered.

"I will not step down," Lanfeld blurted. "It is a mild illness and I will be up about my business tomorrow, next day guaranteed." He looked to Innead. "Is that not true, my trusted advisor? Tell them."

"We will see, my king," Innead whispered. "Rest and sleep for now. Where is Namo-Ke? What is taking her so long?"

"I am here, mighty magician," Namo-Ke sneered. "I have brought what you requested and what I thought more appropriate."

Innead frowned, as did Raliton. Lornear appeared innocent of the words. Namo-Ke only smiled the enigmatic smile she used since her arrival, the one where she appeared to be looking not at you, but through you to some point beyond.

"Here is your mint," she said and handed Innead a bag of rustling leaves. "You would want that in hot water and I told the servants to bring... ah, here they are now."

Two young girl servants hustled in with pots of boiling water while a young boy entered with a crock brimming with cold water.

"Ah, yes," Innead said. "First some of mint." He looked around. "Oh, you brought this along. Good. Good." He grabbed a couple of leaves from the second bag in with the mint and crushed the leaves in a mortar by pounding it with the pestle. A scent of mint and eucalyptus filled the room. "Good," he said. "Now a little cold water in a goblet, some of this mixture." He carefully shook the powder into the goblet. "A quick stir, and now we strain it so King Lanfeld can drink the elixir." He carefully wrapped a cloth about the goblet's mouth and poured the concoction into another goblet. He handed it to Raliton. "Have him drink all of this; it will help. Lornear, if you would, please help me with this poultice."

Lornear scowled.

"Namo-Ke?" Innead asked. "Would you assist me?"

She stepped forward, bent down to the little man hovering over his potions. "I will assist," she whispered in the softest voice. "But you must remember who is the teacher. Tomorrow, something special." She smiled and held a bowl for Innead.

"Let me add the mustard, sage, poke root, and mullein together," he said.

"Add slippery elm and lobelia," Namo-Ke hissed. "Add it now."

Startled by her demand, Innead grabbed the two powders and added a pinch of each.

"That should suffice," she whispered. "It will help with the congestion more than the mint. It is good for the chest ailments."

Innead added a small amount of hot water to the mixture and stirred, creating a paste with an even consistency, almost dry, but still somewhat pliable.

"Please open the king's garment so I may place this on his chest," Innead asked.

Raliton pulled back the nightshirt revealing the curled gray chest hairs.

"Lornear, please place a towel down so I may put the poultice on it. I do not want the king to be irritated by the herbs."

The younger twin grabbed a towel and spread it over his father's chest.

"Is that to your liking, Innead?" Lornear cocked a questioning eye to Innead.

"That is fine," the advisor said. He scraped the bowl with his hand, letting the mixture fall onto the towel covering King Lanfeld. Just as quickly, he spread the concoction out and grabbed another towel to cover it, then pulled bandages from his pocket to tie the poultice plaster securely in place. "This should help in combination with the potion he drank. Now, we should leave the king to rest." He waved his hands to usher the gathered group from the room.

"I will stay to watch my husband," Masia whispered. "He is my love and I will tend to his healing. Raliton?"

"Yes, mother?" he said, stopping and looking back at her.

"I fear your father will not be able to perform judgment tomorrow. Would you please hold judgment?"

"Yes, mother," he replied and turned to Lornear. "I will have my brother assist me, if he will join me?"

Lornear smiled and nodded.

CHAPTER 18: Nos'Nevel Dawn

The snow that lay about is gone
Nos'Dovel pass, Nos'Nevel's dawn
The king lies failing and dying
Two sons he calls, both them crying
One in truth, the other unsure
See the potion, beware the cure

from The Ballad of the Fire

The celebration of Nos'Dovel still wore heavily on King Lanfeld. He fretted it had not been properly handled and felt his illness was the reason. The king's health rallied but still had bouts of a lingering sickness which caused him to require rest and seclusion in his chamber. Raliton assumed most of the duties of his father but still deferred to the king's wishes. Nos'Nevel approached. No'Dva was a busy Moon with planting being very important for the kingdom. The residents scurried in the field to assure all was finished except for the tenderest of plants when Nos'Nevel was celebrated. Those plants would be quickly planted after the celebration. Traditions were upheld as the farmers worked their fields, seeds planted and the month of Po'Dva passed to Po'Nom. The Full Moon was close, which meant so was Nos'Nevel.

Namo-Ke and Innead spent many hours together in Innead's workspace. Many of the servants avoided that portion of the castle. Some even fled down the hallway when forced to pass the great oak door due to the sulphureous scents and hideous laughter. Raliton was present when Innead came racing out the door, his face pale and his body shaking in fear. Raliton heard Namo-Ke's laughter; it started in a low husky voice, but soon climbed into a maniacal and hysterical screech. A shiver coursed down his spine.

"What happened, Innead?"

"An experiment, my lord prince."

"Whatever are you two doing to cause you to be scared? May I see?"

"I shall ask Namo-Ke," Innead said, his eyes down and head slightly bowed.

"I see," Raliton said. "Actually, I don't. This is my father's castle and I feel I should be able to visit any room or chamber as I see fit."

He strode to the oak door and pushed it open. The stench was horrendous and Raliton stepped back.

"Namo-Ke? Are you safe?"

"I am fine, my husband's brother." Her voice was cold. "All is well."

Raliton peeked again into the chamber and saw the curling smoke. Namo-Ke emerged from the clouds to approach the door. Her hips swayed as she moved lithely toward the door.

"I shall visit your wife, Princess Enyra," she said in a sultry voice. "I am sure she is playing with Namo-Hoj." She cocked her head to Raliton. "I do hope my son will soon have a cousin to play with." She leaned in close to Raliton's ear. "If you wish, I can speak with her about certain things to aid in..."

"You speak boldly beyond your position." Raliton glared at Namo-Ke. "That which is between Enyra and I is that, between us only. You need not worry."

"My lord prince," Namo-Ke said softly. She looked at the young man before her but with her usual gaze of looking through and beyond. "I only mention this because a Full Circle has passed and Enyra is still barren."

Raliton's eyes flared. "We will not stand in this hallway and speak of such. If you wish to visit my wife, so be it. Otherwise, our business is finished." He turned to Innead. "We need to discuss a potion. Follow me." He walked into Innead's workspace.

"I am sure a potion may help," Namo-Ke offered snidely then sauntered down the hallway toward Enyra's chambers. "It helped your father." She snickered.

"My father's health still fails, Innead," Raliton spoke loudly so those in the hallway could hear him as the great oak door closed. "I need a potion to help him."

A screech startled Raliton and he looked to the corner and its source.

"In the name of Bre, what is that, Innead?"

"Namo-Ke calls it a falgon." Innead cowed slightly. "It is part falcon, part dragon beast. I usually just ignore it when I am here alone."

"Is it safe?" Raliton edged away from the closeness of the beast and made sure the table was between them.

"It is a pet. She calls it Namo-Jal and I have found it to be, for the most part, very peaceful, content to find any small creature that happens into the chamber here. My rodent issues have become minimum."

"A falgon." Intrigued, Raliton eased around the table to approach the beast.

"I wouldn't, m'lord." Innead put a hand on the prince's arm to stop him. "I said he is peaceful. It is best to just ignore him. Now, what kind of potion do you wish?"

"The king's health continues to fail. Is there nothing you can give him to help him grow stronger?"

Innead shook his head. "I have used everything within my power and I have even asked Namo-Ke for assistance. Together, Namo-Ke and I have concocted the most powerful potions we can find, yet they seem to do nothing. I fear I am not able to help, even with Namo-Ke's assistance."

Raliton gazed upward to the roof of the chamber and noted a cloud that moved, twisted and rolled above them.

"What is that?" Raliton pointed at the churning mass above them.

"Another of Namo-Ke's experiments. She calls it 'Clouds of Visions' but I am not sure exactly what it does."

Raliton watched it, faces formed then dissipated, eyes glared at them only to disappear moments later. "It does not make me feel comfortable," he said. "I feel I am being watched." Raliton grabbed a staff and pushed it toward the rolling clouds. They parted to let the staff touch the ceiling. "Strange," Raliton said. "Very peculiar, indeed."

"Like her pet," Innead said while nodding at the falgon. "I just ignore certain things."

"I never realized my brother's wife was so involved with the arcane arts. She and Enyra seem to be good friends. I will ask Enyra what she has learned."

"My sons," King Lanfeld started. "I ask you to my bedside. My health is failing and I fear I shall soon travel to the Isle of Forgotten Sleep."

Raliton knelt by the bed, holding his father's hand. "You need not talk of such," he whispered. "You are still very strong."

"I am dying, Raliton," Lanfeld said, jerking his hands away to point. "Ask Innead, even that incompetent idiot realizes it. Did you bring me another potion to drink?" He glared at the advisor who stood at the foot of his bed.

"I have, my lord," he replied and handed the king a goblet. "Drink all of it."

"Have you ever given me something and said to only drink half?" Lanfeld sat and jerked the chalice from Innead's hand. He gulped down the contents. "Tastes terrible, as usual. Will it make me well, probably not. Why do I continue?" He lay back and turned to Raliton.

"Raliton, my son, it is time you performed The Challenge. It is time for you to journey to the lords of Adavinya and discharge the rites as set forth by King Arlyon to his son."

"I will accept the path you have decided," Raliton said. "But what of Adavin during my absence?"

"I can watch over Adavin in your absence, brother," Lornear said, he smiled at Raliton. "Have I not been your shadow for many Circles? Have I not been sitting in judgment with you these last Moons?"

Raliton looked up at his brother, surprised by the offer.

"It is a wise decision the two of you make." Lanfeld patted Raliton's hand. "Innead is here to assist Lornear in any issues that may be more unusual. Even in your absence, it will appear you are not absent. The people of Adavin will see a continuity of rule as they have never seen during any previous challenges — even mine." He coughed. "I have removed the stones from the scepter and given the High Priest of Bre the diamond of rule." He held up a bag with the three stones and nodded to the scepter on the small table at the edge of the bed.

"Father, what of your health in my absence?"

"I can keep you abreast of it, my brother," Lornear said. "All will be well. In fact, I think father will be up and about the day you leave."

"Raliton," Lanfeld whispered. "There is another condition I place on you."

"Yes, father. Anything."

"Innead, listen closely and place my words to paper." He patted the opposite side of his bed from Raliton. "Lornear, come closer. Listen, my son."

Lornear moved and knelt by his father, taking the old man's hands into his.

"There is a stipulation I set for Raliton. He will go forth to the lords of Adavinya. He will visit the under-lords of a realm, earning their acceptance. He will attend the over-lord of each realm, obtaining their acknowledgment before moving on to the next realm. So, we all understand, that is part of The Challenge." Lanfeld turned to face his eldest son. "Now, I add, that you, Raliton, must produce an heir in the line of First Borns. If an heir is not apparent within one Circle of my going to the Isle of Forgotten Sleep, you will voluntarily step down and Lornear will rule since he has a first-born son."

"Yes, father," Raliton said. "As you wish."

"Yes, father," Lornear whispered while hiding his smile.

Lanfeld turned to Lornear. "My son," he said. "I know Namo-Ke is with child again. You have produced an heir for me if Raliton fails. You have made me proud."

Lornear bowed his head and placed his forehead on Lanfeld's hand. Raliton repeated the movement on the opposite side of the bed — a mirror image of the two brothers.

"I swear an oath to you, my father," Raliton said. "I will have an heir upon my return to Adavin by next Nos'Nevel." He looked up at Innead. "Place my words also to your paper, my oath."

Innead nodded. "I will place all these words to paper."

Raliton reached up to hug his father. "I will prepare for departure of The Challenge which will be at the end of Nos'Nevel. Today, Lornear and I will ride, together as equals, to open Nos'Nevel."

Raliton didn't see the look which passed between Innead and Lornear — Innead's of fear, Lornear's of sly satisfaction.

CHAPTER 19: Nos'Nevel

The plan is in motion
A fraudulent drinking potion
The king is at Death's door
Allowing Lornear to roar
As Namo-Ke creates
While Innead meditates
The Dark One could not define it better.

from The Ballad of the Fire

King Lanfeld lay in his bed the morning of Nos'Nevel's arrival. The chamber echoing his wheezing and hacking cough. Innead stood at the foot of his bed, Namo-Ke beside him. Miasi sat on the king's right side of the bed, holding his hand.

"Is there nothing you can give me for this?" Lanfeld whined. "My body hurts from all this coughing."

"You gave him the medicine?" Namo-Ke whispered.

Innead nodded. "I reduced the amount of your potion to the mixture." Innead glanced nervously at Namo-Ke before continuing. "Lornear wants him to be of some health when Raliton leaves."

Namo-Ke turned and leaned against the railing of the king's bed. "Now, now," she touted and traced a finger down Innead's arm. "We don't want this old man to be dancing in the hallways."

"No, but..." Innead hesitated. "We want him well enough to see Raliton off." He stooped to pick up the flask at his foot. "After than?" He shrugged. "The king must become more than bedridden. Is that not correct?"

"You learn well and fast, my dear apprentice," Namo-Ke hissed. "You will serve Lornear well." She glanced over Innead's shoulder. "And here comes our next king."

"Are you two plotting, again?" Lornear looked to his father. "Dearest father," he said and went to the bedside to hold Lanfeld's hand. "Do you feel better today?"

"A bit, my son," the old man replied feebly. "Do you prepare for your journey to the lords?"

"Father, it is me — Lornear."

"Oh, my son. Forgive an old man's eyesight and hearing. Is that dirt on your face?" He reached to touch Lornear's face. "You appear different but now you sound the same. There is a newness in you, Lornear."

"I only wished to come in to see you before I joined Raliton for the Nos'Nevel procession. I will return shortly. I see Namo-Ke and Innead are taking care of you for now. I feel you are in good hands. As a future queen, Enyra must participate in the procession."

"They have a lot on their minds," Lanfeld said and patted Lornear's hand. "Go, my son. Join Raliton and do your royal duty."

"As you wish," Lornear said. He turned quickly to Namo-Ke and Innead, nodded to them and flashed the secretive glance at his wife. They all smiled among themselves, but said nothing.

"Lornear!" Raliton called. "I thought you'd forgotten. The stable boy has Nightfire ready for you. Hurry, we're about to start."

Lornear swung himself into the saddle and sat there looking at the pageantry from this new perspective. He turned and saw Maisa and Enyra.

"Mother? Are you sure you wish to do this?"

"It is required," she said softly. "Innead is with your father and being well tended. I will perform my duty before returning to his side."

The heralds trumpeted and the fanfare began. Raliton and Lornear urged their horses forward and the procession to Obera's Obelisk began. The celebration of Nos'Nevel began.

"It is unfortunate Namo-Ke could not join us, my brother, but she told me she was working with Innead to heal our father," Raliton said. He turned and looked back at Enyra. Namo-Hoj rode with her. "Although I do believe your son is enjoying the experience."

Lornear nodded agreement and said nothing. He sat proudly on Nightfire and waved to the townspeople as they passed them. Lornear was able to catch Enyra blow a kiss to her father as they passed the jeweler's store and her old home. He fought the urges swelling in him; he wanted to kick, or lash out in some manner at the old man. He kept silent.

Without realizing how quickly they traveled, they arrived at the obelisk and Raliton was dismounting.

"Stand beside me, brother, as I speak. I want all to see we are equal."

"If you wish," Lornear said. He held back the grin that would reveal his glee.

Raliton rushed up the steps and moved forward on the platform. He turned and motioned Lornear to him. Maisa and Enyra stood to the side, unobtrusive to the business at hand. Raliton raised his hands to quiet the gathered mob.

"My countrymen," he started. "Today, my brother, Lornear, and I bring mixed news. Our father, your king, is ill and rests. I open the celebration of Nos'Nevel for him and with my brother, I now tell you our father's wishes. "He placed an arm around Lornear's shoulders. "Our father has issued a command that I, as first born, shall now face The Challenge and visit the various lords of Adavinya. With our father sick, Lornear will govern the kingdom while I perform my duties in preparation of ascending the throne. For the next Circle, I will be away with my lovely wife, Enyra. When I return, next Nos'Nevel, I have assured my father a son, heir apparent, will be with me."

The crowd cheered at the words that Raliton would return with a son. Again, he raised his hands to quiet them.

"Please," Raliton said. "I now give you Prince Lornear." He motioned for his brother to speak.

There was a small amount of cheering.

"Fellow countrymen," he said. "I stand here, humbled to be in my father's boots, to rule Adavinya during my brother's absence. I pray your assistance during this time." He looked out among the gathered throng. "The fields are planted. I am proud to announce — let the celebration of Nos'Nevel begin."

The crowd broke into a melee of cheers, yelling and music as they burst with a flurry to visit the vendors and begin the three day celebration of Planting Time.

Raliton oversaw the gathering of rations, tents, people and everything else necessary for the journey to the under lords. The three days of festivities blurred and it was time. The morning came and Raliton sat atop Shadowfeet, the red roan prancing ever so nervously. It was then he heard the commotion.

"What is this?" he asked pulling up to the carriage where Enyra sat.

Namo-Ke sulked with her arms folded tightly in front of her. Namo-Hoj stood boldly by her side, tugging on one of her leggings.

"I said to your wife, Enyra, I am to come along," Namo-Ke blurted angrily. "It is necessary but she will not allow it. What will she do if she were to become pregnant. I have the skills. I have the knowledge."

Shadowfeet pranced nervously.

"Namo-Ke," Raliton soothed. "I believe there will be those who know how to midwife at each of the lord's homes."

"But I would be there in an emergency," Namo-Ke pleaded, her eyes flaring red.

"I assure you, Namo-Ke, each over-lord has the necessary personnel to assist in a birthing. Enyra is not now pregnant and it would be a waste for you to journey with us."

Namo-Ke narrowed her eyes and glared at the young prince. Prince Raliton reared back in his saddle at the look.

"My dear sister," he started. "I assure you; all will be fine. Right now, you need to attend to your own health."

She reared her head up and shot him a glance. "What of your wife's? I have been giving her a daily potion to keep her strong. Who will make this if I am not there?"

"Namo-Ke," Raliton said strongly. "Everything will be fine. Your health is more critical at the present. Yes, I've already learned of your condition. We should be more concerned for your health than ours right now. I think it would be best if you stayed with your husband to help him oversee Adavinya's needs."

"But what if Enyra becomes pregnant," Namo-Ke pleaded again.

Raliton held up a hand to quiet her. "We can send for you at that time. Will that not suffice?"

Innead stepped down from the shadows of the archway to stand behind Namo-Ke. He placed a comforting hand on each shoulder. "Hush," he whispered. "All will be fine."

"Besides," Raliton continued, ignoring Innead's actions. "I need you to assist Innead with the potions to aid my father's health. I want him strong when I return so he may play with my son as he has done yours."

"As you wish," Namo-Ke whispered and stroked her stomach. "Your command."

"Prince Raliton," Innead said. "I did not come here to get Namo-Ke, but to bring somebody to wish you safe journey." He motioned back to the archway and two servants assisted King Lanfeld into the sunlight. He held onto a walking stick, wobbling for support. The servants quickly disappeared, leaving him alone to stand proudly.

"Father! It is good to see you about."

"I wanted to see you away on The Challenge. Every king since King Arlyon has seen his first-born journey out the gates. I could not break tradition."

Raliton dismounted and ran up to him. "I am honored, father." He hugged the old man closely. "I shall perform my duty and return by next Nos'Nevel to ascend the throne."

The king looked to Enyra. "My dear, I pray you return to me with an heir. Safe journey."

"Stay well, my king," Enyra said and nodded from the carriage.

"Now, be about," Lanfeld said, waving his hand to dismiss Raliton. "I am tiring already and you've not left yet."

Raliton mounted Shadowfeet and rushed to the front.

"Where have you been?" Lornear asked while grabbing Shadowfeet's reins. "What was all the commotion?"

"Fighting with your wife," Raliton sighed. "She was quite adamant she would journey with us. Since she is with child, I thought it best she remains here. Plus, father was up to see me off."

Lornear frowned at the words then shrugged. "As you wish. Safe journey, my brother. I await your return." He bowed his head slightly and then patted Shadowfeet reassuringly.

"The Challenge begins," Raliton shouted. He stood in the stirrups and motioned for the group to follow him. He sat in the saddle and once again touched the leather bag with the three stones, the Stones of Rule at his side, while in the crook of his arm he held the scepter as he led the procession out the gate and through the city. He nodded silent approval that the diamond was being held by the holy priest in the Temple of Bre.

Lanfeld, standing alone, shaded his eyes with a hand to watch Raliton depart. It was then he heard a voice, one he'd not heard for some time. It whispered in his left ear: "Beware when the son is doubled."

In the distance he heard the dark man titter. He gazed in the sound's direction. The dark man danced precariously on the parapet over the exit where Raliton led his group out of the city.

Lornear smiled — it was not a smile of joy.

CHAPTER 20: The Journey Begins

Into valleys of verdant green
Lush growth of a perfect scene
Goes a prince, duty to a call
An oath by jewels, three in all
By the Lords of Adavinya
Along the Cat King idea

from The Ballad of the Fire

Raliton led the group through the streets of the city, children chasing and singing songs while waving flags and fronds. Soon, the outside the walls were no longer visible and they headed for the large open expanse beyond Obera's Obelisk.

Raliton turned west onto the road toward the sun's nocturnal home. He smiled, knowing soon he would be king and Enyra would be with child as he promised his father. Raliton suddenly frowned at his thoughts realizing when he was king, his father would be gone, or possibly soon thereafter. He rode silently in thought, letting Shadowfeet set the pace.

"Sire, your wife wonders when we will break for the midday meal?"

Raliton turned to face Alson. The man, a few years younger than himself, smiled and his eyes gleamed with excitement. Raliton fretted whether he had made the proper choice in an advisor. Alson seemed overly excited by the adventure, almost immature and childlike. Raliton thought it best to keep Innead until everyone felt Alson had attained the proper skills. Raliton pointed to a cluster of trees. "We will rest and take a meal under those trees there."

"A wise choice, my lord," Alson said. "If memory serves me properly, I believe there to be a small creek nearby to refresh our water supplies."

"Alson, you worry too much," Raliton said. "We will be at our destination before the evening meal. Do you truly feel we will run out of water before then?" He pulled up on the reigns of the horse and Shadowfeet stopped. The rest of the group stopped also.

"Is there a problem?" Alson asked.

"I see movement amongst the trees," Raliton said. "I think we should be cautious."

"I'll send a guard forward," Alson said. "If there is a danger, he will attend to it."

The dispatched guard charged toward the small outcropping of trees. Suddenly the guard started to shout and shake his spear in the air. The activity at the trees stopped and the guard continued to the destination. Just as quickly, the guard raced back to the group.

"Prince Raliton," he shouted. "The trees are now secured. It was only a small group of farmers and their families who were resting, playing and enjoying a meal. They are leaving immediately so you may rest there."

"You immediately return to them," Raliton said. "I do not wish to push others away. Perhaps they will join us, share in our bounty, and I may talk with the men and to learn more about the area."

"As you wish, sire," the guard said. He turned his horse and charged back toward the trees and the families there.

Raliton raised his arm and signaled the entourage to proceed. Alson nodded. "I will be at Princess Enyra's side and call," he said.

"That will be fine," Raliton said and turned to those behind him. "I am going to hasten to our resting place to speak with the farmers before they are overwhelmed."

Raliton urged Shadowfeet forward and soon was charging across the distance. He arrived quickly and dismounted, tying Shadowfeet loosely to a brush.

"Prince Raliton," the guard said. "This is Joalmore, a farmer for Under-lord Laminar."

"Your highness." Joalmore bowed. "My family and friends are more than willing to move on so you may enjoy this area."

"Come. Sit with me farmer Joalmore." Raliton stretched out an arm to place his hand on the farmer's shoulder. "I ask you bring your other friends with you so we may talk. I wish to learn your thoughts."

"Sire," the guard said. "Do you require my services? To be alone with these strangers would put yourself in danger. I promised your father..."

Raliton raised a hand to stop the guard. "My father?"

"Forgiveness, sire," the guard said. "I have been reluctant to reveal my true identity. I am Halsvar, son of Menlo. I have been assigned to protect you and attempt to be inconspicuous." He hung his head. "Of that, I have failed."

"You may rest, Halsvar, these farmers should prove no danger to me," Raliton said. "Assist elsewhere. You are serving me well."

Raliton looked at the farmers, their wives and children. It was strange the whole family was here when they should have been working but still, it was an opportunity for him to learn even more from the people he would come to rule.

"Tell me, Joalmore..." Raliton found a large stone on which to sit. "Why are you here?"

Joalmore stood silently and motionless then sheepishly looked down at the ground.

"My lord," he said. "We were farmers for Lord Laminar. He took our homes and the lands we worked for a tax he placed on them. We are homeless. My brother, Hanilol," he nodded at the man to his left, "also lost his possessions along with our friend, Melniar."

"Then what brings you to this place?"

"We are on our way to Adavin," Joalmore replied.

"To find a position within the city," Melniar added.

Raliton nodded his head, listening to the men talk. He again scrutinized the people about him and noticed the children hiding behind the women.

"My lord?" Enyra called, coming up behind Raliton.

"You've arrived," he said, turning to see Enyra. "Are they preparing the meal?"

"Just starting to get the items around," she replied.

"Tell me truthfully, Joalmore. Have you had your mid-day meal?" Raliton asked while watching the farmer.

"I... we... No, my lord," Joalmore said. "But we will move on so you may enjoy your repast."

"My friend," Raliton said. "I ask you to join us and share of my meal. While the meal is prepared, let us discuss more of your future within the walls of Adavin."

"As you wish," Joalmore said. "My wife and the others will help with the meal." He motioned for the women to assist with the servants.

Raliton raised his hand to stop the women. "Your wives will join my wife and they will discuss that which women find to discuss. The children may continue to play to entertain themselves. Youth passes too quickly."

"You honor us, my lord," Joalmore said.

"What talents do you have?" Raliton asked. "You go to Adavin to work but we have plenty of farmers already there. Where would you labor? Live? Do you have relatives in Adavin?"

Joalmore shook his head, as did the other two men.

"We are but simple farmers. We work with hoe and rake to attend the fields."

"Alson!" Raliton called loudly. "Attend me with pen and parchment."

Alson came running with the required items. He stood to Raliton's right side.

"Place these words to paper," Raliton said. "My father, King Lanfeld, I beseech you to attend my request. The bearer of this parchment, farmer Joalmore, and his brother, Hanilol and their friend, Melniar, I ask you to find positions within my house. These men are farmers and therefore understand the land. I ask you have them to work on the park at Obera's Obelisk, tending the ornamental gardens. Also, within the castle, I request they make necessary additions to the open areas, fountains and floral gardens. They will be royal gardeners."

"My lord," Joalmore said. "You honor us beyond our wonders."

"I offer this in return of a full understanding why you lost your homes to Lord Laminar." Raliton slowly stroked his chin in thought. "I wish to understand this man."

Joalmore nervously glanced at his companions.

"I do not wish to speak ill of Lord Laminar." Hanilol lowered his head and stared at the dust about his feet. "We have lost our homes and land. I do not wish to lose my life or family."

Raliton watched the other two.

Joalmore nodded approval of his brother's words. "I join my brother in his words. I must not speak ill of Lord Laminar."

"I will forfeit the parchment, also," Melniar said.

"Come, let us go eat," Raliton said. "Alson, allow me to sign and seal the parchment. I will give it to Joalmore and I will personally speak with Under-lord Laminar of this incident."

Raliton signed the paper. Alson rolled the parchment and melted the wax to seal it shut. Raliton placed his ring insignia in the warm wax to lock it.

"Seek my father during judgment and offer this parchment." Raliton handed the rolled paper to Joalmore. "If my father's health is still failing, my brother, Prince Lornear will hold judgment and honor my request."

CHAPTER 21: Under-Lord Laminar

The Challenge taken, a challenge unseen,
All neatly woven within verdant green.
A lord in doubt, a prince to find
The duty called, an oath to bind.
An intrigue's veil was hidden well
With two to learn and none to tell.

from The Ballad of the Fire

Raliton bid the farmers a farewell giving each a gold piece for their time and knowledge. Only after much cajoling with the farmers was Raliton able to learn about the man he was soon to visit. Until today, Raliton only knew the Laminar who visited his father and feasted with the other lords of the realm. The image painted by the farmers were of a different color and now he understood the seeming oddness of that particular lord when he visited his father's court.

"I will see you upon my return." Raliton mounted Shadowfeet.

He turned the horse and watched the others finish the last of the packing. He stood in the stirrups and searched the group, noting Enyra smiling at him. Finally, the person he sought popped into view and he urged the horse in the direction of Alson.

"Alson," he said. "Mount your steed and attend me. I wish to discuss..." He hesitated then shook his head. "Attend me." Raliton rode a short distance from the group and waited.

Alson quickly mounted his horse and joined Raliton. They slowly circled the wooded area.

"What troubles you, sire?"

"Did you hear what Joalmore spoke of, Alson? Farming fees? Paid to Laminar?"

"I heard some of it," Alson replied. "Is this a concern for you?"

"It has always been farmers give a share of their crops to the reigning regent in return for the protection he provides. My father even pays the farmers for their services." Raliton turned in his saddle to face Alson. "He has never charged a farmer for toiling in the fields."

"Still, Lord Raliton. It is Laminar's right as regent of the area."

Raliton straightened in his saddle. "You think this proper then?"

"I did not say that, m'lord. I said it was his right."

Raliton stared into the distance, toward the area they were headed.

"I feel there is more than what meets the eye here, my advisor. Laminar has taken the fields of these farmers."

"You believe them, lord Raliton?"

"Alson! Why would they lie to me? I am the future king. They gain nothing by telling me untruths. If I find it to be they have lied, I will have my father or brother attend to the proper chastisements."

"My lord," Alson said, his voice soothing and calm. "You have bestowed upon me the honor of being your advisor. Let me advise. Go to Under-lord Laminar and seek the truth. If the farmer Joalmore has been truthful, the Under-lord cannot keep that secret too long. The whispers of the streets in Alitro will tell me what I need to know."

Raliton narrowed his eyes and watched his advisor. Alson was learning quickly the best viable solution to an issue.

"I see your wife is attempting to gain our attention, m'lord." Alson nodded to the group. "I believe the caravan is ready to continue." He placed a hand over his brows and scanned the distance where the caravan would go. "I think we should reach our destination about late-afternoon."

Raliton nodded in agreement. "Attend my wife. I have much to think about." He raised his arm and the caravan started. He was a short distance ahead of the group when a guard broke out to join the prince.

"For your protection, sire," Halsvar said sharply.

Raliton nodded absently, deep in thought.

Shadowfeet whinnied and Raliton took notice of his surroundings. He and Halsvar rode in absolute silence while Raliton considered the words of Joalmore. The prince gazed at the view from atop the knoll. The road continued down the hill and curved slowly to the left where the first hints of a village could be seen just beyond the trees. Raliton looked to the guard.

"It seems we are almost to our destination," Raliton said and nodded in the direction of the village, Alitro.

"I shall send a messenger to Under-lord Laminar, notifying him of your arrival," Halsvar said.

"No," Raliton said. "I wish to announce myself. Go to Alson and tell him we ride ahead."

The guard hesitated and frowned at the request.

"Is there something you wish?" Raliton cocked a questioning eyebrow in Halsvar direction. "Alson awaits."

Halsvar turned his horse and headed back to the caravan, pushing the horse to top speed. Raliton waited for the guard to almost reach Alson before letting Shadowfeet loose to race to the village.

Leaning down and low to Shadowfeet's neck, Raliton charged to Alitro. He gave Shadowfeet full reign and did all he could to aid in the speedy escape. The edge of the village zoomed into view and soon he was at the village and saw the children playing in the streets. They were thin, frail and in tattered clothing. Raliton frowned at the sight. He saw the stately court where Under-lord Laminar resided. He pressed Shadowfeet forward as fast and carefully as he could, knowing full well Halsvar was close on his heels in an endeavor to protect him.

Raliton raced into the courtyard and quickly dropped from his saddle onto the cobblestones. A young boy ran to grab Shadowfeet's reins.

"Welcome to Alitro and Lord Laminar's castle," the boy said.

"I need to see Under-lord Laminar immediately," Raliton shouted.

"Lord Laminar is napping, sire."

"I care not what Under-lord Laminar is doing. I want to see him now."

"May I tell Lord Laminar who comes?" the boy asked.

A groomsman quickly approached and slapped the boy behind the head. "This is Prince Raliton, you idiot. Take him, now. No sass."

"Forgiveness, m'lord." The boy motioned for the prince to follow. "This way."

Another child was already racing ahead of them. Raliton noted it, knowing the child would notify Laminar of his arrival.

"My lord," Halsvar called loudly. "You must not leave my protection. I have sworn my life to your father."

Raliton turned and stared at the guard. "You will wait here until I return. I am taking care of business. This is official and there is no need of guard protection. Am I understood?"

"But your father—"

"I said you will remain here," Raliton shouted. He pointed his finger down at the marble floor. "That is not a request. It is a command."

Raliton cocked his head and looked directly into the guard's eye, waiting until the man hung his head. He turned and again followed the waiting young boy through the hallways of the court. Three rooms passed and the door was open on the fourth. The child who had raced ahead stood there to welcome him. He bowed and motioned for the prince to enter.

"My lord prince," Laminar said wallowing from the divan toward him. "What an unexpected pleasure. May I ask the reason of your visit?"

Raliton regarded the man before him, searching for what he knew not. He tried to place the person at a royal function. This was not the Laminar he remembered. He was sure he would have remembered anyone dressed as lavishly as Laminar — especially one as short and rotund.

Laminar bowed low, his heavily ringed, thick and stubby fingers holding out the furred cloak draped behind him. The bulky gold necklace with a large, green emerald dangling from it swung freely as he lowered his head. The small, jeweled crown barely stayed on his head, in amongst the myriad of curls.

"The Challenge." Raliton narrowed his eyes and scrutinized the room. "I am here on my year long quest in preparation of becoming the next king," Raliton said.

"Is your father ill?" Laminar stood, his eyes wide in mock shock.

"My father has been ailing, but is as well as can be expected," Raliton replied with nonchalance. "King Lanfeld has decided I should ascend the throne and has sent me on the journey of The Challenge. My father is in good hands with my brother, Prince Lornear."

"Ah, yes." Laminar placed an index finger to his lips. The ruby ring glistened in the sunlight as he tapped his lower lip. "I heard Prince Lornear returned at a most opportune moment." He hesitated. "Oh, and with a wife and child, no less. Having all the family together must be a pleasant thing." Laminar's syrupy voice wrapped in snideness was blatant.

Raliton glanced about the room, it was more lavish than his own quarters at the castle in Adavin.

"My caravan should be arriving shortly. I hope we aren't too much of an inconvenience. All we require is a night with an evening meal." Raliton paused. "And, of course, quarters."

"A meal? Rooms? For how many?" Laminar staggered back, catching himself on the divan. "I am not prepared to host a party."

"We are a small company," Raliton said. "No more than thirty. We had a light mid-day meal and, therefore, many could be quite ravenous. Would you like my servants to assist yours?"

"You brought supplies?"

"My dear under-lord," Raliton said, blinking his eyes in innocence. "You would ask me to share my meager stores with you? I would think you'd open your larder to us, perhaps a fatted calf to celebrate? As to rooms..." Raliton stroked his chin while he considered his words. "A room for me with a guard's quarter, another for my advisor. I would say perhaps a total of five rooms. The servants can set up tents in the courtyard for the evening." He gazed at the under-lord. "Is that too much to ask?"

"Oh, of course not," Laminar replied nervously. "I will see to it immediately."

He motioned to the small boy and whispered instructions to him. The boy nodded and left.

"All will be as you wish," Laminar said. "Shall we go to the courtyard and welcome those arriving?" He turned a nervous eye to Raliton. "Is your wife with you?"

Raliton nodded silently. His first impulse had been to immediately attack Laminar about the farmers and their land. After seeing the opulence of the room and the under-lord's demeanor, he decided perhaps Alson's decision was the better choice. He waited.

CHAPTER 22: The Conflict

Subterfuge is quick to lay hidden
While opulence flowers totally unbidden
Working alone without fail
Laying his plans, to set sail.
The Other plots, working the plan
The downfall of the Cat King clan

from The Ballad of the Fire

Raliton sat silently at the table. He watched the activities of the room. To his right was Enyra and to his left was Alson while directly opposite him was Laminar who continued to be concerned about the possible damages to his luxurious courtyard. On Laminar's left was his so-called advisor, Marnelan and to Laminar's right was his latest companion, a young lady named Tessila. Raliton watched Marnelan who ate voraciously and kept pushing his unkempt, greasy locks of hair behind his ears. Marnelan's extremely hawk-beaked nose and narrow, beady eyes reminded Raliton of a vulture. The advisor's actions only reinforced Raliton's mental image.

What concerned Raliton the most were the two empty chairs dividing the two groups. He knew in Adavin they only placed enough chairs to seat the party at the table. Empty chairs were removed to avoid any awkward isolations. The prince cut his meat and slowly chewed on it, extracting the flavors and savoring them as the juices chased a path down his throat. Raliton could only think this was Laminar's crass decision.

"M'lord," Enyra whispered. "You seem so distant tonight. Is there a problem?"

"No, my dear," he replied, smiled and patted her hand which she had moved toward him. "Everything is fine. Are you enjoying the meal?"

"Yes, Princess Enyra," Laminar spoke up. "How do you find the meal? I know it could never match the culinary expertise of Adavin, but one tries." He tittered.

Enyra swallowed. "The meal is excellent Under-lord Laminar. I don't believe I've ever tasted the yellow fruit before. May I ask its name?"

Laminar giggled. "We call it Yellow Fruit and it grows on a limited number of trees at the edge of the forest."

"Strange," Raliton said. "I don't believe I've ever seen this at court." He glared directly at Laminar and controlled the urge to stand. "Have you never offered the king this treat?"

"Sire," Laminar cried. "There is so little of the fruit."

"I understand," Raliton said.

He closed his eyes and breathed deeply as he'd been taught, remaining calm was important. Raliton quickly opened his eyes and smiled at the gathered group around the table.

"Let us finish our meal," Laminar said. "Then we may move to the Judgment Hall for entertainment."

Raliton and Alson cocked an eye at Laminar's words. *Judgment Hall?*

"Gentlemen, please," he said. "It was short notice but I was able to find a few performers in my humble village to entertain such honored guests tonight. It should prove quite enjoyable."

"Lord Laminar manages to squeeze the best from his people," Marnelan said between bites. "It is a lord's right, is it not?"

"Intriguing question, advisor Marnelan," Raliton said while glancing about the room. "What Under-lord Laminar has done to wrap so much comfort about him is interesting."

"My lord," Alson whispered. "This is neither the time nor the place. I beg you to seek my consul before continuing this line of discussion. I have learned much."

"My lord prince," Laminar said. "I have only surrounded myself with that which any lord should have. Are you saying I must deny myself these pleasures as a lord?"

"The meal is pleasant," Raliton said. "Let us not foul our mouths with a possibly distasteful discussion. There is time for talk later."

"Favor a silly princess, my under-lord," Enyra said. "May I ask what entertainment you have scheduled?"

"Lord Laminar has" Tessila started.

"Shush, my dear," Laminar said, frowning at Tessila and patting her hand. "Princess Enyra directed the question at me. I am the lord here, allow me to answer."

"Under-lord," Raliton said under his breath. "Under-lord."

"Sire," Alson said. "We will talk before the entertainment begins. Wait."

"Did you say something, Prince Raliton?" Laminar asked.

"I'm fine," Raliton replied with a false smile. "You were saying?"

"Oh, yes," Laminar said. He placed his elbows on the table, cupped his hands together and placed his double chin on them. "We have a few jugglers and they will perform some acrobatics."

Tessila clapped her hands excitedly.

"Also, I have a performer who will set a sword aflame and swallow it."

Enyra reared back. "Is that not dangerous?"

Laminar sat there, smug and smiled at her. "It is all part of the show." He eased back into his high-backed chair. "I'm sure you find it all enjoyable."

"Remarkable," Raliton said. "If you will allow, I would like a few minutes to consult with my people before the entertainment to make sure all is ready for tonight and tomorrow's departure."

Laminar absently waved his hand to dismiss him. "As you wish, Prince Raliton."

Prince Raliton noted the gesture and fought the urge, gritted his teeth and forced a smile at Laminar before departing.

"Have you ever seen such arrogance?" Raliton yelled, stepping into his room with Alson. "The man is full of pomp. He even has the audacity of having a Judgment Hall. Only the king has such."

Alson sat on an ottoman and waited as Raliton paced the room, letting the anger depart his body. He listened to the prince rant.

"If you will," Alson finally said. "Lord Laminar..."

"Under-lord," Raliton screamed. "Under-lord. Do you hear me, Alson?"

"Under-lord Laminar has taken more presumptuous steps than any other under-lord or lord, for that matter. I am sure you've noticed the extreme show of wealth."

Raliton eased onto the bed's edge and gazed at Alson.

"My lord prince," Alson continued. "My eyes have noticed more than you suspect by visiting the village before the meal. They have reported certain things to me from this kitchen, the streets of the village and from the fields beyond."

"Your eyes?"

Alson shrugged a shoulder. "Spies, if you will. I call them my eyes since they see and report to me. Are you curious to what they gleaned?"

Raliton nodded for Alson to continue.

"You are right, m'lord," Alson said. "Laminar has commanded his subjects to call him lord, not under-lord. He has taken the liberty of creating a Judgment Hall to distribute justice to his subjects so they don't bother the king. Most of the populace are in fear of him, yet at the same time they loath the man he has become. Now, as to the farmers we met earlier. It is true he sent them from their land and does enforce a fee to all for their labors. In fact, all the inhabitants he rules over are subject to this labor fee, as he calls it. This money is used to allow him the comfort he feels due him. As to the land, it was confiscated to allow him to create groves of this yellow fruit tree."

"Where did you learn all this so quickly?" Raliton asked in utter amazement.

"You assigned me to be your advisor," Alson said. "I was talking with Innead initially, but he was busy with Namo-Ke. I finally came to work with his two assistant advisers to learn all the tricks of the trade."

"And what do you advise me?"

"You cannot leave this man in rule here," Alson said. "He is a thorn and his subterfuge goes unchallenged. He mocks the royal court of Adavin. At your wedding, he attended and appeared the shabbiest of all those in attendance. What I tell you next, I say only to protect my lord. I fear he plots against you, my lord. My eyes tell me he favors your brother, Prince Lornear, as ruler. I've discovered he has visited Adavin unnoticed to talk, possibly plot, with him."

Raliton raised an eyebrow and silently watched Alson.

"Enough," Raliton said while raising his hand. "We will not discuss this further. I have heard your words. I will sleep on them tonight, and tomorrow, in the new light, I will make my decision."

"As you wish, m'lord," Alson said, stood and started for the door.

"Wait," Raliton said and held up his hand to stop Alson. "Tell me, my good advisor, if I were to remove Laminar from his position, who would I have to replace him?"

"My lord," Alson said with a bow. "I am an advisor, not a soothsayer. Laminar has no close relative nor does he have an apparent heir. To pick a replacement, chose anyone you wish or..." Alson started grinning. "Give the deed of replacement to Over-Lord Balneor. Is this not his realm?"

"You will make an excellent advisor," Raliton said. He placed a hand on Alson's shoulder. "Let us go now to this so-called Judgment Hall and be entertained."

Alson smiled, the honor and sarcasm had not been lost on him.

"Ah, Prince Raliton, you return," Laminar said as the two entered the chamber. He lay on a cluster of pillows and patted for them to join him. "We can let the festivities begin." He clapped his hands. "Tessila and your wife have been giggling over there for some time. I have no idea what is so funny."

Raliton walked over to the empty pillows, wrinkled his nose then plopped down to set cross-legged on a large pillow.

"I eagerly await your entertainment, Laminar."

"You will find the sword act especially interesting," Laminar sneered.

"Perhaps it is a good thing my personal guard is nearby," Raliton said and nodded his head to an area just behind Laminar.

Laminar rolled back and turned his head to see where Raliton motioned. The body's tension movement of shock by Laminar amused Raliton. The under-lord returned to his viewing position; his face ashen.

"I did not realize he was behind me," Laminar whispered. "He is very quiet."

"He does his job well, then," Raliton said, stoically. "Very well."

Raliton eased back on the pillow, letting his hands rest on the floor and his arms to prop his body to watch the show. The jugglers tossed a myriad of colored balls back and forth, a veritable rainbow swirling before them.

CHAPTER 23: A Struggle of Power

Hidden in a corner shadow
The Other plots his next big show
Regent and prince in anger bold
Pierces the body as is told
The Other does his dance
To trip one with a lance

from The Ballad of the Fire

The morning sun cast its bright light into the room leaving only one corner in shadows where The Other cringed, waiting, watching. Raliton awoke with a frown; his concerns of Laminar wore heavily on him.

"One day on the journey," he said softly. "One day and already it feels like I have been away more than three moons."

"What is your problem, my love," Enyra whispered. "You tossed and turned much last night. I was tempted to wake you but you'd finally found rest and I saw no reason."

Raliton turned and smiled at Enyra. "It was only dreams, my love. Certainly, no reason for concern."

Enyra frowned at his words. "Concern? Dreams?"

"Let us be about and quickly," Raliton said. "I fear the longer we tryst here, the more chance of an ill omen befalling us. What I must do weighs heavily on me."

Enyra wrapped her night robe tightly about her. She stretched and placed her arms about Raliton's neck and kissed him. "What must you do, my husband?" She lay her head on his chest.

"I wish to do naught and defer my issues to Over-lord Balneor."

"So be it," she whispered.

He held her tightly and caressed the top of her head. "Only if we leave quickly and can avoid any confrontation. I'll call the servants."

The servants entered bearing a breakfast of hard-boiled eggs, assorted breads, pastries, fruits and an herbal tea. Raliton ate then dressed quickly. The handmaidens addressed the issues of what Enyra would wear and how her hair would be done.

"Quickly ladies," Raliton said at the door as he stepped into the hallway.

"The wagons are packed, m'lord," Halsvar said, startling Raliton.

"That is well," the prince said. "Where is Alson? Laminar?"

"Your advisor is in the courtyard awaiting you." Halsvar followed Raliton down the hallway. "I believe Under-lord Laminar still sleeps in his chambers. Do you wish I have him awakened?"

"It would be best if he were in attendance at our departure." Raliton sighed and waved his hand to allow the command to be executed. Laminar must be summoned.

Raliton stepped into the courtyard and saw Alson had indeed gotten the caravan about and packed.

"My prince," Alson started. "I fear today an omen. The soothsayer sought me out early this morning and foretold the death of Laminar by your hand." He shrugged.

"If we leave quickly, the soothsayer's prophetic words will be words in the wind," Raliton replied.

Raliton gazed about the area. They awaited only three people, now two: Enyra and Laminar. Raliton paced, watching the doorway. He smiled. Enyra walked through the arch with her handmaidens following. She nodded to Raliton and they quickly boarded the proper wagons. Everyone waited on Laminar. Raliton paced the courtyard one complete circuit when Laminar appeared.

"My good prince," Laminar said. He stood atop the stairs of the archway leading into the courtyard. "As lord of this realm I wish—"

"You, Laminar, are an under-lord," Raliton shouted. "You are not a lord."

Laminar pulled himself to a full stature, sucking in the rotund stomach, his eyes flared.

"Prince Raliton," he said calmly. "I am regent. I am lord of this realm. I say and do as I please within the walls of my home and my village. Do you deny me my rights?"

Raliton walked slowly and deliberately toward the over-stuffed man. He held his hand on his sword. Laminar stepped back.

"Retreat in fear, little weasel," Raliton said. "You have over presumed your position. You answer to Over-lord Balneor." He raised his hand and pointed a finger at Laminar. "But you answer to me for all your transgressions, whether through Balneor or not."

"I do as I see fit for my realm," Laminar said in a trembling voice.

"Do you deny you stole land from a group of farmers?"

"I took that which was mine," Laminar spat. "These are my lands."

"No," Raliton yelled. "These lands are my father's, not yours. These lands belong to the those who work the fields. You are but an under-lord to oversee the execution of the king's requests via your over-lord." Raliton ceremoniously pulled his sword and pointed it at Laminar's protruding belly. "Do you wish to do combat to retain your rights? If these are truly your lands, then I must defend my father's rights and fight you to the death to reclaim or lose them."

"My lord, Prince Raliton," Laminar stammered. "I only meant I control the usage." He clasped his hands before him. "I beg your mercy."

A shadow moved to Raliton's right.

Laminar stepped forward, his foot tangling in his nightshirt. His eyes flared wide in surprise. He tripped, impaled himself on Raliton's sword which was held less than a forearm's distance away.

Raliton pulled the sword back and tossed it to the side. He grabbed Laminar and helped ease him to the ground.

"Forgiveness, my Prince Raliton," Laminar whispered. "It was my fault."

"My sword did not pierce your heart," Raliton said. "Perhaps a healer will be able to mend the cut. I do not think it to be fatal."

"Relay to Over-lord Balneor my wishes he supports you as king," Laminar whispered. "I was wrong to think your brother, Prince Lornear, should be king."

"Carry Under-lord Laminar to his bed," Raliton commanded. "Call a healer immediately." Servants scurried about. He turned to Laminar. "I must be about my challenge. I will forward your wishes to Over-lord Balneor. I will think strongly on your words I have heard."

"At least in my death I will know I have done proper," Laminar said. He gasped for air and blood continued to spread on the nightshirt, even though a servant pressed firmly on the wound.

"As you say," Raliton said. "I will consult with Over-lord Balneor and have another placed in charge of this realm, whether you live or die. It seems you have been less than honorable in your actions to the king. I will address this conversation with my brother upon my return to determine the full impact of your actions…" He paused. "And his."

"I pray I die now than face the shame that is to come," Laminar said.

Raliton nodded and the servants carried Laminar to his chamber. He stood and faced those in the courtyard which had filled with the news of Laminar having been injured.

"I will leave a messenger here to relay me the final fate of Under-lord Laminar. You!" He pointed at one of Alson's assistants. "I command you to stay and be in charge until a final resolution has been commissioned by Over-lord Balneor. You temporarily now have all the rights of an under-lord and your word is final unless overruled by Over-lord Balneor, myself, or the king. Is that understood?"

The man nodded his head in acknowledgment. "As you command, m'lord."

"Fine. What is your name?"

"Reestan, m'lord," the man replied.

"Halsvar!" Raliton yelled.

"Yes, sire," the guard said.

"Select a man, a well trusted guard, to stay and protect Reestan, the new under-lord I have assigned. Also, select a messenger... no, two messengers. One will be sent immediately to Over-lord Balneor informing him of the current state of mayhem here. The other messenger to Adavinya to Prince Lornear."

"Immediately, sire," Halsvar said.

"To all within my hearing, this is a temporary measure, one meant to last no more than three or four nights. I am sure Over-lord Balneor will act immediately upon this instance and a new under-lord will be assigned. At that time, I fully expect all my staff to join me on my journey. To the villagers I say this, go forth and spread the news Laminar is no longer the under-lord of this realm. Under-lord Reestan will serve to oversee only. All judgments must be brought either to Adavin or Vishalia. I, Prince Raliton, have mandated such."

Raliton turned and noted Alson standing near and walked to him.

"Has the healer arrived?"

Alson nodded solemnly.

"Will he live? Why, in Bre's name, did he fall?"

Alson placed a comforting arm over Raliton's shoulder. "All is as it should be. You did no wrong. The soothsayer's words came true."

"My brother? Lornear? Could what Laminar say be right? Is there truly a subterfuge in the castle of Adavin or even within the realm of Adavinya?"

"I will speak no evil of your brother, Prince Raliton," Alson said. "But, still, he has a son and you have none. The rule of the Cat King must continue; therefore, I suggest you spend more time with Enyra and less time being a proper prince or want-to-be king." He smiled impishly. "I believe you understand my hidden meaning."

"Trust me, Alson," Raliton said. "I made a promise to my father and I will uphold it. I will have a son before I return to Adavin."

"My lord prince?" a small voice called.

Raliton turned to the young girl standing a short distance away.

"M'lord," the girl said. "The healer says that Laminar's wound will heal. There may be infection, but he will live."

"Thank you," Raliton said and waved a hand to dismiss her.

"I am sure Over-lord Balneor will request Laminar's presence very soon," Alson said.

"Write down the words necessary to inform Balneor of the incident and send it immediately." He removed his ring and handed it to Alson. "Seal it. I will visit with Enyra. Our group will depart for Under-lord Viov's village before the sun reaches its zenith." Raliton stared into the distance.

"As you wish, m'lord." Alson offered a knowing smile and bowed.

CHAPTER 24: The Forest Over-Lord

Hidden with the forest glen,
Deep within lies Vishalia men
Over-lord Balneor to rule
To see the emerald, a fool.

from The Ballad of the Fire

The group trudged into the compound of Vishalia under the watchful eye of Over-lord Balneor, who stood on a balcony above them. It was late, the sun was practically set and the shadows were long. Alson was the one who had called for a stop to eat a meal. Raliton wanted to continue, to arrive at the over-lord's city but realized that Alson was right — they would arrive during or after the evening meal. Shadowfeet's hooves clattered on the cobbled stones, then were silenced as he stood, waiting. Stableboys came running to gather the horses and Balneor's staff assisted in getting things sorted.

"Prince Raliton," a voice said. "Over-lord Balneor seeks the favor of your presence in his chambers."

Raliton turned to face an older man who was obviously Balneor's advisor.

"Shall I have my wife in attendance?" Raliton asked.

"I believe Nialisha, Over-lord Balneor's wife, has already found the princess." He pointed to the cart where the two women spoke. "I believe he wishes to speak with you alone."

Raliton nodded and motioned for the man to lead the way.

"My name is Priestos and currently Over-lord Balneor's favored advisor," the old man said. "Follow me."

Contrary to this appearance, Priestos scurried quickly into the castle and Raliton hastened to follow him into the tower and up the stairs.

"I do hope your travels today were not too exhausting," Priestos said. "There will be refreshments in Over-lord Balneor's chambers. Is there anything special you would like?"

"Whatever is available will be fine," Raliton said.

Priestos stopped suddenly and rapped on the heavy wooden door before gently pushing it open.

"My lord," Priestos said, bowing deeply. "Prince Raliton has arrived."

"Thank you," Balneor said and wagged his fingers to dismiss the man. "Leave us."

Priestos scurried backwards out of the room, bowing constantly.

"Forgive me, Over-lord Balneor," Raliton said. "I am curious to the words of Priestos. He says he is the currently favored advisor?"

"Please, my prince," Balneor said with a hearty laugh. "Relax. Enjoy some refreshments." He motioned for the servant to help the prince. "Priestos is an intriguing man and yes, at the present time, he is my favored advisor." Balneor sat, then reclined. He popped a grape into his mouth. "I have three advisers whom I rotate as I see fit. I am a man who enjoys variety and fear I may ruin an advisor with my anger. He picked up a strawberry. "Do try one of these. They are especially sweet this year."

Raliton relaxed and stretched out on the divan opposite Balneor. The servant picked up the decanter and poured a dark ruby wine into Raliton's chalice. The prince reached for a small cake filled with fruits on a tray just beyond his reach.

"So, to keep my sanity, I have a temporary favorite to keep them satisfied. Now, please forgive my presumptuousness, Prince

Raliton," Balneor said. "I really called you here to update you of the situation in Alitro and with Laminar."

"I figured as much," Raliton replied and bit into the cake he held. "This is very good. So, what is the status of Laminar? He did survive, at least, that is what my messenger told me."

"Ah, yes, Laminar. Well, he did, indeed survive the wound. He was here to see me this morning."

Raliton sat up. "Is he here now?"

"Indeed," Balneor said with a sly grin. "Would you like to visit him? I can arrange it."

"Where is he?" Raliton leaned back on the divan, intrigued by his host's tone.

Balneor raised an eyebrow. "Where I can keep an eye on him. This morning he came to me with extreme remorse and babbling about you being the true king and rightful heir. As if there were a doubt."

"Then it matters not to me his whereabouts. Who have you named to Alitro?" He paused. "Are you familiar with his yellow fruit?"

"Ah, yes, the illusive yellow fruit. I have my men checking on that. Now, do you remember my daughter, Shantyra? I have given the post to her husband, Zindrof. I truly believe he will be a firm follower for the new king." Balneor laughed loudly, stood and grabbed Raliton's hand to pull him up into a hug. "If not, my daughter will be in search of a new husband." Balneor gave a small shrug and sly grin. "Let us join our wives in a quiet drink and genial conversation before retiring. Tomorrow will be a day of celebration inside Vishalia. My people have been anxiously awaiting your arrival. So, trust me, Prince Raliton, you did not sneak into my city with the shadows of the evening." He sighed. "If only you could have arrived a few days earlier."

Raliton frowned.

"We could have celebrated Po'Chi with this pageantry." He laughed. "Never mind, my people will enjoy a celebration, no matter the reason. But, this — this is a reason well worth a great celebration."

"Then we are in agreement?" Balneor asked.

Raliton nodded his head and Enyra clapped her hands together. Nialisha smiled agreeably.

"It sounds lovely and the city's courtyard would be the perfect place for such a ceremony," Enyra said.

Raliton placed an arm about Enyra's waist. "I think involving the wives is a good idea since they are the silent partners in all that transpires."

Balneor laughed heartily and stroked his dark beard. "Only a foolish man believes he rules supremely." He bowed to Raliton. "If you will excuse me, I shall have Priestos begin the processes so we may have a proper celebration in two days time." With large strides, Balneor left the room.

"I do wish Namo-Hoj could have joined us for the experience," Enyra said.

"Namo-Hoj?" Nialisha queried.

"Our nephew," Raliton said. "First son of my younger brother, Lornear." He glanced about the room anxiously, unsure of how the conversation would turn. Raliton felt awkward discussing obvious heirs although he had none at the present time. "I do believe we are done here." He placed his hand at Enyra's elbow and pressed in an attempt to escort her from the room. "Perhaps we could enjoy a stroll about the gardens or even amble about the streets of the city?"

"That would be nice," Enyra replied while giving Raliton a strange look.

"Oh, look at me," Nialisha said. "Here I am babbling on with questions when this is your first time to our fine city. Balneor would be..."

"Balneor would what?" he said, strolling back into the room. "Prince Raliton, I have initiated the arrangements we discussed. My astrologer has already promised me fair weather for the event. In fact, I decided to heighten the pageantry. I've dispatched messengers to the under-lords requesting their attendance." He stood there rubbing his palms together, quite proud of himself.

Raliton stared into the space over Balneor's head. "It took us almost two days to arrive here from Under-lord Viov's village. Surely you don't expect his attendance with such short notification?"

Balneor motioned for the group to have a seat. "There is a hawk already dispatched to Viov's residence. It should arrive later today. Viov is always ready to travel at the shortest notice. He will be en route shortly after the evening meal and travel most of the night." Balneor placed a finger to lip. "Off hand, I'd say he should be here by morning's sunrise the day of the event."

"Won't he eat?" Enyra asked, her eyes wide with surprise.

"Under-lord Viov, his lovely wife, and his staff will eat cold meals during the trip." He smiled at the group. "Trust me, Enyra, he won't stop to fix a meal while moving. If ever he were to go to war, I would consider him a very dangerous opponent, if only for his zeal for duty."

"War," Enyra echoed. "What a strange word to invoke so many images."

"King Arlyon," Balneor started. "Now, there was a man who knew how." He glanced at Raliton. "My error, my lord. If any would know about King Arlyon, you, a direct descendant, should explain."

"My grandfather, many times removed, was indeed a great warrior. He knew only a lasting peace would establish his dynasty. He absorbed so many of the small fiefdoms and villages as man grew. Yes, there had been war, but it has been over six hundred circles since there has been any major strife between cities and villages. Even over-lords and under-lords live in harmony." He looked at Balneor and smiled. "For the most part, that is."

"Six hundred circles," Nialisha whispered.

"War is destruction," Raliton said and pounded his left fist into his right palm. It smacked loudly. "There are no winners, everyone is a loser."

"Are you saying the Great Cat King was a loser?" Nialisha asked, her eyes wide in surprise. "He is your ancestor."

"King Arlyon won the battles, Nialisha," Raliton said. "But think of all the men who lost their lives in the conflict. My grandfather lost even when he won."

"But, my good prince," Balneor added. "King Arlyon won the ultimate prize — peace. Imagine, over six hundred circles of peace for your people."

"They're not my people," Raliton said. "They are our people. We are one, together."

Balneor stood and walked over to Raliton and bowed his head. "You will make a good king," he said. "There is none other I would swear my fealty. You are, indeed, the Cat King's grandson heir."

Raliton placed a hand on Balneor's shoulder. "I am honored. Now, do you think we should discuss the finer moments for the ceremony?"

"Is there no precedence for this ceremony?" Enyra asked.

"None, my love," Raliton replied. "My father took this journey when Balneor was still a very young boy." He turned to Balneor. "And, I do believe, if my memory serves me correctly, little boys care little for pomp and the goings on of stateliness." Raliton cocked an eye. "Am I correct?"

Balneor smiled. "You are most certainly correct. I only remember parts, like watching a ship come through the mists. It is bits and pieces, not the whole. If you ladies would prefer, go to the gardens and enjoy the day while the prince and I establish something resembling a ceremony with just the proper amount of pomp."

"I believe we have been dismissed," Nialisha said and reached for Enyra's hand. "Come, m'dear. I do believe we can find something more interesting than this stuffy ceremony." She laughed. "Perhaps a trinket from a street vendor." She led Enyra to the door.

"Please be sure to leave time for me, my husband," Enyra said.

"As you wish, my love," Raliton said and bowed as they left the room.

Balneor snapped his fingers. "Lisnia," he blurted. "Why didn't I think of that sooner? I am sure she was in court the day your father came on The Challenge." He ran to the door and yelled to a person out of sight. "Lisnia. Get her, you idiot. Bring her to us, immediately and as quickly as you can. It is important." He walked back to the chair where Raliton sat. "Would you like some refreshment, my prince?" Balneor poured a light-yellow colored liquid into goblets. "This is sweet, yet sour. I find it very refreshing."

Raliton grabbed the goblet and tasted the liquid. "A fruit juice. Yes?"

Balneor nodded agreement. "It is a lemoned water with honey."

They drank and bantered topics.

"Where can they be?" Balneor asked in an agitated tone. "They should be..."

"Lisnia, as requested," the servant said as the litter entered the room.

Balneor was surprised by the usage of one of his litters for a servant.

"Forgiveness," Priestos begged. "I ordered them to use it for speed. Lisnia can barely walk these days. She is very old."

Balneor waved them away. "Be gone." He walked over to Lisnia and stared at the old hag who reclined on the litter. "Do you know who I am?" he asked.

She studied him with a partially open eye. "I know you, Over-lord Balneor. What is your bidding? I am but an old servant."

"Rest," Balneor said. "Tell me, Lisnia. Do you remember when King Lanfeld came to Vishalia during his challenge?"

"King Lanfeld? Does he still live?"

"Think, Lisnia," Balneor whispered. "Remember back to when you were young. There was a ceremony when Prince Lanfeld came to my father to request fealty?"

She raised a gnarled finger into the air and waggled it. "Prince Lanfeld? Yes, he came here. It was many circles ago. Oh, what a party they had."

"Yes, yes. Go on," Balneor hissed.

"The stone," she croaked and raised a hand as if reaching for some invisible item in the air before her. "So green." She slumped back onto the litter. "The prince gave it to your father." She glanced at Balneor, her eyelids fluttering to stay open. It was obvious the old woman was tired. She breathed deeply, holding her breath mere seconds. "You... You were but a young lad. You had no care for the pompous goings-on. You were scurrying about the chamber, chasing your pet cat."

Balneor nodded his head, remembering that particular incident.

"Tell us more," Raliton whispered, completely immersed in the memories of this old woman. He kneeled close to the litter to hear her weak voice.

CHAPTER 25: **The Emerald**

Held aloft for all to see
The emerald green shines brightly
A plan, a party for all to see
One to make the Over-lords be
Ever mindful of what to do
To make The Challenge show

from The Ballad of the Fire

Prince Raliton adjusted the breastplate then shifted the sword. He shook his head then fidgeted with possible adjustments to make it feel comfortable.

"Is there nothing to happen correctly today?" He glanced at Enyra as she sat before the mirror and attached her earrings. She patted the necklace, then turned to stand and face him.

"Am I presentable?" She turned a full circle, the dark green dress blossoming out in the swirl.

"And very desirable," Raliton said. "You have chosen well with the green to match my apparel. We honor Over-lord Balneor in his forest colors."

There was a knock at the door and a servant hustled to answer. Balneor strode in.

"Do you feel we have the ceremony well practiced?" he asked.

"We have no choice," Raliton replied. "We shall do fine. How many here have attended a challenge ceremony? Lisnia was a young woman when my father came here on his challenge."

"We shall do fine, then. All the under-lords have made attendance except Viov which I find very unusual." He grimaced and looked at Raliton. "Did he indicate his thoughts to you about your ascension?"

Raliton walked over to Balneor and placed a comforting hand on the man's shoulder.

"My good friend, Balneor. I truly questioned if Viov would make the trip. Remember, he is not as young as you and I. Twenty years ago he was formidable. Today? He is a more docile and regal persona. Now, as to his intentions, I felt he was comfortable with my becoming the king. I know for a fact he said he would support me."

"Then it is settled," Balneor ambled to Enyra and took her hand in his then cocked his head to look at Raliton. "It will be full support of my fiefdom to you, the new king." He turned to face Enyra. "Besides, how could I not place my alliance with you, your wife is so breath-taking."

"I turn around and you disappear," Nialisha said, strolling into the room. "Then I find you in a dalliance with the future king's wife. This is not good, Balneor." She laughed, shaking her index finger, admonishing him.

Enyra viewed Nialisha's gown: a leaf green color with silver and gold threads embroidered in a whimsical pattern yet mimicking the forest vines. "You look lovely," she said.

"As do you, my dear," Nialisha replied. She entwined her arm with Balneor. "No wonder this poor lad was tempted to stray."

Enyra blushed.

Raliton stepped close to her. "I shall defend your honor to the end, my love." He placed a protective arm about her waist while placing a fist over the pommel of his sword in a mock threat.

They all laughed.

"Perhaps we should put something of the sort into our celebratory shenanigans today." Balneor struck an aggressor's pose with hand to sword. "You thoughts, Raliton?"

"Only if I win." Raliton grinned.

Balneor bowed. "As you wish, Prince Raliton."

Raliton stepped onto the balcony and watched the changing scene below him. In the courtyard, performers - jugglers, fire-eaters, stilt-walkers, and others moved about the celebrating populace gathered for the ceremony. Raliton took a deep breath. He smelled the distant woods: cedar, oak, cherry, and one he was not familiar with. He frowned at the strangeness of the scent. It reminded him of his youth, of something he had forgotten.

Suddenly, below him, he saw the strange man dancing about within the people. He knew the man. At least, he thought he knew him, yet it made no sense since most of these people he'd never met.

The man gazed up and waved. Raliton absently waved in return. Who was this silly man in black who danced so gaily?

"Enjoy your day, young prince," the man whispered in his ear.

Raliton jerked back to see the strange man standing close to him. *How had he gotten there? Where was his guards?*

"Time is so fleeting." The dark man grinned and tittered. "It is almost gone."

The strange man jumped to the balcony's edge, balanced momentarily before leaping down into the fray below.

Raliton leaned over the balcony to see the man once more dancing among the populace, kicking his legs high in celebration. None seemed concerned.

"Is there a problem?" Raliton was silent. "Prince Raliton?"

Raliton jerked about to face Balneor. "I'm sorry. I didn't hear you join me."

"I should say," Balneor replied. "You were certainly immersed in the activity below. Shall we join the wives and begin the ceremony?"

Raliton nodded, and glanced once more below. The black man was gone.

Trumpets sounded, blasting the air three separate times with their fanfare. With each timed blast, the people quieted more and more. When the trumpets sounded for the third and last time, silence reigned in the courtyard.

A drum pounded a slow cadence.

Two guards moved forward in step with the drums. They opened the way to the center. The crowd separating to allow their passage.

Nialisha followed about twenty paces behind the guard. Each of her steps in sync with the drum beat. Arms held strongly to her side, she moved as if in a trance. She approached the open space, took her place between the two guards and turned to face where she'd entered. The drums stopped.

"I present Princess Enyra." Nialisha's voice cut the air for all to hear.

The drums began, again.

Princess Enyra stepped ceremoniously toward Nialisha, pacing her steps to the drum. Like Nialisha, Enyra moved forward, arms to her sides, strong, with every muscle tightened, ready to spring if necessary. She bowed before Nialisha. The drums stopped.

Nialisha took Enyra's hands and turned her around to face the people. "This is Princess Enyra, wife of King-select, Prince Raliton."

People cheered and applauded.

A single trumpet sounded.

"My lord, Over-lord Balneor," Nialisha announced.

Once more the drums began their rhythmic drumming with a slight alteration of a side beat.

Over-lord Balneor strode forward in time with the tempo of the drums. He moved proudly and with the air of authority. He stood before Nialisha and Enyra momentarily before turning to face the crowd.

"I am Over-lord Balneor." He paused. "I now call forth King-select, Prince Raliton."

There was a full trumpet fanfare as the drums began their beating, again, but with a new double side beat.

Two guards preceded Prince Raliton, as well as two guard behind the prince. The five stepped in perfect syncopation to the drum and with each other as they moved through the group and into the opening with the others.

The leading two guards stepped off in opposite directions before reaching Balneor. Raliton stood facing the over-lord. The following guards repeated the actions of the first guards, each stepping to the side.

Prince Raliton held his position momentarily before dropping to one knee before Over-lord Balneor.

"Over-lord Balneor," he began. "I have visited all your esteemed under-lords, seeking their fealty. I now offer you the Forest Gem, an emerald. I request you to attend me at Adavinya when I finish my Challenge. If you swear fealty to me, return the stone to me for placement in the Staff of Rule."

Raliton reached into a leather satchel at his side, pulled the green gem from its confines, and lifted it into the air before him. The stone glistened in the sunlight, radiating a green sheen.

Silence that had reigned over the ceremony was replaced with a soft murmur of the crowd who stood in utter awe of the stone.

Over-lord Balneor reached out and cradled the stone in his large hands at waist height. "I take this gem as requested. If all my under-lords are in agreement of fealty unto you, I will return it with my oath of undying fealty to you as my king."

A small curl of Balneor's lips indicated his urge to smile.

"Stand, Prince Raliton, King-select. Let us celebrate this occasion." He lifted the stone into the air, holding it in the tips of his fingers for all to see. The stone radiated green beams in the sunlight. "Let the celebration begin. A feast for all to enjoy will be held at sundown." He turned to Raliton. "Please, my prince, let us join together in meeting the people of Vishalia."

Raliton noticed a litter near the front. It was Lisnia.

Balneor placed an arm over Raliton's shoulders. "I felt she deserved a place of honor in fair regard of her assistance to us in this ceremony." He looked conspiratorially about. "Who would have thought there would be so much more to happen before we feast tonight." Balneor smiled. "I look forward to our mock sword battle." Once more he glanced about him. "I've also ordered a little diversion for after the feast. A troupe will portray the beginning of Adavinya and retell the story of King Arlyon."

"You honor me, Over-lord Balneor."

Balneor slapped Raliton on the back.

"I want to make sure Over-lords Zornear and Hasputhner have to up the ante in their celebrations to compete with mine." He gave a full-bellied laugh. "None of this, here's the stone." He handed the jewel to Priestos. "Now, we party. I demand they attempt to outshine our ceremony today."

Nialisha slipped her arm around Balneor's. "Are you going to brag all night or will you be showing me around the courtyard, mingling with our guests." She smiled. "By the way, Under-lord Viov was able to make the ceremony. I noticed his entourage as I turned when I first walked up at the beginning of the ceremony." She hesitated. "Shall we go greet them?"

Enyra slid in beside Raliton. "It would be nice to visit with Under-lord Viov and his wife, again." She snickered. "Actually, it would be nice to revisit all of them…" She paused. "Except, perhaps, Lady Kalay." She turned to Nialisha, ashamed at her outspokenness.

"Don't fret, Enyra," Nialisha said. "I've arranged the seating at the feast so you won't need to endure Lady Kalay. I am quite familiar with her vanity and snobbery." She gazed about. "Shall we attend to Under-lord Viov's needs?"

CHAPTER 26: Plots Appear

The Other dances his steps alone
His plans coming together to bemoan
The Challenge must continue to pass
Yet news from the castle is but crass

from The Ballad of the Fire

Prince Raliton sat atop Shadowfeet, surveying the group, assuring himself everything was ready. He watched Alson approach on his steed.

"Sire," Alson called. "Supplies have been packed. All is prepared for departure."

Balneor walked up to Shadowfeet and placed a calming hand on the horse's neck before giving the forehead a scratching. "A beautiful steed, indeed, Raliton." He cast a glance at the prince. "Ready to depart?"

Raliton nodded.

Balneor and Raliton grabbed arms in a farewell gesture.

"Nialisha and I wish you safe travel. We will wave from the main gate as you pass." Balneor turned and headed to the litter where Nialisha and Enyra said their goodbyes.

Raliton waited, watching Balneor move among the group to the littler. He saw them step aside and head toward the main gate.

"We journey," Raliton said to Alson.

Alson, in return, moved his horse among the group, making sure all was ready to move.

Raliton led the group toward the gate where Balneor and Nialisha waited.

"Safe journey, Prince Raliton," Over-lord Balneor said once more, clutching a closed fist to his heart before moving it in Raliton's direction, palm up.

"Safe journey," Nialisha whispered. A tear welled in her eye. "Until we meet, again."

Raliton kept Shadowfeet's pace slow; he was in no hurry to leave. He maintained his stare at the goal of this journey, to the fiefdom of Under-lord Pahl in the foothills of the Mountain Realm of Over-lord Zornear.

When he was sure the last of group was out of Vishalia, he turned to gaze back at the main gate. There, on the parapet, stood Over-lord Balneor and his gracious wife, Nialisha. They waved.

"The mountains are an illusion." Alson rode beside Raliton. "We have traveled over a half day and they appear no closer than when we first saw them."

"It will be another full day's journey before we reach Under-lord Pahl." Raliton raised a hand to cover his eyes from the sunlight. "With luck we should arrive before meal."

Alson gazed at his companion. "I will send a messenger to notify Under-lord Pahl of this fact." He smiled. "It would be nice to have a warm meal awaiting our arrival." He paused. "And soft linens in which to rest."

Raliton grinned. "I see. Personally, I thought you'd look forward to an evening at a local brew master's establishment."

Alson jerked in his saddle to stare at Raliton.

"I'm not blind," Raliton said. "You are a young man. I cannot expect you to be at my side every minute of the day." He leaned over and patted Alson on the shoulder. "I know you have, at times, been known to sneak out to tarry at a brew house." He gave Alson a knowing look. "I'm not that old I do not remember the soft womanly luxuries of such an establishment."

"Sire, I... uh... It is my duty."

"I have been guarded all my life, Alson. You are my advisor, not my mother. Your assigned night guards are very efficient to cover your actions, but I know of a man's need." He pointed at himself. "After all, I'm a man, too. My question, what of Julenia? What are your intentions?"

Alson frowned and was silent for a moment.

"Do you not favor her, Alson?"

"Upon our return, if she has not found favor with another, I will ask her hand in marriage." Alson took a deep breath, his chest swelling with pride at the finalization of his decision.

"Is that a truth, Alson? You intend to marry Julenia?"

"Yes, sire." He paused. "Would I be too bold to ask you to seek out her father and ask his blessing on the binding?"

Raliton nodded. "I would consider it an honor, Alson. If you would, take lead. I must speak with Enyra."

Alson nodded.

"Enyra, my dear. I have a request of you."

Raliton got off Shadowfeet and strolled along beside the litter.

Enyra pulled back the curtain of her litter and smiled at Raliton. "Request, my love."

"Alson has expressed a desire to marry Julenia. Would you like to see a wedding at Over-lord Zornear's castle?"

Enyra squealed. "Can it be?"

"Am I not a prince? Soon to be king? I see no reason I can't do this."

Enyra leaned closer to the edge of litter. "How can this happen?"

"Alson has asked me to be his go-between with Julenia's father in asking for her hand." Raliton leaned in and kissed Enyra on the cheek. "Give it some thought, my love. How shall we go about this? I certainly don't want Alson to wait until the Challenge is complete."

Raliton stretched and pulled the curtains of the litter closed so the dust of the trip didn't bother her. Once more he got on Shadowfeet and trotted to the forefront of the group.

"Any issues, Alson?" he asked.

"None, sire." He held a hand to his forehead to shadow his eyes. "The sun will soon drop below the horizon. Do you wish for one to ride ahead to find a place to rest for the night?"

"There should be a small stream ahead, not that far. Send Halsvar ahead to check. If it be too far away, we will camp earlier, but I feel we should reach our destination before the sun sets."

Raliton watched as Alson turned his horse around in search of Halsvar. Raliton scanned the distant horizon, looking for any indication of a possible stream. He'd seen the map at Balneor's castle and seen what he believed to be a small stream less than a day's march from the castle. He felt it had to be close.

"My lord," Halsvar said. "You wish me to seek a stream ahead — for camping?"

"Yes."

"But, my lord, who will guard you in my absence?" He smiled shyly. "I have been lurking behind the lead wagon so I may be ready to defend you, if necessary."

Raliton frowned. "Listen to me, Halsvar. There are no enemies. Our realm has had over 600 circles of peace. Guards are ceremonial in most instances. My distant grandfather, King Arlyon, established and assured us this peace."

"I will go as requested." Halsvar, down-trodden, sighed and nudged his horse forward to soon race from sight.

"He means well, Prince Raliton," Alson said.

"I know, but he is young and filled with tales of a time before." Raliton yawned. "I do hope this stream is nearby. I believe the excitement of the last few days has taken its toll on me."

"It must not be far," Alson said and nodded to the distance in front of them. "Already I see Halsvar returning. Look at the dust."

Raliton stood in his stirrups and gazed at the person charging toward them.

"To arms! To arms!" Halsvar rode like a crazed man, pushing his horse to faster and faster speeds. He continued to yell. "Prepare to defend. To arms!"

Alson stood in the stirrups of his steed. "I do not believe he is alone."

"He is not. He is being chased." Raliton turned to the caravan. "Guards! Attend!"

The caravan halted.

Ten ceremonial guards moved forward, bows drawn, swords at the ready at the hip.

Halsvar slowed as he approached.

"Robbers, my lord. They attacked me at the river's edge." He turned his steed around to face the oncoming strangers.

An arrow whizzed by Raliton and thunked into the wagon behind him.

Ten bow strings twanged in unison as their arrows released. They sailed through the air toward the galloping attackers. Of the seven attackers, three fell from their charging steeds. They were dead.

"Halt!" Raliton yelled. "You dare attack a royal caravan?"

The remaining four attackers slowed and paced at a distance away.

Once more Raliton shouted. "You dare to attack a royal caravan?"

"We attack whomever we please, my lord. You are not our ruler."

"I am the King-select on my Challenge journey. How dare you..."

"We dare what we want in this area of the Clondine realm. You are the trespasser, not us. Prepare to give us your valuables."

"We'll not give in to these thieves, my lord," Halsvar whispered. "I will see them dead first."

The lead man of the thieves leaned forward on his horse, resting his arm on the pommel. The cloth which covered his lower face flapped in the light breeze. Only his eyes, dark and calculating, stared back. "You, my young lad, underestimate my skills, and, I would say, overestimate your skills. You'll not see me dead for I will be standing over your body with my sword in hand. It will be your last vision."

"Over-lord Zornear will hear of this," Alson shouted.

"Ah, yes, the Challenge. Let me think. You are coming from Over-lord Balneor's palace, headed for Over-lord Zornear's castle. That means you must have, at minimum, the ruby gem from the Staff of Rule." He grinned. "Maybe the blue sapphire gem, too?"

The man to the left of the leader of the thieves leaned closer to him. "With this being a royal caravan, Jenix, just think of how much jewelry, gems and gold should be with them." He sat in his saddle and glared at Raliton. "Perhaps we should just kill them all and take what we want."

"Lower your voice," the leader snapped.

Raliton heard the bow strings stretch taunt.

"You are no longer moving targets," Raliton said. "My bowmen have you in their sights." He paused. "These are royal archers and swordsmen of the court. Their accuracy is uncanny, especially with still targets." He waited, letting his words be weighed for truth. "Go. Leave us and my guards will not harm you."

"Ah, you must be Prince Raliton." The lead thief performed a mock bow. "Is it true? Did you steal the birthright from Prince Lornear, the rightful heir?"

"Prince Lornear is my younger twin. I'll not discuss the royal ascension with the likes of you. Now, do you wish to leave or fight?" Raliton moved in his saddle attempting to not show his nervousness of the situation.

Again, the lead thief bowed. "As you wish, my lord. We shall leave you. If you kill us, it will be with arrows in our backs like the cowards you are."

"Do not cross our path again." Raliton threatened. "I do not give such grace all the time."

The four thieves turned their horses in unison and trotted away, picking up speed as they departed.

Raliton turned to Halsvar. "My apologies. You are correct. I need a guard."

"Nay, my lord," Halsvar replied. "Your diplomatic abilities surpass my swordsmanship, but I will be by your side at all times."

"I take it you found the stream?" Raliton asked.

"Yes, it is a short distance from here. I will speak with the guards and arrange protection for the night." Halsvar glanced at the small dots of the retreating thieves. "I do not believe they are going to leave us alone. I may be wrong..."

"Do as you feel needed, Halsvar. I trust your judgment." Raliton turned Alson. "Do you have anything to add?"

"No," Alson said. "Did the thieves have a camp at the stream?"

"I don't believe they did. I will take two guards with me. This time I will survey the area to be sure they are gone." Halsvar glanced at the sun. "You should reach the stream before the sun has traveled half the distance to the horizon."

Raliton sat beside Enyra as they finished the last of their meal. The stream babbled in the distance.

"Have you given any thought to Alson's wedding proposal?" Enyra asked.

"I will write a request to Julenia's father asking for her hand in marriage to Alson."

Enyra squinched her nose. "Is that the best you can do?"

"I can't leave to do it in person." Raliton sighed.

"Send one of your guards," Enyra suggested.

"Would not Alson be curious? He is my advisor... why am I sending away a guard, especially back to Adavinya." Raliton gazed about the area. "And we have robbers?"

Enyra's eyes widened. "I will send one of my maidens back. She will need a guard to protect her." She smiled. "Especially after today's encounter. Your guard can take the message to Julenia's father." Enyra patted a wrinkle from her skirt. "Better a guard than a simple messenger."

"And what, pray tell, will I tell Alson your maiden needs?"

"I've not been feeling well in the morning. You may tell him I'm sending her back for some of Namo-Ke's potions." She scrunched up her face and shivered. "Not that I'd really want to take the terrible tasting stuff. I'm so glad to be away."

"I see I will need to take more precaution with you, my dear. You're very sneaky." Raliton laughed. "Let me compose the letter. You pick a maiden."

Enyra leaned in and kissed Raliton. "Our plot thickens. I do hope Julenia agrees to the marriage... and her father." She laughed and left to find a maiden to send.

CHAPTER 27: Under-lord Letiman

Discreet plots and plans are made
Namo-Ke's potions have gone to fade
Enyra's health has changed indeed,
To fulfill Raliton's challenge final need.

from The Ballad of the Fire

Raliton sighed. "It has come to my attention, my wife, Enyra, needs a potion only Princess Namo-Ke prepares." Raliton motioned for Alson to have a seat near him by the fire. "She wishes to send a maiden to fetch such from Adavinya." Raliton stared into the fire so he wouldn't make eye contact with Alson. "I need a guard to send with her. Is Reestan, I believe that was his name — the one I had watch over Laminar's affairs when we left. Could he go with her for protection?"

"Perhaps I could have the potion made for her. What are her ailments?"

Raliton looked to the sky, studying the crisp starlight in the almost moonless night. "Enyra is sick some mornings and Namo-Ke created a potion to help her. I don't know the ingredients..." He finally stared at Alson. "You know Princess Namo-Ke does not share her secrets." He grinned. "Is there a problem sending a guard?"

"I see none if they leave in the morning, early before we even begin to prepare for our final day's journey." Alson paused. "The only issue would be the robber thieves, but again, they would carry little of value."

"Fine," Raliton replied, standing in preparation of leaving. "I will notify Enyra. You will notify Halsvar of this action."

"My lord?" Alson held up a hand, begging the prince's attention. "You say Enyra is sick in the morning, is that correct?"

"She claims to have an upset stomach and has trouble keeping her meal." Raliton cocked his head in question.

Alson nodded. "I would have her see Under-lord Letiman's healer when we arrive or perhaps the next day. It may be good news."

Raliton shrugged. "As you wish." He walked away, grinning at his cleverness over Alson.

Halsvar stood behind Under-lord Letiman at the main gate to the village.

"Welcome, your royal highness," Letiman said with a full flourish bow. "Allow me to share my humble abode with you. It is late, but I have a meal prepared and waiting for you and your group." He spied Enyra. "Ah, Princess Enyra. You grace our lowly abode with your beautiful presence." He turned to lead the group into the village of Evanal. "Come."

Under-lord Letiman's residence was similar to most of the under-lords in the Vishalia realm. Raliton smiled at the memory of the lavishness of Under-lord Laminar's palace. This was nothing like that.

"Thank you, Under-lord Letiman," Raliton said while passing the reins of Shadowfeet to Halsvar and joining the older under-lord. "A nicely prepared meal and fresh quarters will be a welcome relief from last night's stay by the river."

"Yes, I heard about the fracas by the river. Robbers? In my area? I never knew. I will have my advisor check into it immediately." He glanced about, searching. "Where is that man? He seems to disappear too often." Letiman stopped and stretched, searching the whole area of the open market. "Jaren!"

"Yes, my lord," the man said, appearing from a doorway. "I was checking a price for entertainment tonight."

"Jaren," Under-lord Letiman started. "This is Prince Raliton. He is here on the Challenge journey. Please have them shown to their quarters and bring them immediately to the dining hall." He turned to Raliton. "I will have the servants be ready to serve when you attend."

"Again, I thank you, Under-lord Letiman. Your attention to detail is admirable."

Letiman turned to face Enyra. "Until your beauty graces my dining hall." He bowed, turned and departed.

Enyra leaned into Raliton. "His has a silver tongue, his wife must enjoy the compliments."

"Under-lord Letiman has no wife. She passed a half-moon ago." Jaren bowed his head as he spoke.

"Forgiveness," Enyra replied. "I did not know. We have been on Challenge."

"Yes, I understand," Jaren said. "One tends not to hear the current gossip when traveling. May I inquire as to how long you will be staying with us?"

"We will stay a full day so I may have the proper amount of time to discuss matters with Under-lord Letiman. We will depart on the second morning if all goes well."

"I understand, Prince Raliton." Jaren said, his voice enunciating the name distinctly.

Raliton frowned at the response, unsure how to react. They walked in silence across the courtyard until they arrived at the Letiman's residence.

Three maidens appeared and Jaren spoke with them.

"They will take Princess Enyra and the others to their quarters." Jaren turned to Raliton. "Please follow me. I will take you to my lord's chambers. He awaits you."

Raliton frowned again, unable to remember Letiman discussing such actions.

"Tell me, Prince Raliton, how was your journey from Under-lord Balneor's realm? A pleasant journey?"

"Yesterday, just before we prepared for the evening, we were beset by a group of common thieves. Robbers, no less. My guards killed three of them, the other four were turned away."

Jaren stopped and stared at Raliton, his face denoting total shock.

"There have been no roadside robbers for… for… before Under-lord Letiman took his position. I find it quite strange. Robbers." He shook his head.

"Let us continue, Jaren. It is of little bother. It was barely a nuisance to our day."

"Perhaps," Jaren replied. "Still, intriguing."

"Ah, Prince Raliton," Letiman greeted as Raliton entered the chamber. "What brings you here? Ready to eat, already?"

Raliton frowned and turned to ask Jaren. The advisor was nowhere to be seen.

"I was under the impression, per your advisor, you awaited to speak with me. Jaren brought me here."

"How strange," Letiman replied. "I came here to freshen and join you in the dining hall." He turned a circle. "I've put on my best for the future king. I hope it meets your approval." He paused. "I've none to assist me since my wife passed."

"I beg forgiveness, Under-lord Letiman. I was unaware of your loss. Now may not have been the best time to arrive. Is there anything I may do to assist?"

Letiman giggled and placed a finger to his lips. "Shh. I'm color blind. Aveena always made sure my clothing was appropriate." He sat in a chair. Tears came to his eyes. "She was everything to me." He sighed. "Now, she is gone."

"Was Aveena the only one to know your secret?" Raliton sat in the chair opposite him.

Letiman nodded. "I'm sure there are those who suspect, but only she knew the truth." He breathed a deep sigh. "Maybe my advisor, Jaren, is very suspicious or knows."

"Under-lord Letiman." Raliton stared at the man until he looked directly into the prince's eyes. "There is no reason to hide or be ashamed of this secret. You are not the first." Raliton stood. "I think the first thing you need, at the current time, is a male servant to assist you. Take him into your confidence. There is no reason to share your secret, but you could tell him you will make him responsible for your appearance." Raliton smiled. "That should scare or intimidate him, at first. Let the servant decide what you will wear, at first with your guidance, then release him with full charge of your apparel."

"Perhaps Jaren could assist?" Letiman's eyes sought approval.

"I think not. I would not trust my advisor with too much free reign." Raliton gazed at the floor. "I don't trust Jaren," he mumbled.

"Did you say something, Prince Raliton?" Letiman stood.

"Just mumbling to myself — nothing to concern yourself with, Under-lord Letiman."

"If this clothing meets your approval, we shall join the others in the dining hall." Letiman moved to the chamber's door.

"You appear finely dressed. Do you wish me to assist in the selection of a male servant?" Raliton followed Letiman to the door.

"I have two in mind. I will introduce them to you during our meal. You may decide which you feel would be the best choice." Letiman faced Raliton. "Do you mind?"

"I would consider it an honor, Under-lord."

Raliton and Letiman entered the dining hall where the Challenge group stood awaiting them.

"Ah, Prince Raliton." Jaren noted the entrance. "I have arranged the seating so you will be next Under-lord Letiman. I have placed your wife, Princess Enyra on his other side. I will sit beside you."

He gazed at Halsvar. "He informed me he will eat after so he maintains a proper guard. I'm not exactly sure of his intention, but..."

"It will be fine, Jaren," Raliton said. "My guard feels since the attempted robbery I should be under surveillance at all times."

Jaren's eyebrows knitted together in a frown. "Fine. I have suggested Under-lord Letiman's daughter sit beside your wife so she may have another to speak with."

"Daughter?" Raliton glanced at Letiman.

"Yes, Belova is young, not quite twenty circles in age." He waved his hand as if dismissing the thought. "I am sure they will find a common thread to discuss."

Raliton studied the table. "May I make one minor change? I would prefer to have my advisor at my side. If the under-lord and I discuss something, I would like my advisor close so he may know what is happening."

Jaren bowed. "Of course, Prince Raliton. Whatever you wish." He paused and looked at the table. "I will place myself to the other side of Belova where I originally had your advisor." He smiled. "The others will find their own seats." He took a deep breath. "There. That is taken care of."

Under-lord Letiman spread his arms out to the group. "Let us share a meal together. Please, sit and enjoy the humble foods my cook has to offer."

Raliton and Letiman sat in unison to honor each other. The others followed and a low murmur filled the hall as conversations began.

Alson leaned close to Raliton. "I was quite content to be at Enyra's side, if need be."

Raliton lifted a chalice which a servant immediately filled. He gazed at Alson. "I have my reasons for you beside me. Mainly, I don't trust Jaren. Something stirs awkward within me when he is around."

"Tell me more about these robbers," Letiman asked while holding a steaming piece of chicken between his fingers. He popped it into his mouth and chewed with a smile.

"Yes, of course, but first, may I ask why you do not ask your daughter, Belova, to assist you with your clothing issue?"

"What?" Alson asked.

Raliton ignored him.

"Ah, yes. Belova. Do you not think it would be awkward for her enter my chamber with me in possible undress?"

Raliton nodded. "I understand. I look forward to viewing your choices."

"And the robbers?" Letiman asked, again.

"There is not much to tell. We were accosted by the bandits. My archers killed three. The remaining four considered my options and left. Their leader was very bold, even when he realized he was dealing with royalty." Raliton paused to enjoy the seasoned potato cube. "By the way, the food is delicious, Under-lord. I only mentioned the robbers to make you aware of the danger out there. They are a danger to travelers."

"Jaren! What do you know of these bandits?"

"Pardon, my lord?" Jaren held his napkin to his face as he hastened to finish the food he was chewing. It covered the lower half of his face from nose to chin, only his dark eyes showed.

A shiver coursed down Raliton's back.

CHAPTER 28: Jaren

A face is seen
A face is hidden.
The truth comes forth
From life unbidden.
Can life be fair?
Can truth be told?
One seeks the truth
The lie is sold.

from the Ballad of The Fire

Raliton stared at Jaren, every muscle in his face taunt at the realization. He tried to look away, but still his eyes were drawn to the napkin-covered face of Jaren.

"Prince Raliton says we have bandits, thieves or robbers within our boundaries. Are you aware of such goings on?"

"My lord," Jaren replied. "I keep my eyes and ears open to any news. I've not heard of any robbers in the vicinity." He leaned out over the table to see Raliton better while he dabbed away any crumbs from the sides of his mouth. "Did they steal any valuables?"

"Oh, no," replied Enyra. "Our guards protected us. Prince Raliton was able to convince them to leaving us or die. They chose to flee like silly maidens finding a spider."

"Did they?" Jaren sneered. "Perhaps they weren't really robbers."

"They attacked us. An arrow narrowly missed me." Raliton glared at Jaren. "Their leader was extremely haughty, but he realized he had met his match."

"Of that, I'm sure, Prince Raliton." Jaren smiled as innocently as possible, yet his voice belied his action.

Raliton was sure, there was unbridled loathing in Jaren's reply. He turned to Alson. "Do you feel the bandits were more of a bluff than a threat?" Raliton gave Alson the knowing look and wink.

"I would say they might scare a simple farm lad or fair maiden, but any average man could certainly overcome them easily. More show than action. The leader was a buffoon."

"A buffoon, you say?" Jaren controlled himself. "I will have some guards look into this immediately. If this leader character is such clown, perhaps they can capture him quickly." He stood. "If you don't mind, my lord, I'll have such action taken immediately. Excuse me."

Jaren exited the dining hall, his robes rustling loudly in his haste.

"You need to excuse Jaren," Letiman said. "When his authority is tested, he tends to take immediate action to counteract. Any bandits near Evanal would indicate a failure on his behalf. If I were the bandits, I would leave the district."

"I don't think the bandits will leave, Under-lord." Once more Raliton lifted his chalice. "Let us discuss other matters."

Letiman pointed to a servant and motioned him forward.

"What is your name?"

"I am called Pinster."

"You will be asked questions, answer them as honestly as you can."

Letiman nodded to Raliton. "You can question this servant, my prince."

Raliton asked several questions, some of which the servant was unsure and wondered why a prince would ask such a question. Raliton finished and excused the young man.

Letiman scrutinized the area before finally seeing the other young man he had chosen.

"You, come here."

Raliton again asked the same questions before letting the lad be excused. Raliton then considered the answers of the two.

"Call Pinster. I think he will make the best choice for your needs." He turned to Halsvar. "Go to the plaza and find a proper tunic in this lad's size. He will be Under-lord Letiman's personal servant. He shouldn't be wearing scullery attire."

"Yes, sire."

Within ten minutes, Halsvar returned with a light-blue tunic with dark blue trim and a silver thread at its base.

"Pinster," Raliton began. "Go and clean yourself. Put on this tunic and return here to stand behind him. You are now his personal servant. I will explain more tomorrow morning."

Pinster stared at the fine fabric, his fingers absently feeling the silver thread. "At once, your highness." He disappeared.

"Now, Under-lord Letiman, shall we finish our meal?" Raliton smiled at the host. "I do believe I heard Jaren mention getting entertain possibly. Is that true?"

"Bring in the performers. We wish to be entertained." Letiman retrieved a chicken leg from the large platter and ate with gusto.

"Now that Letiman is being entertained in discussion with Enyra..." Raliton's voice trailed as he attempted to get Alson's attention.

"Yes, m'lord?"

"Do you recognize Jaren?" Raliton asked.

"The under-lord's advisor?"

"How many Jarens have you met today? Yes, the advisor!"

"Like you, I met him this morning as we came into Evanal." He frowned at the prince.

"You didn't meet him yesterday?" Raliton stared at Alson. "Think."

Alson searched his memory, his eyes flashing back for, seeking or reading unseen notes. He shook his head. "I can't remember him. Was he in Vishalia?"

Raliton took a deep breath and slowly let it escape. "Have I made a mistake in my choosing of an advisor? Does the name Jenix sound familiar?"

"Jenix... Jenix...the leader of the robbers?"

"Exactly. If he returns to this meal... or in the morning, have him caught off-guard where he will bring the napkin to his face to cover his eating. Look closely."

"I will."

"Also, listen to his voice. Remember how Jenix mocked me and slurred his references to my being a prince?"

Alson nodded his head.

"I am taking Enyra for a walk in the village tomorrow." He snagged a crispy edge of chicken breast meat from the platter. "I will learn what I can. In the meantime, allow your "eyes" to wander the village and learn what they can. We will talk again later." Raliton chewed, a slight frown to his face. "I wish to be prepared when I enter the village."

"What did your eyes learn, Alson?" Raliton eased the door shut to the room and glided to Alson who sat by the wall window.

"The village is in turmoil and has been since your birth, it would appear. There are many here who feel Prince Lornear is the true heir of the throne, not you."

"After all these years?" Raliton stared out the window at the moving populace below.

"Also, the bandits are new. Only a few have had any interaction with them. They, the bandits, were non-existent prior to Aveena's death. Only since her death have they made themselves apparent, and, with the audacity, they seem to rob mainly the rich, leaving farmers and such alone."

"Are they stealing from the rich and giving to the poor?" Raliton turned and leaned against the wall. "Is that a possibility?"

"Not from what I've learned. At least, no farmer or poor person came forward with such information." Alson laughed. "I'm pretty sure the bandits are keeping the plundered loot for themselves." He hesitated. "But, it seems, since Aveena's death, Jaren has become more powerful, and, surprisingly, a bit more affluent monetarily."

"Why does that not surprise me, Alson?" Raliton paced the room. "There has to be way to force his hand. To make him reveal his alter-ego."

Alson stared at Raliton. "You are positive this is the same person as Jenix, the bandit?"

Raliton sat before Alson. "You're not?"

Alson shrugged. "I was not able to see him as you did last night. Perhaps at mid-day meal."

Raliton nodded. "I think I shall take Enyra for a stroll in the village." He cast a wary eye to Alson. "Am I safe or need I take Halsvar with me?"

"I don't believe you will be in any true danger, but you might wish to have Halsvar with you. I would suggest Reestan but he hasn't returned from Adavinya." He frowned and grimaced. "I do hope he returns soon." He smiled. "I asked him to check on Julenia, to see if she has found another." He held up a hand. "I made sure he didn't bother her, but only watched to see if she had another."

"Would you prefer to go to Adavinya and seek her hand?"

Alson paled. "No, my lord. We still have several moons to finish this Challenge. If she finds another, then so be it."

"Fine. Tell Halsvar we will meet him at the main gate and spend the day in the village."

"Only if you promise me you will take Enyra to the healer to confirm her illness. I do not wish to be the one who is responsible for the royal family on this trip and have the wife of the future king in less than perfect health." Alson stared at Raliton, waiting for a confirmation.

"I swear," Raliton replied, opened the door of the chamber and left.

Enyra was ready, standing, waiting outside their room.

"Is all well, my dear?" she asked.

"As can be expected. Let us see what Under-lord Letiman's village holds." He grabbed her hands. "I promised Alson I would take you to the healer. He has concerns about your health."

"It is nothing, Raliton. My stomach is just upset with all this travel. Nothing more, I assure you." She released his hands and wrapped her arms in his as they headed for the main gate.

Halsvar stood ready.

"Please try to stay a few paces behind so the people of Evanal may approach me. I do not want to seem aloof or unapproachable."

"As you wish, sire." Halsvar nodded acquiescence.

"Also, our first stop will be the healer."

Halsvar offered a questioning look to Raliton.

"It is for Princess Enyra. She has not been feeling well of late."

Halsvar nodded.

Raliton and Enyra began down the cobblestone road which quickly changed to a dirt road between the various stores. Halsvar followed a solid ten strides behind.

"There's the healer's shop," Enyra said and pointed to a building. She scurried forward and dashed in, leaving Raliton and Halsvar outside.

"Are you going in?" Halsvar asked. "I will wait for you here." He leaned against the building, folding his arms across his chest. "Perhaps something will catch my eye."

Raliton nodded and entered the building.

The healer stuck his head through the curtain covering the doorway to the next room.

"Is there an emergency?" he asked.

Enyra smiled. "There, I have seen the healer. We have fulfilled Alson's request and will not be caught in an untruth if asked." She headed for the exit.

"My wife is ill in the mornings after a meal." He cocked an eye at Enyra. "I have discovered she is also ill sometimes after other meals, too."

"Are you not Prince Raliton?" the healer asked.

The prince nodded.

The healer held an index finger up. "One moment." He disappeared behind the curtain. The sounds of turmoil and stumbling ensued.

A man burst through the curtains, a tunic partially pulled over his head and body. He bungled to get the tunic on properly.

"Come back tomorrow," the healer yelled and pushed the man through the room and to the exit. "The salve will dry. Now, begone!" He turned to Raliton and Enyra. "Your ladyship has been sick." He hobbled up to her and held her chin in his gnarled fingers. "How long has this sickness been with you?"

Enyra flushed. "Perhaps a week, no more."

"Sit," he commanded, indicating a stool for Enyra. "Your eyes." He scowled and scrutinized her eyes closer. "What potions have you been taking?"

"None, healer," Enyra said, before pulling away and staring at him. "I was taking a potion given to me." She glanced at Raliton then lowered her head. "There was one given me by my sister-in-law. It was to aid me."

"Aye," the header mumbled while nodding his head. "Aid you in what way?"

"To bear a child, a male child." Once more she glanced at Raliton before hanging her head.

"You've taken nothing else?"

Enyra shook her head.

"Strange." The header once more cupped her chin and stared into her eyes. "I see indications of black-bane in your eyes." He looked to Raliton then back to Enyra. "Are you sure the potion was to aid in pregnancy?"

Once more Enyra flushed. "Yes."

"It is very unusual for one to use black-bane in a potion to aid in pregnancy." He leaned back and twirled a lock of straggly hair while he thought. "Are you sure it wasn't to stop you from getting pregnant?"

Raliton moved forward. "I truly believe the potion Namo-Ke made was to aid my wife. I remember upon our departure, Namo-Ke, even though she was pregnant herself, was concerned for my wife's health and the possibility of her getting pregnant on the Challenge journey."

"If I may," the healer said and indicated his desire to touch Enyra's stomach area.

"Yes," Enyra replied.

The healer felt, moving his fingers gently across and around Enyra's mid-section. He smiled at Raliton.

CHAPTER 29: News, Good and Bad

A surprise for Enyra, a truth to unfold
Happy news for Raliton, a promise foretold
Subterfuge unfurls to be told
Secrets come for, some too bold.

from the Ballad of The Fire

The healer stood to face Raliton and leaped back, startled when a person plunged into the building. The stranger straightened to face the prince.

"Forgiveness, my lord," Reestan stumbled to regain his standing. "I came immediately from Princess Namo-Ke with the potion when I found you were coming to the healer upon my arrival back. She was quite adamant that Princess Enyra should not take any other potion." He paused to catch his breath.

Raliton saw Reestan shiver.

"Are you cold?" Raliton asked.

"Nay, my lord. It was Princess Namo-Ke's words. She said I would be damned and burn in the flames of Unholy Bre if I failed to give your wife this potion." He held out a bottle.

"Let me see that," the healer said, snatching the bottle from Reestan's hand. "The purple color indicates to me it may contain black-bane." He realized his action and stared at Raliton. "Forgiveness, my lord. I have overstepped my bounds." He held the bottle out to Raliton. "If you would allow me to verify its contents, I may be able to assist you."

Raliton nodded and the little man scurried behind the curtain.

"You made very good time, Reestan," Raliton said. "The two of you rode hard to make it back so quickly."

"Again, forgiveness, my lord. I returned, leaving Princess Enyra's maiden at the castle. Princess Namo-Ke was quite adamant I get the potion to her as quickly as possible."

"And what of my request?" Raliton asked.

"Good news, sire. Julenia's father has blessed the union and she agrees. They will await us at Over-lord Zornear's keep in the mountains. I told him it would be approximately two or three circles of the moon until our arrival. Julenia's father hopes the ceremony could be part of the celebration of Nos'Hanlah."

"That would be perfect," squealed Enyra. "A wedding at Nos'Hanlah. Wonderful."

"Is Alson aware of this news?" Raliton asked.

"Nay, my lord." Reestan reached into his pocket and retrieved a letter. "This is for Alson from Cardin."

Raliton frowned as he took the parchment.

"Cardin is Julenia's father's name." Reestan shrugged. "He asked if he should address his response to you or Alson." Again, Reestan reached into his vest and pulled out another smaller parchment. "This one he addressed to you." He nodded to the larger parchment. "That one is for Alson."

"Are you aware of what they say?"

Reestan stood to attention. "Nay, my lord. They are not addressed to me and Cardin did not make me privy to his intentions other than to tell me he agreed." He smiled. "I also have another letter to Alson — one from Julenia to him." Once more he pulled another parchment from his vest.

"Excuse me, Prince Raliton?" The header's bodyless head stuck out through the curtains. "May I ask your attendance within?" He moved the curtain to the side and motioned them in.

"Please wait with Halsvar," Raliton said and escorted Enyra to the back room.

"This way," the healer said. "See this? This is black-bane. This is blue-bane. If I mix them together in a small amount of water..." He mixed the two ingredients. "Now I add some honey, some sesame oil and a pinch of this purple flower." He held up a weed and pinched off a couple of buds. He handed the concoction to Raliton. "I'll not ask your wife to taste this, but you can smell it, my lord, and a taste to the tip of the tongue."

Raliton lifted the goblet and sniffed. It was pungent and he grimaced at the scent. Raliton carefully tipped the drink and let his tongue touch the liquid.

"You drink this stuff?" he asked Enyra.

She smelled the concoction. "It seems the same as Namo-Ke's."

"This is what your guard brought." He handed the bottle to Raliton. "Smell the similarity and also, the taste."

Raliton repeated his actions. "They seem the same."

The healer held the bottle up to Raliton. "This is used to stop a pregnancy. This is not good if your wife has been taking this in the past."

"I've not taken it since the first night of our Challenge journey." She smiled at Raliton. "It has been over two circles of the moon."

The healer smiled. "Your illness will soon ease, Princess Enyra." He held up the bottle, once again. "Never take this vile potion again. You are pregnant. I would say you will deliver a child near the end of the Quiet Time."

Raliton grabbed Enyra and hugged her.

"We're going to have a son," Enyra said.

"Or a daughter," the healer added. "There is no potion to define the baby, a girl or a boy." Once more he lifted the bottle from Namo-Ke. "But there is a potion to stop a pregnancy."

Raliton frowned. "Why would Namo-Ke do such a thing?"

"Let us be about our business," Enyra said. "Let us not fret about what she has done."

"Are you sure you don't mind cutting our visit of the village short?"

Enyra smiled. "My dear Raliton. We are to have an heir as you promised your father. I am so happy, even bad news won't spoil my day."

Raliton grinned. "Shall we visit Alson and let him know what we've done?"

Enyra grabbed Raliton's hand and raced up the street toward Under-lord Letiman's residence. Behind them, Halsvar and Reestan ran to keep up.

"Alson!" Raliton called. "Attend me, immediately."

Alson ran into the chamber, out of breath and flustered.

"Is there a problem?"

"No, my good friend. I have good news." Raliton sat in the chair by the window, a proud grin on his face. "Sit. Sit."

Alson crossed the room and joined Raliton, sitting in the chair next to him.

"We saw the healer." Raliton leaped from his chair. "Enyra is pregnant!"

Alson slumped back in the chair. "She is?"

"You seem shocked."

"I am happy for you, my lord." Alson stood. "I should have known. An advisor should be aware of these fact, all facts. Why did not somebody tell me? There had to be signs."

"Don't fret it, my friend. I shall have an heir. I promised my father an heir before we returned to Adavinya — and I will have one. Is that not good news?"

"Yes, my lord."

Raliton strode to Alson and placed an arm over the man's shoulder.

"Don't feel so downtrodden, my advisor. I believe I have good news for you."

Alson cocked his head to gaze at Raliton. "Good news for me?"

Raliton stepped back and neared the table covered with papers.

"I have sent a message to Cardin..."

Alson frowned. "Who is Cardin?"

"Let me finish. He is the father of Julenia. I asked for her hand in marriage to you, if she was not already seeing another."

Again Alson frowned, his thick eyebrows knitting together. "And..."

Raliton picked up the first parchment. "This is his response to you." Raliton handed the sealed letter to Alson. "Read it."

"You've not read it?" Alson asked. "Why would he reply to me?"

Raliton smiled. "This is Cardin's personal reply to you. Now read."

Alson broke the seal and curled the letter open. Raliton watched as Alson's eyes flashed back and forth reading the letter.

"He has given his blessing." Alson held the letter to his body. "This is wonderful news. When we finish the Challenge, I will seek Julenia's hand and we shall be wed."

"Wait, my good man." Raliton retrieved the smaller letter from the table. "There is more."

He handed the second letter to Alson who ripped it open in haste.

"It is from Julenia." His eyes widened. "She says she will meet me at Over-lord Zornear's keep in Clondine." Alson stepped back. "We are to be wed?" Eyes wide, he shifted his gaze from the letter to stare at Raliton in shock. "I will be married?"

"I would say you need to return to Adavinya immediately and place a proper bauble upon her hand to claim your bride-to-be."

"There is the Challenge. I am your advisor. I can't leave your side."

"Alson, you are a man first. If you leave with Reestan in the morning, you will be back in three days. That will allow you some tarry time Julenia." Raliton spread his arms and turned a full circle of the room. "This will suffice until your return. Under-lord Letiman and I can spend time together and I can socialize with the subjects of the village." He paused. "Now, go, prepare yourself for departure. If Reestan wishes to leave earlier, you may, but please be thoughtful, the man has only just returned and is probably in want of sleep."

Alson rushed from the room, a letter held tightly in each hand.

CHAPTER 30: True Colors

Twins who are not, but one
Live together to all as done
Jaren and Jenix are two
But appear as one to do

from The Ballad of the Fire

Searching the room, Raliton spied who he sought. "Jaren," Raliton called. "May I speak with you?" He motioned to the man.

"Are you not the king-select?" Jaren replied with a cocked eyebrow in Raliton's direction. "If it is your biding." He shrugged.

"Fine." Raliton gave him a cursory look. "Let us retire to my chamber where we are assured privacy from wandering ears."

Jaren grinned. "If you think that, my lord, you are foolish." He glanced around the hallway. "Even here there are ears listening, even as we speak."

"If that is so, then we shall take a ride beyond the village." Raliton turned to walk away, down the hallway. "Join me at the stable." He paused and glanced at Jaren. "It is a beautiful day and a short ride would be invigorating."

"As you wish," Jaren replied and followed.

"What is so important, Prince Raliton, we find ourselves alone on this road?" Jaren endured the clip-clop of the horse under him. He sighed. "I find horseback riding too discomforting to enjoy. I prefer a litter to carry me when I travel."

"We'll not be long," Raliton replied, pulling up on Shadowfeet's reins. "If we keep our voices low, none should hear us, not even the trees."

Jaren rode up to Raliton.

"What do you wish to discuss."

"Please do not take offense. I only wish to discover the truth." Once more Raliton glanced about to assure there were no others. "Do you have a twin brother? An identical image, like I have with my brother, Prince Lornear?"

Jaren pulled back and sat straight in his saddle. "Nay, my lord. You and Prince Lornear are the only twins ever to be born in Adavinya to my knowledge."

Raliton stared into the distance, thinking. "It is strange. When the bandits approached us on our way to Evanal, the leader…" Once more Raliton paused, thinking. "I could only see his upper face, his eyes. Do you remember our first night here, the evening meal?"

"Yes," Jaren said with cursory glance at Raliton. "What is your issue?"

"When you brought your napkin to your face—" Raliton stared directly into Jaren's face. "Your eyes were the same eyes of their leader, Jenix. Do you know of him?"

"I have never heard the name Jenix used in our village." Jaren tightened the reins of his horse. "Is there more or may we return to the village?"

"Just one more question. Are you the bandit, Jenix?"

Jaren turned to stare at Raliton. "Now, my lord, you insult me with the insinuation I am a common bandit."

"I only asked, Jaren. I am the king-select and it is my duty to protect the citizens of Adavinya."

"I am not the bandit!" Jaren dug his heels into the horse's flanks, urging it forward and rode away, headed to the village.

"My lord," a young boy knelt before Raliton as he rode pass. He held a parchment up.

"What is it, lad?"

"A man gave this to me at the edge of town. He told me to seek out the prince and give it to him." He stretched a little more to offer the parchment to Raliton. "This is for you."

Raliton got off Shadowfeet and stood by the lad, taking the proffered scroll. He opened it.

I wish to meet with you to discuss a proposition. Jenix.

Raliton re-rolled the scroll. He frowned at the prospect. Even if he were agreeable to such a meeting, how and when. Once more he looked at the young boy.

"Did he expect an answer?"

The boy stood. "The man said to shake your head yes or no."

Raliton shook his head in agreement.

An arrow whizzed and impaled itself into the ground between them. Raliton jumped back. On the shaft was a note.

One hour after the evening meal.

Raliton pulled a coin from his belt and offered it to boy. "For your efforts."

"I did nothing, my lord. I do not deserve such a treasure." He turned and ran, disappearing down a narrow passage between two buildings.

Once more Raliton read the original parchment. *What type of proposition could a bandit offer a king?* He wished Alson was present to these ramifications. He was about to consider Halsvar when he realized the guard would want to be present. Raliton decided against it.

"You seem distant, my husband. What are your thoughts, Raliton?" Enyra leaned against Raliton as they dined on the meal spread before them. Under-lord Letiman fussed about with his new servant as they re-arranged his garments.

"Do you not enjoy this meal, Prince Raliton?" Letiman noticed the prince's reticence to the meal and activities of entertainment. "Is your stomach not well?"

"You honor me, Under-lord Letiman." Raliton shifted and faced Letiman "I have several thoughts in my mind." He smiled. "I am sure you understand I fret about my future duties."

"If you are questioning my loyalty, Prince Raliton. I will tell you now, I support your ascension to the throne. I have no hesitations. You are my choice."

"Your decision pleases me, Under-lord Letiman." Raliton took another beef slice wrapped around a grape and dipped it in the spicy lemony-honey sauce before popping it in his mouth.

"I will convey my thoughts to Over-lord Zornear in the morning." Letiman sipped from his goblet before munching on a cracker.

"I am hoping my advisor returns within the next two days." Raliton lifted his goblet.

"This action intrigues me," Jaren said. "Your advisor has left you… and with your blessing it appears, to return to Adavin. Is this customary for your advisor to do?"

"I arranged for his betrothal the other day. I was honored to be his go-between in asking Julenia's hand of her father."

"Would that have been the guard and hand-maiden who departed?" Jaren again wiped his face with a napkin and Raliton was once more reminded of Jenix.

Raliton attempted to stifle the goosebumps coursing their way up his spine. He smiled and cocked a wary eye in Jaren's direction.

"You seem quite familiar with the coming and going of my staff, Jaren."

Jaren fluttered his fingers into the air. "All part of my daily work. I pride myself on knowing the affairs within..." He cast his glance about the room. "And also outside the walls of Under-lord Letiman's dominion." Jaren grinned then yawned, barely covering the action with his hand. "If one doesn't know, how can one advise?" He paused. "And, now Alson is in Adavin."

Raliton felt the viper's bite in the conversation.

"Then you know about the arrow during my return to your village?"

"Arrow?" Jaren immediately sat upright; his eyes wide. "You were attacked within the walls of this village?"

"Raliton!" Enyra stared at her husband. "Why did you not tell me of this earlier?"

Halsvar moved closer. "I will be at your side until we leave this place."

"No. No, you won't." Raliton stood. "I am going to my quarters to contemplate my affairs. I do not wish to be bothered for the next three hours." He glared at those who surrounded him. "Am I understood? No person shall approach me until I come back out of my quarters."

"I will stand guard at your door, my prince." Halsvar clicked his heels together. "None shall pass the portal of your quarters."

Raliton placed a hand on Halsvar shoulder. "You, my friend, will spend your time in the compound with my staff." He held up his hand to silence Halsvar. "I have spoken."

"As you wish, my lord." Halsvar stepped back to blend into the shadows.

"What am I to do?" Enyra asked. "Am I also banned from the quarters?"

Raliton smiled at Enyra. "You will go about the compound, checking for any who can assist you on the remainder of this journey. I do not want my..." He paused and grinned. "My regent should be attended to properly. Do you understand?"

Enyra stretched up to kiss him. "Yes, my dear husband. I will attend to these details at once."

"Under-lord Letiman and guests." Raliton bowed. "I will now retire to my quarters. I thank you all for a wonderful day and delightful meal." One more he bowed. "Please, remain, enjoy your meal. Until morning."

Raliton left the hall.

Raliton sat at his chair by the desk. He watched the fire, thinking, wondering exactly how Jenix would sneak into his room. His gaze flicked to the balcony. He considered walking to it when there was a knock on the door.

He waited. Again, there was the knock. Raliton answered the door to see Jaren.

"I told everyone at the meal, I didn't want to be disturbed."

"You misunderstand, Prince Raliton. I am not Jaren."

Raliton stepped back. The voice was deeper, the eyes slightly different.

"Jenix?"

He bowed. "At your service, my lord."

"So, you do know you appear as Jaren. Are you twins, like my brother, Lornear and I?"

"No. We are more complicated than that. I do not wish to discuss that. I have a proposition to offer you as the new king of Adavinya. Are you interested?"

Raliton waved his arm to the table and chairs. "Shall we sit to discuss this?"

Jenix took a seat and reached for a nutmeat on a platter.

"I find it amusing. In homes of the wealthy, they will place such..." He held up the nutmeat. "They offer it to their guests. If the guest doesn't eat it, it will be thrown out and fresh will replace the old the next day." He sighed. "Such a waste."

"Your point?" Raliton joined Jenix at the table.

"In my home... when I am allowed such a luxury as to be in my home, the nutmeat is kept within the shell, holding its freshness until it is needed. None are deigned too worthy not to break the nutshell for themself." Jenix smiled. "In other words, my lord, it is not a job for the servant." Jenix popped the nutmeat into his mouth.

"Thank you for explaining how special my life has been." Raliton grabbed a couple of nutmeats to eat. "May I ask, to what purpose does the nutmeat serve in our discussion tonight?"

"Notice the nutmeats." Jenix placed two nutmeats on the table. "They all appear very similar. Which of them should rule?" He cocked an eyebrow in Raliton's direction. "Which is the true heir and which is the second?"

Raliton leaned back in his chair. "I see you are questioning my right to ascension to the throne as the rightful first-born."

Jenix nodded approvingly at Raliton's assumption. He grabbed one of the nutmeats and nibbled. "You have proof you are the first-born?"

Raliton leaned toward Jenix.

"Can you see the light birth-mark? It is in the shape of a cat. As a child it was extremely prominent, but now, it is barely noticeable."

Jenix reached to Raliton's forehead.

"May I?"

Raliton nodded.

Jenix slid his thumb across the light blemish in an attempt to remove a possible smudge.

"As foretold," Jenix said. "When the son is double." He laughed. "I often wondered at the legends. How could we have a double sun? When I learned of the twin heirs, it was then I realized the word 'sun' was wrong." Jenix leaned back in his chair. "And, now the trouble."

Raliton frowned.

"I'd not thought of the legend in that regard."

"Then I shall tell you of what I have learned from Jaren. Your throne is in question. There are those who doubt you to be the real heir. Also, although you love your brother, he is not being faithful to you. He plots his own reign."

"I have no fear of Lornear, Jenix. He is attending to my father and the ruling of Adavinya in my absence."

"Here is my proposition, my lord. I have men, men who will follow me and if I follow you, they will follow you, also. If you need me, notify Under-lord Letiman and I will quickly learn of your need and attend you at full haste."

Raliton fingered the nutmeat in his hand, scrutinizing Jenix and evaluating his words.

"You seem very alarmed."

"You, my lord, have been involved with two issues, of which both are directly connected to your ascension to being the next king."

Raliton frowned. "Two?"

"This quest for approval of the Over-lords and..." He paused. "A royal heir of your loins." He smiled. "I know Princess Enyra is pregnant so now that aspect is no longer a sword at your neck. But, still, you will fret about this during the whole of the pregnancy until your heir is in your arms." Jenix bowed his head. "This, I understand. Now, I believe all the Over-lords will accept you as the next king. It is tradition. Not once in the history of Adavinya has the heir-apparent been refused."

"Ah, but never has there been twins, either." Raliton held up his hand to make that note.

"My lord, Prince Raliton." Jenix lowered his voice. "I had a dream... nay, a nightmare. Your heir will be born but you'll never be king. I saw death and the destruction of Adavin."

Jenix eyes glazed.

"I do not fear my brother," Raliton said.

"Perhaps when your adviser, Alson, returns, he will be able to..." Jenix shook his head and placed a hand to his forehead. He blinked his eyes profusely.

"Forgive me, Prince Raliton. I must leave immediately."

Raliton stared at Jenix and his sudden desire to leave.

"I will contact you another time." He stood. "I apologize..."

Jenix voice broke and changed.

Raliton watched the man stand and drop the nutmeats from his hand.

"I detest nutmeats." He wiggled his fingers, removing all crumbs from them as he fled the room.

CHAPTER 31: Curiosity

The Other has played his hand
Two sons and now two stand
Raliton surges forward with a fix
Confusing The Other with his mix

from The Ballad of the Fire

Raliton stared at the closed door, wondering about the sudden change in demeanor with Jenix. He frowned as he considered the action.

There was a soft rap at the door.

"Raliton?" Enyra's voice but a whisper. "May I join you now?"

Raliton dashed to the door and opened it.

"Come in, my love."

He hustled her through the doorway, leaned out and gave a glance in each direction. There was nobody to be seen.

"Did you meet anyone in hall?" he asked.

"Just Jaren mumbling to himself." She giggled. "I believe I startled him when I greeted him. He jumped to the side of the hallway before bowing and asking forgiveness for not noticing me." A small wrinkle creased her forehead. "Was he here with you?"

"Come. Sit. I'll tell you what has transpired."

He helped her to the divan and then joined her, grabbing her hand into his.

"I was visited by Jenix. Remember him? The bandit?' He softly patted her hand. "No need to worry, he is not about to kill me. In fact, it may have been Jenix whom you noticed in the hall." Raliton paused. "Before he left me, he... well, he seemed odd and suddenly distant. In fact, he sat with me, discussing issues and all the while, he was eating nutmeats. Just before he left, he stood and was like a completely different man. He said he despised nutmeats."

Enyra smiled. "Jaren despises nutmeats. The other day a new servant offered him a tray with nutmeats and he flew into a rage, knocking the tray from her hands. Are you sure it was Jenix? Could it have been Jaren? They do appear to be similar in looks."

"I ask Jenix if they were twins - like Lornear and I. He claimed it was more complicated than that. I'm not sure what he meant, but I plan to find out and..."

There was a series of hard raps on the door.

Raliton stood, hand on sword.

"Enter," he said calmly.

Halsvar stepped in. "My lord, Alson has returned. Do you wish to see him?"

"Immediately," Raliton replied. "Have him attend me here."

Halsvar disappeared behind the closing door.

"Stay with me, my love. Alson's news of his engagement is part of your doing."

Within moments, there was a soft rap at the door and it opened. Alson entered the room.

"My liege," Alson said while bowing. "I found my Julenia the most beautiful of stones possible. We are officially engaged." He frowned. "I stopped at the castle to visit your father and brother." He pulled a chair near the divan. "Your father's health continues to fail, but he was still of good mind and happy to hear an update of your Challenge journey." Again, he frowned. "I spoke with your brother. Lornear was aloof, seeming to have no interest in your affairs. When I asked how morning judgments went, he informed me the people no longer require judgments and he has banned the action from the court."

"He has done what?" Raliton stood and paced the room. "What is my brother thinking? Since the beginning, my great-grandfather, King Arlyon, has always held court for judgments to deal with both minor and major issues within the kingdom." Raliton shook his head at the thought. "I must remedy this immediately. I will return..."

"You cannot return, Prince Raliton." Alson stood to face Raliton. "You must continue and finish your Challenge. To return at this point would be an affront to Over-lords Zornear and Hasputhner. You don't want to embarrass yourself. I understand your issue, but there is more. I found the farmers from Alitro - Joalmore and his brothers. There were begging at the gates of the city. Your brother did not honor your request, it seems."

"Immediately send a guard to Adavin to locate Joalmore, his brothers and their families. Send them back to Alitro to ask their original lands be given back to them at my request." Raliton nodded to Alson. "Make an decree to that account, give the order to the guard and have him take it to Joalmore." Raliton stopped pacing to stare at Alson. "I'll not have my brother overruling my requests. He is not the king."

"One more item, my lord," Alson said. He looked at Enyra and grimaced. "I attempted to purchase my jewels at..." He paused and hung his head. "The store was not open and nobody has seen the jeweler for several days."

Raliton stared at Enyra. "Has your father closed business?"

"My father is still young," Enyra replied. "Perhaps he has gone on travel to search for more inventory." She forced a smile. "Since I no longer live with them, I am sure my mother decided to travel with him."

"Perhaps," Alson agreed. "Although, there was a certain air looming over Adavin. It didn't seem to be the same happy place I remembered. But, then again, my mind was elsewhere. We shall be in Clondine at the beginning of Ha'Chi? Am I right?"

Raliton nodded his head while grinning. He lifted a chalice of water.

"Will you be able to contain yourself that long?"

Alson composed himself. "Sire, I am your advisor. I will maintain the proper decorum." He paused, noticing the three chalices.

"One is yours; one is Enyra's — a third chalice and it is not mine. May I ask who has visited?"

"Jenix," Raliton replied with a slight disregard. "He proposed a plan, one I might need to consider."

"Jenix!" Alson stared at Raliton with total disbelief. "You allow a thief to walk the halls of Letiman's home?"

"I believe he roams these halls more than you think, my dear Alson." Raliton popped a nut meat into his mouth and chewed. "I saw him up close. I could see no difference between him and Jaren. He claims they are not twins like Lornear and I." Raliton smiled, his eyes glistening in the room's light. "He claimed it was more complicated. When he left, Enyra met him in the hallway, but she is positive it was Jaren, not Jenix. Strange, indeed."

Raliton stood and walked to Alson.

"Sit," he commanded while pushing the younger man into a chair. "I believe you've just returned and very exhausted from your quest." He massaged Alson's shoulders. "I am sure you will need, at minimum, at least two days rest before we can move on." He paused, staring into the corner, his hands frozen in time on Alson's shoulders. "Plus, we must await the guard's return so we have a better understanding of that which is happening in Adavin."

Raliton strolled to the window and turned, leaning against the wall beside the window.

"Is that not a wise move? Let us say it will be another three days before we move out." He nodded his head in approval, more to confirm his thoughts than to receive agreement from those in the room. "We have a plan."

He clapped his hands and moved to Enyra.

"Shall we prepare to retire?"

"I shall prepare the message to Joalmore and have Halsvar select a guard." Alson stood. "This order will be on its way within the hour."

Alson bowed and headed for the door.

"Trust me, Alson," Raliton said. "We shall be in Clondine in plenty of time for your preparations to wed."

"Thank you, sire." Alson bowed and slipped out the door.

"Sire." The street urchin turned his eyes toward Raliton. "A message, my lord." He proffered the scroll toward Raliton.

Raliton took the parchment and unrolled it.

"If you agree, my lord, I was instructed to tell you to raise your right hand into the air. If not, then you are to ride on." The boy turned and disappeared into the market.

Raliton read and raised his right arm. Above him flew an eagle which cried to its mate. Some of the market patron's thought the young prince to pointing toward the bird and watched it momentarily. Raliton lowered his arm and rode toward Under-lord Letiman's stables. Shadowfeet was getting restless and wanted to run.

Realizing Shadowfeet's urges, Raliton turned and headed out the main gate and let Shadowfeet have full rein to run free.

Within moments, a horseman rushed toward him from the right.

"My Prince Raliton," Jenix yelled. "I thought you agreed to meet in your chambers."

Raliton laughed. "It seems my horse had other plans. Will this not work?" He reined in Shadowfeet to a trot as Jenix joined him.

"This will be fine. Did you adviser inform you of what is happening in Adavin?"

"The news was disconcerting but nothing to alarm me, as yet. My father's health is waning but from what Alson could tell, he is still of strong health to survive my challenge."

"I told you of my nightmare. Last night, I had another and it was almost exactly like the one before. You will gain a son to be king but you will never be king." Jenix, once again, bowed his head. "I offer you my services."

"I have considered your offer, Jenix. I am confused by you, yet I am willing to take a chance and accept your offer. But, on one condition. Will you stop your thievery of those who travel the road?"

"Yes, my lord, if you are willing to pay my men and me a small sustenance so we may live with some dignity."

"Will ten gold pieces per man per month be sufficient?"

"More than enough, my lord." He turned his horse away. "I will relay this information at once."

Jenix rode away, yelling. "If you need me, notify Under-lord Letiman and I will know and be at your side."

Raliton watched Jenix ride away, wondering how it was that Under-lord Letiman knew nothing of the thief, and yet, the thief knew everything that happened within the court.

"My lord," Halsvar rode up. "Why did you not request an escort for this excursion from the city." He turned to watch the distant rider disappear over a hill. "Who was that?"

"That was Jenix, the so-called thief of the area," Raliton replied. "He is no longer such and is now in the service to me. Treat him fairly when you next meet him."

"Your service?"

"My service," Raliton reassured him. "Now we shall return to Evanal and although I doubt your guard has returned, yet, we shall prepare for departure to our next destination." He smiled at Halsvar. "There is need to be in Clondine by…"

"I know the reason, my lord," Halsvar said. "Alson has been less than discreet about his engagement. I believe all of Evanal knows of it." He shrugged. "Will tomorrow morning be a timely departure?"

"We shall leave shortly after the morning meal." Raliton nodded approvingly.

Halsvar rode silently as they made their way back to the village. He casually glanced around and finally swung to face Raliton.

"My lord," Halsvar started. "Forgive me for speaking out of turn, but I must say something as your adviser regarding this agreement you've made with Jenix."

Raliton reined Shadowfeet to a halt and leaned on his saddle's horn.

"What is your issue, Halsvar?"

"Why have you aligned yourself with this thief? To what advantage is his service? To be honest, Prince Raliton, I am totally perplexed by your action." He paused.

"There is more?" Raliton asked.

Halsvar set his chin with a grimace and glanced at Raliton.

"You hesitate." Raliton watched Halsvar with a curious stare. "Why is this?"

There was a long pause, finally broken by the sound of Halsvar taking a deep breath.

"My lord." Halsvar chose his words carefully. "I am your adviser, yet you entered into this association with Jenix without consulting me. Actually, I don't believe you consulted anyone, even Enyra."

Raliton leaned over and put a strong hand on Halsvar's shoulder.

"My friend, my dear adviser. There will be times I will make a decision without you. It is not that I don't value your thoughts, but because I have a gut feeling. Something tells me Jenix would be a better adviser to Under-lord Letiman than Jaren." He smiled at Halsvar. "At present, I am studying my options and bringing Jenix under my jurisdiction may serve my ultimate goal better."

"Ultimate goal?" Halsvar cast a questioning scowl.

"Your news of Adavin has disturbed me. At the same time, Jenix has revealed to me details that I have tended to ignore." He paused a stared directly into Halsvar eyes. "There are those who feel my brother, Prince Lornear, is the true heir." Again, he paused. "Do you not remember Under-lord Laminar?"

Halsvar nodded.

"Plus, I am curious about the duality between Jaren and Jenix. I have a plan."

Raliton nudged Shadowfeet. "Race you to the village gate," he yelled while allowing Shadowfeet to gallop away at full speed.

"You take the advantage, my lord," Halsvar replied, taking the challenge.

CHAPTER 32: The Plan

Raliton and The Other dance together
Each adopting a plan to confuse the other
The Other stays hidden, sight unseen
Raliton moves forward, a changing scene

from The Ballad of the Fire

Raliton slowed Shadowfeet to a trot as Halsvar rushed past him. Halsvar pulled up his horse to a stop and waited for Raliton to join him.

"Is there a problem?" Halsvar asked. "Or did you decide on a different finish line?" He paused. "Surely you didn't let me win by default, did you?"

"I've been thinking on my plan and realized it wouldn't work." He smiled at Halsvar. "Of course, I have a new plan — a much better plan." He straightened in his saddle. "I do believe it will work."

"What is this master plan, my lord?"

"Watch and learn," Raliton replied, narrowing his eyes and grinning. "Watch and learn."

Raliton passed through the gate into the village, all the while he scoured the village people, searching for one person in particular. He was sure he would find him.

"You, there," Raliton called. "Lad, come to me."

The young boy hurried to Raliton.

"You called, my lord?" He kept his head bowed.

"Let me see your face." Raliton slid off Shadowfeet and immediately lifted the boy's face. "Yes, you have your father's eyes. I can see that now." Raliton cocked his head to the side and again examined the lad's face. "Are you not the young boy who communicated Jenix's wishes to me?"

"I gave you the parchment given to me by…"

"It matters not, lad." Raliton knelt to the boy's level. "I want you to take a message to the person who gave you the parchment. Do you understand?"

The lad nodded.

"Tell him I wish to meet with…" Raliton paused, thinking perhaps Jenix had passed the parchment to another for delivery. "Tell him, I wish to meet with Jenix tonight in my chamber, an hour after evening meal." Raliton pulled a copper from his belt. "Can you do that?"

"I believe so, Prince Raliton. You wish to meet with Jenix an hour after evening meal." He hesitated. "Yes, in your chamber. Is that correct?"

Raliton gave the boy the copper coin. "Be about the task, lad." He watched the boy scamper down a narrow path between two buildings, turn and disappear.

"This is the great master plan?" Halsvar asked as Raliton got back on Shadowfeet.

Raliton shrugged. "It is the start." He urged Shadowfeet forward.

"How do you know he will show?" Halsvar rode beside Raliton, smug in his question.

An arrow whirled through the air to impale itself a few feet forward of the horses. Raliton gazed in the direction the arrow came and saw a man, perhaps Jenix, on a rooftop. The man waved and bowed, turned and disappeared.

"There is your answer," Raliton replied. "He'll be there."

Halsvar stared at the arrow. "He could have killed you."

"Yes," Raliton replied. "And, you, too... but he didn't. Doesn't that strike you odd?"

Halsvar frowned in thought as they continued to ride in silence. Exasperated, Halsvar broke the silence just before they approached the stables.

"What is the next move in your plan?"

Raliton got off Shadowfeet and handed the reins to a stableboy.

"Quite simple," Raliton said. "After the evening meal, I'll ask for Jaren to join me, along with you, to discuss our plans for tomorrow. I'll have Enyra entertain Under-lord Letiman, or least attempt to distract him from joining us."

"Deceitful. Then what?"

"When Jenix joins us, I will then be able to confirm my plans of Jenix within my royal entourage." Raliton paused. "I must have all the players in one location."

"For what purpose, my lord?" Halsvar followed Raliton up the stairs to the quarters.

"Very simple, my dear adviser." Raliton placed an arm over Halsvar's shoulder. "When I have both Jaren and Jenix in the same room, then, and only then, can I learn the truth about their similarities. Neither of them seem very forthcoming as to their twin appearance." Again, he paused. "Perhaps, when I have them both together, I will see they are not identical in appearance."

So, tell me Jaren, how long have you served Under-lord Letiman?" Raliton stretched out on the chaise in the room. He spied the nutmeats and fruit on the table but realized, even though he wanted some, he'd just finished the evening meal and was full. He turned his attention back to Jaren.

"I was raised within the walls of the courtyard, Prince Raliton. I have known Under-lord Letiman since my birth. I was a playmate to the prior adviser's son who had no interest in what his father did. I, on the other hand, when not playing with Lenox, would sit at his father's feet and listen to him drone on about how he decided this or that. When he passed to the Isle of Forgotten Sleep, I felt I had lost my only friend. Lenox declined Under-lord Letiman's offer as adviser. I meekly offered my services and he accepted me on trial and I have been in his service ever since." He paused and stared at the upper corner of the room. "It has been almost five Circles now." Jaren turned to Halsvar. "How long have you served Prince Raliton?"

Halsvar glanced to Raliton. "I have been in his service as adviser approximately one Circle. I am learning my duties in the tutelage of King Lanfeld's adviser, Innead." He smiled. "Of course, now that we are on The Challenge, I am basically gleaning my skills via experience."

Raliton waved his hand. "May I ask, Jaren, how long has Jenix been a nuisance? I don't want to use the word thief since he's yet to steal anything from me." He laughed.

Jaren frowned and Raliton could see the muscles tighten beneath his garments.

"Jenix... Jenix has been a thorn in my side for the past three years." He immediately glanced up to Raliton. "Of course, he has only been actively plaguing the countryside for the last few months."

"Curious," replied Raliton. "Three years. Perhaps tonight we may settle some issues for I have requested his presence. He should be here shortly."

"I don't think Jenix will appear." Jaren stood. "He will be arrested when he shows his face within the halls." He stepped away from the chair and stumbled. "I... My lord..."

Jaren crumbled to the floor, collapsing like a tower of water.

Halsvar responded and rushed to his side. Raliton sat on the edge of the chaise, observing every movement and action by Jaren.

"Here, take a drink of water," Halsvar offered.

Jaren sipped the water then proceeded to stand.

"How peculiar." There was a new air about Jaren. "I seem to awaken and find myself on the floor more often than not."

Raliton noticed a voice difference. There was a deepness and ring of authority. Gone was the nasal whine Jaren spoke with.

"Jenix?" Raliton cocked his head and stared at the man before him.

"At your service, my lord." He bowed low with a full flourish of both arms extended out.

Raliton slipped back on the chaise, placing an elbow on knee and chin in hand. A crease of the eyebrows above the nose revealed his concern.

Jenix stood from his bow and took the chair where Jaren had sat. A small curl at the edge of his lips revealed his amusement of Raliton's befuddlement.

"It appears you have stumbled upon the truth of my little secret."

"What is this trickery?" Halsvar stepped away, staring at Jenix with an occasional glance to Raliton.

"It is not trickery, my good adviser," Raliton replied. "It is possession. I heard Innead discuss it one night with Namo-Ke. She explained this happens when two souls are trapped within one body. Many consider Lornear and I to be such but we have two bodies." He nodded to Jenix. "They do not, they share a body." Raliton sat back and stroked his chin. "She also claimed there are times when more than two souls get trapped. She said there was one time where five different souls were in one body. It was three men and two women which caused much concern for the village and they stoned the person to death."

"I thought this to be complicated for you to comprehend, Prince Raliton." Jenix stood and paced the room. "I see I am wrong." He faced Raliton. "What will you do, now that you know the secret?"

"Nothing," Raliton replied.

"Nothing?" Halsvar stared at Raliton. "This man is dangerous. He hides within the body of another and you do nothing?"

Raliton stood and walked to Halsvar. "Exactly which man hides within this body? Is it Jenix or is it Jaren? Who truly owns this body?" He placed an arm over Halsvar shoulder. "How would you treat me if both Lornear and I shared this body?"

"That is not the question," Halsvar spat. "This man—"

"Is Jenix and now controls the body. I will make Jaren's life much easier. I will explain to Under-lord Letiman there will be times when Jaren will not be available and it is quite acceptable and not to fret." Raliton strolled to the table, plucked a grape from the plate and popped it into his mouth. "I believe it will allow Jaren to be more relaxed." He turned to Jenix. "Is Jaren aware of your existence?"

Jenix smiled. "He fears there might be a demon within him. He has trouble understanding the slight lapses in memory and location changes. My wife has learned to cope with this strangeness and my son is learning."

"Your son," Raliton repeated. "The young boy who has been our go-between — yes?"

Jenix nodded. "Halbeor. He is a good lad."

"Would you allow him to travel with me? To be my future son's friend and confidant?"

"The honor would be mine, my lord, but first, I must discuss the issue with his mother."

"Be assured, Jenix, your son would be allowed to visit home at least once each moon and your family would always be welcome to visit each festival, or any other time."

"As you wish," Jenix said with a bow. "I will—"

He stumbled forward toward Halsvar who grabbed him before he fell. Halsvar held him as Jenix twitched and Jenix blinked his eyes repeatedly.

"Are you okay?" Halsvar asked.

"Yes, yes, I do believe I am." Jaren's nasally voice replied. "I must have fainted."

"We have much to discuss, Jaren," Raliton said, coming to assist Halsvar. "Let us sit at the table as we explain.,"

"Explain?" Jaren reached out to grab the table for support. "Forgive my fainting, Prince Raliton. I must have consumed something during the evening meal..."

"I shall explain," Raliton said taking a seat as Halsvar sat Jaren at the table. "Perhaps a little drink to help clear the mind." He smiled. "This explanation is going to be extremely complicated, but I do feel when it is finished, you will be relieved."

"So, it is understood, Under-lord Letiman, that your adviser may be missing at times for an uncertain length of time and all is well. Correct?"

Letiman nodded. "Will this Jenix person come to my court?"

"Perhaps, in time," Raliton replied. "If so, please show him respect and hospitality.

"So be it," Letiman said and stood. "I will do as you wish."

"I shall be on my way, Under-lord Letiman.

CHAPTER 33: The News

Within the mountains born of the fire
To visit the village of Gautiner and the sire
Under-lord Sasjaq and then to Over-lord Hasputhner
The plan is made, but not by The Other.

from The Ballad of the Fire

Raliton rode Shadowfeet to the litter with Enyra and Halbeor in it. He found the two huddled together in an attempt to keep warm.

"We approach the mountain stronghold of Under-lord Sasjaq." He smiled at Enyra who rubbed her swollen stomach. "Then we go see Over-lord Hasputhner and move on to the eastern shore and the realm of Yorela with Over-lord Zornear." He sighed. "The journey is almost over."

Enyra winced. "Yes, the journey is almost over. My journey." She hesitated. "Have you considered a name for your offspring, be it a boy or a girl?"

"I fear the name of Arlyon for a boy would be too pretentious. I do like the name Ralson." He raised a hand to stop any comment from Enyra. "Yes, I know, that was the name of Arlyon's first-born grandson." He paused. "Of course, I also like the name Norance."

Enyra frowned. "Whatever does that mean? I've not heard of such a name."

"Halbeor is a good name," Halbeor mumbled and quickly hid his eyes so he wouldn't see Raliton's reaction.

"Indeed, it is a good, strong name," Raliton said. "But, consider the consequences. If I were to call my son and his name is the same as yours, who would answer?"

"I understand, sire," Halbeor mumbled.

"Learn to speak up, Halbeor. You are to be my son's aide. I can't have you constantly mumbling. Yes, I will be king, but I am a man, just like your father."

Halbeor gazed into Raliton's eyes. "As you wish."

Enyra pulled a cloak around her. "It is getting cooler."

"We will spend a day or two with Under-lord Sasjaq." He gazed at the sun and the misty moon in the opposite direction. "Ha-Chi is near." He examined the passage before them. "We pass over and down into the valley. "It will be warmer."

Enyra winced. "We'd best be to the Under-lord Sasjaq's soon. I don't think your heir will wait must longer."

"We will be over this pass within the hour," Raliton said, reaching down and grabbing her hand. "Will you be able to make it?"

She closed her eyes and nodded. "Yes, my husband."

Raliton spurred Shadowfeet and raced to the front of the caravan. Hustling the wagons and people, Raliton was true to his word as they pushed over the mountain passage and into the valley where it was warmer.

As they approached the main gates of the city, Raliton gazed back at the passage.

"Another moon and there will be snow on that passage." He nodded. *Best we be on our way as soon as possible and out of the mountains before the Quiet Time.* He smiled. *Enyra will enjoy the Eastern Shores where the Quiet Time is mild. We should be finished with the Challenge before Nos'Dovel and back in Adavinya to celebrate it.*

"Prince Raliton," Under-lord Sasjaq bellowed as he approached on foot. "You honor me. Come. Welcome to my beautiful city. Gautiner is at your disposal."

"You have a beautiful city, Under-lord Sasjaq," Raliton said. "Gautiner is a hidden gem within the Iron Mountains. May I ask how often Over-lord Hasputhner visits?"

Sasjaq grimaced. "He definitely makes the obligatory visit each Circle." He narrowed his eyes in thought. "It has been..." He paused. "At least four Circles since he made more than one visit during a Circle."

Raliton gazed back at the narrow mountain passage and considered the bleak outskirts of this city-state in the far reaches of the Iron Mountains. A cloud of dust caught his eye.

Halsvar leaned in. "You see it, too, sire. Whoever it is, they ride like the god Bre chases them."

"Whoever it is; they should be here shortly." Raliton smiled at Halsvar. "There is no reason for alarm." His eyes scanned the top of the high wall surrounding the city. "We are protected. Make sure everyone is inside."

Halsvar nodded and departed to perform his duty.

Enyra moaned and followed it with a soft scream. "It is time, Raliton," she said. "Get me a healer."

"This way," Under-lord Sasjaq said noting Enyra's swollen stomach. "My personal healer will see to your needs." He offered his arm to her. "Can you walk?"

"I will help," Halbeor said and stood beside Enyra.

Sasjaq grinned. "The two of us will take the princess to the healer."

Enyra placed her right hand on Halbeor's shoulder for support, and her left arm wrapped within Sasjaq's arm. "I will make it," she whispered as her knees gave out and she began to slip to the ground.

"Enyra!" Raliton shouted and grabbed her, holding her before she reached the ground.

"Litter!" Sasjaq yelled.

Raliton placed Enyra on the litter and the men scurried off with Sasjaq and Halbeor following.

"My lord, Prince Raliton," a voice called.

Raliton turned to see a horse nearly upon him and an Adavinya guard dressed in mourning leaping from it to fall on the ground, one knee bent. Behind the horse, dust followed to envelope the group.

"Forgiveness, my lord," the guard said. "I have been riding for three days to find you as requested by your mother. I stopped at Clondine to see Over-lord Hasputhner in my search. He said you were in Rastin. I hastened there to find you had left. I have followed you, always a day or two late. Under-lord Alzon assured me you were headed here, to Gautiner, to visit Under-lord Sasjaq."

The words came broken and between deep breaths.

"I regret to inform you, your father, King Lanfeld has gone to the Isle of Forgotten Sleep. King Lornear ordered that none should contact you since you were on The Challenge and not to be bothered." He bowed his head. "Your mother sent me. If I have done wrong, take my life."

"You have done right," Raliton said then paused. He frowned. "King Lornear?"

"Yes, King Lornear," the guard muttered. "It is rumored when King Lanfeld died, he gave explicit instructions that Lornear would be the new king."

"I leave as soon as I can get the supplies needed." He turned to Halsvar. "I travel alone."

Halsvar stepped forward. "You will do no such thing, my prince. Enyra is in labor. You have an heir coming. Come into Under-lord Sasjaq's home and rest."

"No, Halsvar," Raliton said. "My father has died. I must seek out my brother and..."

Halsvar began to speak.

"Alone," Raliton said, cutting off any words from the guard. "And we both know I can travel faster by myself. None will bother me." He turned to the guard. "Refresh yourself. Rest. When my wife delivers, you immediately come to me in Adavin to let me know whether I have a male or female heir."

"Yes, Prince Raliton," the guard said.

Halsvar motioned the guard toward the stable. "I will have some food brought to you."

Raliton jumped on Shadowfeet and a servant brought a bag of foodstuffs.

"There is plenty there for three days," the servant mumbled as he handed Raliton the sack of goods. "In case you are delayed."

"I will not be delayed," Raliton said. "I will reach Adavin in less than two days."

He turned Shadowfeet toward the main gate, spurred him, and in a flurry of dust, disappeared.

CHAPTER 34: Adavin

The Other dances with none to see
Raliton views Adavin and questions to be
This is not his city, not his realm by rule
Who has changed this? By what tool?

from The Ballad of the Fire

Shadowfeet trotted near the walls of Adavin. It was late. Raliton was surprised to discover the main gate closed. Normally, the castle had lights; tonight, there were none. It was dark.

Raliton turned Shadowfeet toward Obera's Obelisk. Again, Raliton was surprised. The grounds were unkempt. Two vendor stands wobbled in the light breeze, questioning their stability. He pushed the tall grasses around the obelisk and created a small space for him to sleep. Raliton leaned against the obelisk, facing to the east so the sun would wake him. Shadowfeet nuzzled into the tall grass, getting the shorter, sweeter grass below. Raliton stared at the distant walled castle. If he'd not known the city was there, he would have passed it during the night.

The sun shone on Raliton's face and he raised a hand to shadow his face. He stretched. In the distance, the gates of Adavin were open, yet there was no activity.

Strange, Raliton thought. *The city should be bustling with activity. Vendors should be hawking their wares.* He frowned. *What has happened?*

Opening the bag of supplies, he made a breakfast of crackers and cheese. He gazed at the red apple and decided to give it to Shadowfeet.

Tying the bag of goods and hooking it to Shadowfeet's saddle, Raliton prepared to enter the city. He immediately noted the startling changes inside the gates.

The vendors who normally bellowed their services and wares were quiet and covert. They averted their eyes and watched him over their shoulders. As he rode through the streets, the inhabitants, they couldn't be called villagers, stared at him with blank, glassy eyes as they scurried out of his way, all the time bent over, arms held up to protect themselves.

What has happened during my absence? It has been almost a full Circle, Raliton questioned as he sauntered the streets toward the castle. *Surely, if the rumors had been true, someone would have sought me, to advise me, or give me council.*

Suspicions ran rampantly through his mind.

As Raliton entered the castle grounds, a young man scurried out to grab Shadowfeet's bit.

"Prince Raliton?" the lad questioned. "You live?"

"Yes," Raliton said as he slid off the saddle. "Why do you question that?"

"It was rumored you were killed." He dropped to his knee. "I beg forgiveness, Prince Raliton. I speak out of turn." He looked both ways before gazing up at Raliton. "I am babbling rumors to the true king." His eyes widened. "I have said too much."

The lad stroked Shadowfeet's muzzle and forelock. "It is good to see you, again, Shadowfeet." He led the horse to the stable.

Raliton walked the passageways. They were empty. Even the chambers he remembered filled with activity and light were dark. The only sound was that of his soles on the marble. He made his way to the throne room.

Prince Raliton entered the Hall of Rule and all his suspicions were confirmed. The massive black onyx throne with its inlays of gold, silver, and semi-precious stones should have been empty.

Prince Lornear sat on the throne with his son, Namo-Hoj, upon his lap. Princess Namo-Ke stood to one side, nursing their new daughter.

Innead, the sorcerer, stood on the opposing side of the throne from Princess Namo-Ke.

"Our father has, indeed, passed to the Isle of Forgotten Sleep six days ago." He eased back into the big throne. "I am now king. This was the last instruction of our father, King Lanfeld, before making his journey. His words were 'You, my son, are now the king' and then he expired."

The shock of the situation was great, but Prince Raliton stood firm against them.

"As first born and the one on The Challenge, I am the rightful heir of the throne."

Prince Lornear leaned forward. "You have no heir. I have two."

"I am here to inform you that my wife, Princess Enyra, has delivered me an heir.

Namo-Ke paled at Raliton's words and backed into the shadows.

Lornear, jumped to his feet, spilling Namo-Hoj to the floor like an immense festering lump of flesh, and turned on his wife, shrieking, "Witch, you have failed me. You said it would be a still-birth." His eyes flared in anger. "Take your demon spawn and return to the bowels of Bre from whence you came." Lornear grabbed a spear from behind the throne and had it impaled through Princess Namo-Ke before any could move to stop him.

A high-pitched wail and black smoke issued from Princess Namo-Ke. When the smoke cleared, Namo-Ke and her offspring were gone. Only the voice of Namo-Ke could be heard.

"You are not easily rid of me, worm of Adavin. I have your vow, remember it well."

The room filled with darting shadows and echoes of hideous high-pitched laughter.

Raliton stares at his brother as Lornear's skin lightens a shade.

As the laughter fades, Innead, the sorcerer, shakes his head and gazes about as if just awakening from a drunken stupor, the mind spell placed by Princess Namo-Ke now broken.

The huge doors of the hall abruptly break open and an Adavinyan guard, the one who sought Prince Raliton in Gautiner stumbles into the great hall.

"Forgiveness, m'lord, on this intrusion." He falls forward to the floor in front of Prince Raliton. He utters the words that bring a smile from the older twin. "You have a son. Princess Enyra requests your presence. Return quickly, a name must be given."

A high-pitched shriek from the dais warned Prince Raliton, but not quickly enough. The spear pierces, and passes full length through Prince Raliton. As the blood spews from the open wound, Prince Raliton falls to the floor. The only thing he hears is his brother's maniacal voice screaming that only he, King Lornear, will rule the realm of Adavinya. He will rule with Enyra at his side as his queen.

The older twin stares with disbelief at his wild-eyed younger brother. Again, Lornear's skin lightens yet another shade.

In the corner, a shadow dances and titters.

Prince Raliton's lips move as he silently whispers the name of his son. None hear the naming. Prince Raliton lies gasping for life in an expanding pool of blood.

Innead, who has stood transfixed during the action, attempting to understand the situation, now quickly moves to Prince Raliton's side.

A voice fills the room. "Two deaths, worm of Adavin!"

Both Innead and Prince Lornear search the air above them for some embodiment from whence the words are spoken.

Innead leans down and picks up the spear that had been used to slay Prince Raliton. He stands there, bloodied spear in hand, looking at the fallen prince. He glares at Lornear.

"This is wrong," Innead says as he lifts the spear into the air. "Our pact never alluded to Prince Raliton's death, only the..."

The spear falls from Innead's hand as he clutches the one now protruding from his abdomen. Innead stares wide-eyed at Prince Lornear. The young prince stands on the dais, hands on hips, gloating over the scene of his actions. Innead slumps to the floor, dead.

Once more, Lornear's skin lightens to his original white skin color. The gold emblem on his forehead drops to the floor and clatters down the steps of the dais. Only the scars on Lornear's face differentiate him from Raliton.

"Revenge is mine, mortal. Oh, Lornear, you corrupt slug-worm. The citizens of Adavin allowed you this! You have broken your vow of three consecutive non-battle deaths. I call you to the lower realms of Bre. Let the Fires of Bre be upon you and your puny mortal kingdom!"

As the voice of Namo-Ke echoes through the air, a shriek emits from Prince Lornear as flames envelop him and disappears in the dwindling flames.

"Namo-Ja," Namo-Ke's voice commands. "I call you to spew your destruction."

The falgon flew into the chamber, enlarging, filling the room with its body. The flames flickered along its feathers. The falgon lifted into the air, a trail of fire following its flight. Soon, the entire falgon was flames and the flames grew larger and larger.

Namo-Ke watched as the falgon grew to almost five hundred strides high. Flames of destruction covered everything. The walls of Adavin were molten lava, running in each direction. Citizens attempted to flee but were caught in the melee of fire.

The falgon stretched and opened its beak. Fire spewed forth, igniting the ground to the north where the Iron Mountains were. The villages of Over-lord Hasputhner were in flames. Only the small realm of Gautiner survived the onslaught, snuggled in its valley. To the west, Over-lord Balneor's realms were almost completely destroyed. The Eastern Shore was caught in the flames but only a small edge. The southern forests burned to the Lost Mountains.

Namo-Jal spiraled upward in the flames to disappear, leaving only a continuing burning pillar of fire from the bowels of Bre where once stood the throne of Arlyon.

Namo-Ke smiled. A dancing shadow caught her eye and she tried to focus on it.

"Only he who walks within the flames of fire will be allowed to rule," Namo-Ke whispered.

"I have won," The Other mumbled. "Chaos rules."

"Until," the Council of Creation whispered.

THE END.

This page left blank.

A Tease Read – Book 2: The Lost One

(This is a work in process and can change in the final version of the book.)

Prologue ~ The Lost One

T he Under-lord stood on a precipice at the edge of the mountainside to gaze over the valley below. "Come," Sasjaq called. "You must see this to understand." The winds blew and Under-lord Sasjaq pulled the furs closer to him.

Princess Enyra nodded and Halbeor pulled back the heavy fabric of the litter's curtain. She snuggled the furs around the baby and stepped out into the snowy cold. Young Halbeor huddled close, pulling his jacket open to help protect the baby as they walked.

"See?" Sasjaq pointed out over the mountain cliff. "That is what is left of Adavinya. He swept his arm from the east to the west to encompass everything below the cliff.

The wind curled up from below, a warmness hidden within the cold. Snow swirled around Enyra and the baby whimpered.

"If you wish," Halbeor offered. "I can take Ralson back to the litter."

"Look!" Sasjaq demanded. "See the pillar? Still a fire burns where the castle of Adavin stood. Do you see your prince out there? It has been two full moons and Prince Raliton has not returned. Yet, foolishly, you hold true to him, hoping he will come back." Sasjaq leered at Enyra. "He is dead, my princess. Even Halbeor realizes his home is gone, his parents dead." Sasjaq pulled his fur cloak about him as a gust of wind burst from the valley below. "I have been benevolent, but I can no longer allow you to continue to stay here and live in the style of a princess. You are no longer a princess of Adavinya."

Enyra stared out at the burned plain, watching the distant pillar of flame stretch upward into the wintry sky.

"So, I am no longer a princess of Adavinya," Enyra said. "What do you propose?"

"You have two choices." Sasjaq grinned evilly. "Get rid of the abomination you hold. He is heir to nothing. Throw him over the cliff to the fires of Bre below and become one of my wives." He shrugged. "Or, as you can see, I made sure your whole retinue was with us today." He pointed to the east. "There is the path to Yorel. Take your tale to Over-lord Zornear, if he still lives."

"Come, Halbeor," Enyra said, pulling the furs tighter around her and the baby. "We are leaving."

"Before you leave, Enyra," Sasjaq said. "I ask you give me the ruby since Over-lord Hasputhner no longer has use for it. I, as King Sasjaq of Gautiner, will use it."

Prince Enyra turned to face Under-lord Sasjaq. She smiled. "The stones were given to my husband to give to the Over-lords. He had them, so, I assume, the stones were destroyed when he was…" She left the sentence unfinished.

"I take it you will be leaving my fine city of Gautiner?"

Enyra nodded. "I feel it is time for me to move on." She proceeded to the litter. Halbeor followed.

"But…" Halbeor whispered. "I thought…"

"Hush, little one," Enyra whispered back. "All will be revealed as needed." She turned to the two guards who stood by the litter. "Reestan. Halsvar. We go to Yorela, if it still exists. We will no longer stay here." She glanced back to Sasjaq. "We have overstayed our welcome."

Halbeor held back the heavy curtain fabric for Princess Enyra to enter the litter. Enyra turned to face Alson.

"Please make sure that King…" She slurred the word. "Sasjaq has given us enough food for at least part of our journey."

Alson bowed and excused himself to be about his duties. Enyra entered the litter and Halbeor joined her.

"The stones," Halbeor whispered.

"Are safe," Enyra replied. "The stones are for Over-lords, not a lame want-to-be king."

"My princess," Alson called. "I have checked the supplies. They are meager but I am sure Sasjaq will not allow any more to us. We will, with proper allocation, be able to make the trip."

"Then we leave," Princess Enyra said. "On to Yorela."

"A short journey," Halsvar said. "There is an overhang where we can safely stay under its protection from the wintry cold for the evening and the next day make our way in the realm of Yorel." He gazed about. "Away from this wintry mix." He pulled the furs around him closer.

Alson stepped into Princess Enyra's tent. "My princess," he whispered. "We have been visited by thieves during the night. I fear they have taken most of our foodstuffs and several of the horses. The guard Halsvar set was pummeled with a stone and knocked cold."

Princess Enyra gazed to the corner where the baby's cradle should be.

"The prince is gone," Enyra screamed. "They stole my baby."

Alson gazed at the close corner where Halbeor had slept. "Halbeor is also missing, but from what I see, he did not got peaceably. Note the mussed sleeping area and there is some blood. He fought them, but they won."

"Ralson is missing," Enyra wailed. "They have the cradle with the stones and the scepter. The king-to-be is lost."

"We will go directly to Yorel and notify Over-lord Zornear."

Princess Enyra sat huddled, crying.

Chapter 1: The Fire Reading

To those who weave another man's life;
Trust my word as true.
For when I forced my friend to talk;
His soul was taken, slew.
And as time went, we were apart,
For how could I have knew.
The Silverhawk will ever talk,
And tell what's in the brew.

from The Ballad of the Fire
"Song of Linnell"

The early fall season night sky was clear as stars glittered in the black space. The full moon cast silver highlights on a darkened forest. The trees encircling the clearing were emblazoned with the golden glow of reflected firelight. Shadows danced among the trees as the flames flickered hypnotically across the logs. A grayish plume of smoke languidly wove a path upward to the stars.

Trel sat cross-legged near the edge of the fire. A stable groomsman in the king's service and assigned companion to Prince Linnell, he wore a simple woven tunic revealing a well-muscled body. He stared intently at the fire in front of him with his hazel-colored eyes. A curl of smoke separated and he tilted his head to watch it drift and diffuse into nothingness. Trel shook his head, his black mane of hair shimmering as it brushed back and forth across his shoulders. He pushed the locks of his hair back into place and absently reached with his left hand for the pile of sticks lying near him. He glanced at the prince sleeping at the edge of the small clearing, assuring himself the boy was asleep. His fingers played with the special cluster he'd assembled: oak for strength, willow for submission, pine for timeless, rose bramble for beauty and tied together with string to represent the thread of life that binds. He held the bundle and reached for his knife, and with one quick glance, assured himself that Prince Linnell slept. Trel pricked his finger, adding a drop of blood to the cluster, adding the life force needed and dropped it into the flames. Sparks of ash and cinders flurried into the night sky. Trel's concentration was now on the bundle as he watched the string twist and curl in the heat and flames. He bent his head to side, questioning the view. Trel's vision followed a flame as it flickered skyward, splitting and blending to dissipate to nothingness. Once more he stared into the blue heat of the fire and surveyed the embers glowing embers as they the shadows of heat danced across the surface. The string burnt and crumbled as a wisp of smoke spiraled upward, curling on the heat waves toward the stars.

"No!" he yelled then quickly looked to where Prince Linnell should be.

The prince sat, cross-legged, watching him, a smile on his face. "You're doing a blood-fire reading!" An arm reached out toward Trel with an ominous, threatening finger pointing at him. "Blasphemy!"

The area shaded in a bilious color as the fire's flame changed green and flared, surging upward in shades of yellow and blue.

Trel forgot about Linnell and watched the flames as they revealed the future he so wanted to know.

The colors intensified. A single red flicker twisted toward the sky and Trel scrutinized its every movement. His shoulders slumped and he sighed.

The prince stands up from the shadows. He is near eighteen Circles of Seasons in age. His blond hair in a light disarray, he slides his open hands over the tops of his ears, then behind them to push the long locks back. The gold buckle, the only emblem that bears witness of his royalty, reflects the firelight as the prince wraps it about his waist. He approaches Trel. His simple tunic matches that of Trel's, and reveals young muscles still in development.

"Tell me, Trel. What did the fire say?" Linnell queries as he approaches. The prince's voice is not arrogant, but has a full richness to it. A voice that commands.

"Say? Fires don't say anything, they only crackle occasionally." His voice maintains a tight composure, even as he attempts to make a humorous response to the young prince. "Why ask me what a fire says? Why are you not sleeping?"

"Don't fool with me, Trel. In the Winter Season I will have reached my eighteenth Full Circle. I know of fire-readings. Many times, the sorcerer, Zalran, has performed fire-readings for my father. I have even been allowed to witness one being performed." The prince appears to swell with pride in this proclamation of accomplishment.

"*Zalran! That name!*" Trel thinks to himself. "*If only Linnell knew the full truth of Zalran's past and of his true ambition.*" The current events cause emotions of buried hatred to swell through Trel. The guilt of being caught by the prince cause childhood memories to flow through his being.

"*Caught! Just as Zalran had caught me years ago doing a fire-reading, now this young prince has caught me. I was Zalran's servant from my turning of my seventh full circle. My mother died during my childbirth; I had no father. I was given to some distant relatives who claimed they knew my mother. When no inheritance was forthcoming, I became a costly burden. They sold me into servitude when I was seven; although I was already a servant to these so-called relatives. They thought I would enjoy becoming an apprentice to the locally known mighty Zalran. The gold denyas he offered assured them that I would be properly cared for; as if that was a concern to them. Since I was the wizard's boy, I was always shunned by the other village children and not allowed the same privileges as freedmen. None can count the number of times he placed me into vile situations during his sorcery, causing me to retch my stomach. Especially loathsome was the cleaning of his hut after he had performed his great magic for some of his fellow initiates. The smell of death hung in the air about his forest compound, sometimes strongly, sometimes very faintly; but always ever-present. Zalran! You are a curse upon the royal house. You used your sorcery to assist King Ariello gain the rule of Yorela. You play your games to help others; only to help yourself in the end. Your bony fingers will never lie upon my shoulders, and your black beady eyes will never mesmerize me to do your bidding again. You may think you rule the royal house, but your time will come and you will not have dominion over the king. I thank Great Bre that King Ariello would not allow you servants when you entered into his service. I also thank Great Bre that I was only twelve circles, one less than necessary to be an apprentice. My loathing of you is so great!"* The voice of memory screams within Trel. *"Never has it diminished over time, even now that I am almost twenty-four circles of age. Thank Great Bre that Lady Teloive is my friend and has tempered me over the seasons."*

A quick shift and memories of Lady Teloive begin flooding his mind. *"She's so old, at least seventy-five Full Circles. My first thought when I met her. There she was, leaning on her staff, catching her breath. She was dressed in shades of gray and black. A shawl was across her shoulders; even in the heat of summer this did not seem unnatural."*

"Lad, how would you like to earn a copper coin?" she whispered to me between breaths. A smile crossed her weathered gentle featured face; her eyes twinkled brightly. The mottled sunlight played different colors, almost rainbow like, into her hair of silver.

"Oh, yes, revered mother." I quickly responded, using a title of honor for one so aged and forgetting that my first loyalty should have been to Zalran. A young boy of seven lets everything slip memory when a smile is given and a rare

pleasantness is being offered. My mind quickly forgot that the sticks I carried for Zalran bundled over my shoulder and onto my back could also be used to beat that same back until it bled.

"Then move quickly to assist me. Can you not see that this sweet old lady is in urgent need of some young lad to carry this load of firewood?"

"But, what wood, revered mother?" I answered eagerly, not seeing the wood that she referred to. My hands released the ropes that held the sticks that I carried for Zalran. They fell to the ground behind me; a haphazard pile of sticks, carelessly abandoned.

"This wood laying right in front of me." Moving her hand in a graceful arc to the ground, with her index finger pointing straight down, the wood suddenly appeared from out of nowhere.

"Oh, revered mother, are you a sorceress?" I questioned her. I was already in trouble with a sorcerer, as my mind raced to remind me; and now I stood in the presence of what appeared to be a very adept sorceress.

"I am not a sorceress; nor a witch. Now, fetch the wood, and follow me. You shall get your silver coin shortly." She then proceeded down the trail; her staff leaving small indentations in the ground, the only trace she left, as she walked.

"Yes, revered mother." I replied, hastily picking up her neatly stacked pile of firewood, bunching it under my arms and running to catch up with her.

"Please don't call me revered mother. My circles are many, but I am not a relic to be honored and have some young lad stand in awe of. My name is Teloive. You may call me 'Lady' Teloive." Her voice was pleasant, but it commanded.

"My Lady Teloive, where do you live? Do you share this forest with the mighty Zalran?"

"Zalran? Mighty?" She laughed, a tinkling chime to her voice. "So, little one, he is mighty. What do you know of him. You cannot be more than seven circles, eight at most. He is not allowed to apprentice anyone under thirteen full circles of seasons, and if he was to have a servant, he would surely choose an old village hag to do his bidding. Just who are you lad?" Her questions and answers were hurled toward me as she turned to appraise me again with severe scrutiny.

"I am servant to Zalran, sold to him by relatives for a few coins. My real parents are dead, or so I am told. How much further do you live from here? I must hurry, or I shall be punished by him for being late upon my return."

"Hmm..." Her voice now had a different tone, one of almost seeming to care, as if she knew something. It carried a promise. "I live right here." Just as she had abruptly started scrutinizing me, she now was pointing a finger to a small hut with a thatched roof. A small garden lay to one side of the hut. A light wind jostled the herbs, flowers and spices growing in the garden, creating a light fragrance for the pleasure of breathing. Lady Teloive's hut was very similar; and yet, very different than Zalran's. Here a smell of sweet scents to lift the spirit; while at Zalran's a loathsome smell of death and foulness filled the air. "Come in lad." she ordered. "Quit gawking about."

I didn't hesitate. I immediately went into the small, seemingly dark hut. Inside, the hut glowed with an inner light. It was impossible for the windows to allow that much light into the hut. Truly this lady was a sorceress. I lay the wood by the stove and started to exit.

"Here, lad. Your silver coin as promised. Come fetch it from the table. Also, there is a refreshing drink for you." She lay the coin on the table beside the drink, turned, and was gone.

She hadn't disappeared, nor had she walked out of the hut; she just ceased to be there by the table. I was not afraid; it seemed natural. I took the water. It was flavored with mint-grass; definitely refreshing me. I looked about the inside of the hut. The decor was simple and everything seemed to be ordered. I finished the water and decided that I would probably find her outside in the garden. I looked at the coin; went to reach for it; hesitated, then turned for the door; leaving the coin on the table where it had been placed. I didn't feel I had truly earned the silver coin. I walked through the doorway.

I was on the path; no hut, no garden, just a scent of honeysuckle in the air. My previous pile of sticks lay before me bundled very neatly. The hut of Zalran was just in the distance. How strange it seemed; but that was Lady Teloive.

As the seasons passed, I secretly grew to love Lady Teloive as my own mother. She was not a witch, nor a sorceress. I do not know of any one word to describe her. She claimed to be the daughter of Time. She was very capable with spells and magic. She also had a very thorough understanding of the woods and of things that grew. She also seemed to have some power over Zalran. When I was forced to explain my obvious absences, I finally explained my friendship with Lady Teloive. It appeared that Zalran was truly in fear of her. Of course, that fear was not so great as to stop him beating me when I did not respond with the speed he wanted. She was able to stop the bleeding and take the pain away when I could find her. She was unique in that manner; she could only be found when she wanted to be found. She seemed to live in her own time and world, crossing occasionally into the drab world that I existed in.

It was she who taught me how to do certain magic and spells. Fire-reading was one of the hardest to do and she had taught me well. Fire? Prince Linnell!"

The reverie stops.

"Tell me what the fire-reading is, Trel. Trel? Are you listening to me? Trel?"

"Fire-reading? You accuse me of fire-reading? Even the king's son should know that it is treason for anyone but the royal sorcerer to fire-read for one of the royal family. Many a witch has seen death for attempting to fire-read in public to ridicule or threaten the king. Now you accuse me of fire-reading? Does my young companion also accuse me of sorcery and even worse, an insubordination to the king?" Trel attempts to change the conversation topic.

"Trel, please don't treat me as a child." The young man bows his head to look at the ground, eyes averted, his left foot lightly fidgeting. He then begins again slowly, stumbling for words. "You know... I... I have seen you fire-read before tonight. You can do fire-readings." It is not a question, but instead a simple statement. He snaps his head up, a determined look on his face and stares at Trel. "I wasn't sure then, so I vowed to stay awake until you also went to sleep. If you had read the fire before, you might read it again. And you did. Please, Trel, tell me what you saw in the flames." The young prince's voice pleads. Trel is moved watching the petulance of youth fight with the knowledge of manhood; a need for acceptance, a desire to trust, the power of royalty and the strength of friendship swirl in conflict within the prince.

"My lord, you have known me as your companion for five Circles of Seasons. You say you have seen me read the flames before. Do you think that I would perform such a treasonable act to the king, my master, and read the fire for one of the royal family? I have been a loyal subject in service to your father almost eight full circles; and now, my friend, you ask me to read the fire and flames for you. Only your father has the right to know what the flames say; and only Zalran can read the fires for him." Trel's voice is now harsh.

"Trel, did we not share an oath of shield-sworn. With that pact I promised my life to your protection; even above my kingdom. Would I ask a friend to commit treason? Even though I am the son of a king, I do not command you to tell me. I ask as shield-sworn; the truth. Do not keep secrets from your shield-sworn. Did you not read the fire?"

Trel sits with his back to the fire appraising his young companion as the firelight flickers fleeting shadows across Linnell's face. "*This young man will make a very good king. Never demands or commands of his subjects what he wants; instead, he uses a tactful method to retrieve the information he desires.*" Trel thinks to himself while the inner battle between treason and shield oath blazes like the fire near him.

"As shield-sworn, my friend, Prince Linnell." Trel's voice is slow and deliberate. "Yes, I truly can read the flames of fire. But, also, as shield-sworn, I implore you not to ask me what the prophesy reading is, or of my blunt indiscretion tonight."

"Trel, my dear friend, I will not ask the prophesy. I only wish you reveal to me why you shook your head so vehemently as you watched the smoke go into the air?"

"Lin," starts Trel, using the most familiar of names, "I can only say this to you. It unveiled that my betrothed, Nori, will marry a man other than me. A man of royalty and she will bear him a child." Trel's voice dwindles into the darkness.

The pain and guilt of being caught in the fire-reading is strong on Trel. He seems resolved that what will be, will be. His lovely Nori, beside another man. A vision of Nori moves through Trel's mind. An albino, with long white flowing hair, sometimes worn braided up as other palace ladies, ivory cream skin, long delicate fingers tipped with pink painted nails. The graceful vision dances through his troubled mind.

"And when does this occur, oh mighty soothsayer of gloom? Nori and you are to wed at the full moon after the Festival of Nos'Rovlah." Linnell attempts to bring Trel out of his misery. The young prince's voice taunts.

"Mock not my reading, Prince Linnell!" The anger and humiliation build within him.

"I do not mock you, my friend, nor your reading. I only wish to point out what Zalran told my father; not all readings come to pass."

"And now you are an expert, after only one reading with the mighty Zalran. Trust me, Linnell, I have read the flames correctly. Street hags and charlatans may misread the flames, I do not. What could be, can be; what would be, will be." There is a fire in Trel's eyes; anger flows with the blood in his veins.

"So, you have read the flames correctly. Then, tell me, when does this happen?"

"I cannot tell you. The prophesy is tied to..."

"Cannot? Or will not?" Linnell cuts off Trel's explanation. A new boldness swells in the prince. "Which is it, my friend? Surely, you can reveal something of the time when all this happens without telling me the prophesy."

"Cats! I can tell you about the cats!" There is almost a

little boy quality in Trel's approach to the subject. His eyes are alight with the chance to speak as if this will set him free of the guilt.

"Then tell me, oh mighty soothsayer." The prince struts his way to a nearby tree. "Tell me of the cats since they are of my heritage and ruling." Linnell leans back. "The great cats belong to my father and someday to me." This new persona of authority and near arrogance in the prince irritates Trel.

Trel glares at the young prince, then with his head hung down as if in shame, he begins. "I saw the Snowcat running with the Junglecat. A strange new cat, unknown to me, appears in our land. The cats..." Trel's voice stumbles. "The cats become fire. A fire so enormous, then they are one large cat of flames. They..." Again, Trel's voice fade. He watches the young prince eyes move quickly about in thought. He heaves one big breath then lets his head slump forward.

"Ah ha!" Linnell jumps up startling Trel. "As you know, the Snowcat is only seen in the winter months north of here beyond the Iron Mountains in the Arctic Plains. The Junglecat is only visible during the summer in the Southern Hills near the South Pass. The fire? Hmm, that is obviously..." His voice hesitates. He turns and faces the Trel. "A cat of fire? Trel! You speak of the Firecat!" Linnell's voice almost shouts the name. The young prince paces back and forth in front of the fire. "Your cat of flames is the Firecat. It is just a fantasy, a legend. The Firecat is not real. It is the Fire Prophesy, a myth of long ago. It is said that the Firecat is the..." Linnell's voice fades as his hands wave into the darkness above in exasperation. Trel can now see that the young man is obviously fretting. "How can you say that the Firecat is part of your fire-reading?" Linnell's voice is almost to the point of sounding incredulous. "How can you put your faith in a fantasy? That there is not in existence such a beast should prove you wrongly reading about Nori wedding another. One of royalty? With her currently betrothed to you?"

"Firecat? I saw the Firecat? The Fire Prophesy?" Trel thinks to himself as he now realizes why Linnell is so agitated.

"Believe me, Prince Linnell, that is why I spoke aloud and shook my head. The reading does not make sense, but the flames told me twice the same story. The cats and Nori are tied together as part of the fire-reading." Trel watches Linnell pace about the campsite. "I beg forgiveness, m'lord." he says to the young prince.

"No fear, Trel. The Firecat is just a legend. There is nothing that you should be worried about. Prophecy is just prophecy. What could be, can be; what would be, will be. A scholar taught me that!" Linnell watches Trel grin at the phrase Lady Teloive had drilled to Trel over the years.

Another set of eyes and ears have watched and listened to this tale. The Silverhawk lifts from the branch where it has sat in silence spying. The wings flash their silver in the moonlight as it flies in the direction of the castle-keep. The bird's exit has not gone unnoticed. Trel watches the Silverhawk escape and glimpses the four stars that streak across the dark sky.

Linnell turns to look at what has caught Trel's attention and caused his friend's face to pale. A Silverhawk! A Silverhawk that obviously belongs to Zalran. Prince Linnell is filled with remorse. He has forced Trel to speak and now he must live with this forbidden knowledge.

"Did you see them? The shooting stars? An omen?" Linnell's voice is falsely excited in an attempt to bring Trel out of the moodiness.

"Yes, Lin, an omen." he responds. *"An ill omen. As fast as the stars fell, the Silverhawk will be to Zalran. No later than mid-day tomorrow, Zalran should have the king's orders for my death."* he thinks to himself.

The Silverhawk lands on its perch in Zalran's room. The sorcerer glides over the floor toward the bird. His robes flow with a slight rustle, the arcane embroidery of silver and gold on the royal sorcerer's habit glitter in the candlelight.

"Ah, what is this my little one? Has Trel committed a transgression against his royal master? Oh! So, he still thinks he can read the flames of fire." The voice is deep, yet sweet. There is power in the voice; also, sarcasm. "Well, let me see. Cats, you say? Hmm... No fear, my precious one, these cats are but fantasies of Trel's vivid imagination. Teloive has ruined his mind to the truths of life. Firecat indeed! If the Firecat could be invoked, I would have already had done so. So much for Trel's reading of the fire. Yet, the fact still remains, he has read the fire for one of the royal family. A very dangerous prospect. Treason is punishable by death. And death he shall have." The voice of Zalran is full of vindictive laughter. The idea of ruining such a good friendship between Trel and the prince makes this fortuitous moment glorious for Zalran.

"At last! Sweet revenge. I lost you as my servant; now the prince will lose you as his companion. A thorn for many years in my movements for the dominion of the young prince, you now shall be removed. How you can remain so innocent and continue to fight my will after all these years is a credit to you, Trel. Nonetheless, death will be quick for you and then Prince Linnell will be mine. I will assign a proper companion-teacher for the future king. When King Ariello is finally dead, I will have complete dominion over Linnell and all the power I need. First the beginning of a potion, then I must make sure the king is awakened and warned of this foul deed. Dalliance is for fools; quick action is for the strong. All I have to do is just make sure..." the voice trails off as Zalran starts his preparations for Trel's return. He quickly moves about the room. Vials of potions send their decadent odors into the air as Zalran creates the proper spells. The Silverhawk quickly flees the room and their odors; again, it flies toward the Great Desert Forest.

About the Author

My name is Robert S. Nailor but most people call me Bob.

I'm retired from the federal government. I was a computer geek and still do some programming yet today. One would think I should have plenty of time to write, but I actually seem to have less now. So, to make sure that things work out correctly, I force myself to sit down and write. That doesn't always work. Today, writing is fun and I find it relaxing. I get to visit those fantastic and strange places within my mind and well, if I don't come back right away, there is no longer somebody behind me writing on a pink sheet of paper.

I live with my wife, Violet, in a ranch home snuggled into a small wooded acre in NW Ohio. I was born in Sioux City, Iowa but my parents moved to Ohio in 1953. I have four sons and currently have ten grandchildren - 7 granddaughters and 3 grandsons. Plus, I have 11 great-grandchildren — 5 great-granddaughters and 6 great-grandsons.

My interests are camping (have RV, will travel), gardening, music, cooking and reading. So where do I travel? I've been in 46 of the 50 states and strangely, Hawaii is one of the states I've visited (U.S. Navy) but not Alaska. I have also visited two of our territories - Puerto Rico and the Virgin Islands. Traveling allows me to add the ambiance to my stories and also to some of the characters. Gardening is a bit gamey since we live in the country and have the wildlife visiting us constantly — deer, rabbits, raccoon, birds, squirrels plus many others. So, vegetables don't always make it to harvest, but what does is more than tasty. There are flowers, sometimes too many, to keep me busy. Music? I love New Age music and my favorite group is Mannheim Steamroller... and not just because of their fabulous Christmas albums;

I was hooked on them before that. I also have created some of my own electronic music which I've been told is pretty good. Should I mention cooking? I love to cook and do gourmet cooking. Having worked with Boy Scouts for several years, I have taught many boys the basics of cooking beyond hot dogs and beans. I have won quite a few contests. As to what I read; well, obviously a lot of science fiction, fantasy and some Christian. Horror, romance, adventure and other genres are also great reads when they catch my attention with an intriguing tag line or cover.

Bibliography

Novels:
The Secret Voice ~ Book 1 in The Amish Singer series
The New York Voice ~ Book 2 in The Amish Singer series
The Amish Voice ~ Book 3 in The Amish Singer series
The Vietnam Voice ~ Book 4 in The Amish Singer series
The Family Voice ~ Book 5 in The Amish Singer series
The Englische Voice ~ Book 6 in The Amish Singer series
Eternal Blood ~ Book 1 in the Barry Hargrove detective mysteries
The Babbling Sphinx ~ Book 2 in the Barry Hargrove detective mysteries
Dragon Feast ~ Book 3 in the Barry Hargrove detective mysteries
Pangaea, Eden Lost ~ a Barclay Havens, relic hunter mis-adventure
Three Steps: The Journeys of Ayrold ~ an Irish fantasy for today
2012 Timeline Apocalypse ~ the Mayan calendar comes to an end
At Death's Door ~ a collection of "light" horror stories about death
The Emerald ~ Book 1 in The Shiyula Realm series

Coming Soon...
The Scepter of the Fire Cat, The Lost One ~ book 2 in the series
The Topaz ~ book 2 in The Shiyula Realm series
Mommy Missing ~ book 4 in the Barry Hargrove mystery series

Anthologies I Am In:
52 Weeks of Writing Tips ~ tips to improve one's writing ability
Telling Tales of Terror ~ essays on how to write horror and dark fiction
Mother Goose Is Dead ~ a collection of favorite fairy tales, fractured
Dead Set: A Zombie Anthology ~ a collection of unusual zombie tales
The Complete Guide to Writing Paranormal-Vol 1 ~ various essays
Nights of Blood 2 ~ different takes on the vampire story
Guide to Writing Science Fiction ~ essays on writing science fiction
Firestorm of Dragons ~ an eclectic collection of dragon stories
Fantasy Writer's Companion ~ essays on writing fantasy
13 Night of Blood ~ 13 amazing vampire tales
Spirits of Blue & Gray ~ a collection of Civil War ghost stories

PLUS more at www.bobnailor.com

www.ingramcontent.com/pod-product-compliance
Lightning Source LLC
Chambersburg PA
CBHW030109260626
47156CB00008B/2583